DEATH
by
ACCORDION

DEATH
by
ACCORDION

Cheryl Miller Thurston

Acknowledgments

THANK YOU TO Shirley Wilsey and Susan Malmstadt, whose suggestions, ideas, and enthusiasm helped keep me going and were absolutely invaluable.

Thank you to my husband, Ed Armstrong, for never, ever saying "You're writing a book????" or indicating in any way that he thought I might be crazy to take on such a project.

Thank you to Zach and Shanna Miller for their help with medical questions, to Annet Wollan for help with police procedural questions, to Eric Wollan for drum questions, and to Scott Wheeler for questions about both EMTs and trombones.

Thank you to Teresa Stockley for letting me volunteer in her classroom so that I could learn about being a kindergarten teacher.

Thank you to Mark Heffron and many other friends and family members who answered all kinds of questions as I tried to get the details right.

And, finally, thank you to my late father for making me take accordion lessons as a child.

Cheryl Miller Thurston

For my friends, accordion-loving or not

CHAPTER 1

MORE THAN ONE PERSON wanted to strangle Judith Pence Friday night. I was not one of them.

Okay, I lied. I was one of them.

And my thoughts weren't limited to strangling.

After two hours of rehearsal, we weren't even halfway through Act One of the musical *Carnival.* Nothing, I mean *nothing,* was making our director happy. "It's community theater!" I wanted to yell at her. "Not Broadway!"

I am not a yeller, though.

I just sat quietly in the orchestra pit, adjusting the weight of the accordion—yes, accordion—on my lap and thinking mean thoughts. Later I would feel a little guilty about those mean thoughts, but at the time they were therapeutic.

Suddenly Judith's voice was right behind me. "When are you two going to learn those lyrics?" she yelled.

I turned around cautiously and saw her standing at the railing of the orchestra pit. She was glaring up at the two actors on stage.

"Sorry!" said Feleesha Farnsworth, the blonde playing Lili, the lead. Rumor has it that she had changed the spelling of her name from "Felicia" to "Feleesha" when she went to New York City to make it big. She obviously hadn't made it.

"I know I screwed up, too," said Joe, the male lead.

"That's an understatement," said Judith.

Joe bristled. "I'm working on it! I just haven't had time to get that song down yet."

"When the blazes do you intend to *find* the time? We open this weekend." Judith rested her script on the metal pit railing, took her pen from behind her ear, and clanked it against the metal over and over again. She was clanking a little too close to my head for comfort, so I leaned forward a bit.

Finally she said, "Go to the greenroom, both of you, and work with Erin on your lines. *Again.*"

Joe joined Erin, the stage manager, but Feleesha lingered. She crossed her arms in front of her, giving herself a little hug. Finally she said, "It's just that we've got so *many* songs, Judith."

"That's what happens when you're the lead. Now go."

She went. Quickly.

Judith shouted, "Celeste! Victor!" The two understudies scrambled from the wings. "Fill in for Feleesha and Joe, and see if you can do it off book." She looked down into the pit at Becky, our conductor and musical director. "Play that song again, and slow it down."

Becky took a deep breath and fingered the cross around her neck for a moment. Then she lifted her baton, and we played "I Hate Him" again at exactly the same speed as before. Celeste and Victor sang flawlessly.

Judith had not one word of criticism, and Judith always had at least one word of criticism.

An hour later, after yet another lecture about responsibility and commitment and honoring our implied contract with the audience to provide high quality entertainment, Judith finally dismissed us.

I slipped my accordion, Tillie, off my shoulders and settled her carefully onto the wooden stand next to me. (I have a tendency to name objects I love. My accordion. My car. My favorite purse.) I always leave Tillie in the pit for the duration of a show, alongside the drums, because she's too heavy to lug up and down the stairs and lift in and out of the car every day. I hate to go home without her, as she is such a nice accordion, but the theater is always locked when we aren't there. Besides, as the other musicians tease me, "Who would steal an accordion?"

I stood up and pulled back my shoulder blades, then stretched both arms overhead, getting the kinks out of my back. Next to me, Gordon put his trombone in its case and snapped the locks. "A flute," he said, continuing his nightly routine of suggesting instruments I might play that aren't "the size of a small refrigerator." He picked up his case. "No back problems with a flute."

"But no one knows what to call you," I said, continuing my routine of rejecting his suggestions. "Flautist? Flutist? Fluter?" I stretched my neck from side to side. "A little yoga before I go to bed, and I'll be fine."

I would probably pop a couple of Advil, too, but I wasn't about to tell Gordon that. I am a bit sensitive about my instrument of choice—well, not my choice exactly. My Polish great-grandfather is the one who decided to enroll me in accordion lessons when I was six. Jaja loved the accordion, and to everyone's surprise, I soon did, too.

There isn't a lot of modern accordion sheet music in the world, so my teacher gave me music from the decades when the accordion enjoyed more popularity—the 1930s, 40s, and 50s. Like a duckling, I imprinted. Then in high school I discovered musical theater, and show tunes took their place beside the old standards in my brain.

"Thank God you have us," my two older brothers reminded me often. They taught me to beat-box, saving me from, as they put it, "complete musical nerd-dom."

"What in the Sam Hill is beat boxing?" my grandmother had asked when she learned about it. When I explained that I could use my voice to imitate the sounds of a drum machine, she looked skeptical. When I demonstrated, she was not impressed. "Too much like spitting," she said.

Gordon gave me a wave. "I'm outta here." He and I had become friends a couple of years earlier during a production of *Fiddler on the Roof.* He's one of the dozens of people who have given me copies of the Gary Larson cartoon: *Welcome to heaven…Here's your harp. Welcome to hell… Here's your accordion.* I could paper a wall with them.

"Say hi to Annalise and the kids," I said.

I pulled my purse out from under my chair and then looked over at the drummer. I hesitated, then said, "See you, Stan." He muttered a crabby, "Yeah," as usual. Was he *ever* going to get over my turning him down for more dates?

Carefully, I made my way through the orchestra pit toward the steps, trying not to dislodge or trip over all the cords snaking across the floor, and saying goodbye to other band members. I went up the steps out of the pit and was heading up the stairs to the stage when Judith yelled, "Ella!"

What now? I stopped midway up the stairs, momentarily enjoying a sense of power from standing above her.

"I'm just not happy with that opening," Judith said. "It doesn't look like Aiden is really playing the concertina."

"That's because Aiden *isn't* really playing the concertina." I managed to hold back a "Duh!"

Carnival opens with a lone figure walking across the stage with a concertina and playing the beginning of "Love Makes the World Go Round," the only song anyone ever recognizes from the show. But in our show, Aiden just pretends to play while I actually play the song from the orchestra pit on my accordion. I play because, despite my best efforts to teach the teenager the simple melody, Aiden can't begin to do it. He has the musical talent of, oh, a coffee table. I have not even been successful teaching him to *fake* play the song believably.

"You've got to try again to teach him to play it himself. I don't like this fake business."

"But…"

She gave me what Gordon and I call her "Mama Morton" look, a reference to the prison matron in *Chicago*. "Just do it," she said. Then she turned and walked away.

I wasn't about to do it, but I wasn't going to tell Judith that.

I am not a confronter.

Poor Aiden. I suspected that he was in the show only because his mother wouldn't have agreed to be musical director unless Judith found a part for him. In addition to his brief appearance walking across the stage with a concertina, he also plays a tightrope dancer in the ensemble. That hasn't gone well either. He has a decent voice, but he is uncoordinated.

The choreographer has tried to help him blend into the background with easy steps, but an awkward fifteen-year-old with a bright shock of red hair doesn't blend easily. His costume of purple Spandex doesn't help.

When I went to the greenroom to get my sweater, I saw that Feleesha and Joe were still going over their lines, only now it was Feleesha's mother, Paula, coaching them, not the stage manager. As wardrobe mistress, Paula sews, organizes, and maintains the many costumes for the show. Did her responsibilities now include coaching?

"I have to go," said Joe, closing his script and getting up. "Really."

"Not exactly committed, are you?" sniffed Paula.

"I'll get the lines. But now I need some sleep." He took his script and walked away.

I heard him mutter "bitch" as he left. I wasn't sure if he meant Judith or Paula.

CHAPTER 2

THE NEXT NIGHT, I pulled into the theater parking lot a little early for rehearsal. The Juniper Theater is part of a thriving downtown in our small community along the foothills of the Colorado Rockies. Juniper has become known as an artist's community, with downtown businesses and galleries hosting pottery workshops and exhibitions that have gained a national reputation.

Nothing seemed out of the ordinary as I parked the car. It was just another night in a string of rehearsal nights. If I'd known that I'd later be asked to reconstruct every detail of the evening, I'd have taken notes. Or pictures.

But as it was, I just headed for the greenroom, hoping the lasagna I'd grabbed at Whole Foods wasn't cold yet. I remember seeing two teenage cast members—dancers—already sitting at the mirrors piling on makeup. They never appear without heavy eyeliner, blusher, and perfectly blown-dry hair, even for rehearsals. One of the girls, Helena, wears camisole tops and brightly printed leggings that outline everything she has, and what she has is definitely worth outlining. Everyone knows her name, but not the name of her not-so-spectacular-looking friend.

Then I sat down at a table beside Feleesha, who was carefully eating five carrot sticks and some hummus. She had wrapped an orange and blue Broncos fleece blanket around her shoulders to take off the chill. "Not exactly a big supper there, Feleesha," I commented. She weighs maybe 100 pounds. Surely she wasn't dieting.

"Not supper. Just a little snack to keep me going. Gluten-free, of course."

"Of course." I gnawed on the giant roll I'd slathered with butter to go along with my lasagna.

Feleesha looked around. "Is Judith around?"

"I haven't seen her," Stan said, sitting down with a cup of coffee and a granola bar.

"Good." She reached inside the small cooler beside her and pulled out a packet of string cheese.

Joe sat down beside us, sucking down a chocolate shake. "Keep an eye out for her, Ella. You're facing the door." Judith has a policy forbidding all singers from eating any kind of milk products before a show or a rehearsal—something about it causing phlegm. But Joe, among others, says that theory is nonsense.

I remember that Noreen, the woman who runs lights for the show and is in charge of the facility during rehearsals, came in late. Although she is much easier to get along with than Judith, it's not a good idea to cross her. She has rules, and she expects us to follow them. She also has a temper.

Stan asked her to borrow a music stand light because his was acting "kind of wonky," and she said she would go up to a storage room in the balcony area to get one. I remember that bit of conversation because I love the word "wonky." I zoned out for a few moments, thinking about other "w" words I like—wheeze, willowy, wriggle . . .

Then I noticed Caleb coming in late, too. He works for

the theater and runs sound for our show. He collapsed in a chair and pried open a Styrofoam container.

"You seem a little stressed," I said.

"I'm late. My wife got tied up at work, and I had to pick Jamie up from soccer practice and feed him," he said. "Guess what kind of take-out an eight-year-old won't eat."

"Sushi?" I hazarded a guess, looking at his chopsticks.

He frowned at me. "How did you know?"

"Seaweed . . . kids . . ."

"Of course I didn't get seaweed. It was California rolls." He slid a piece of chicken off a stick and onto his rice. "Tonight he says he hates California rolls. Two weeks ago he loved California rolls." He shook his head.

Then Noreen came back and handed Stan a light. She picked up a waste basket and slammed it on top of the table. "Smell this, everyone!" No one seemed eager to sniff. "You're supposed to put the food trash *only* in the green trash bin because it is the one Caleb and I empty every night. But somebody used this one!"

"It smells like rotten beef," Feleesha shuddered. I didn't smell anything, but then I didn't have Feleesha's nose, or Noreen's. If anyone put on even a tiny spritz of perfume, they smelled it, and we would get a lecture about respecting the sensitivities of others.

Noreen continued. "You guys have got to remember to clean up after yourselves. If you sit in the auditorium when you're not onstage, don't leave your gum wrappers or sweaters or notebooks or Kleenex packs or whatever in the seats or on the floor. Same with you people in the pit. And if you're leaving stuff in the greenroom, put it in a bag, not scattered all over the damn place."

She was on a roll. "And for God's sake, act like you were raised in civilization. I found sunflower seed shells in a pile on the floor last night, still slimy. Have you never heard of wastebaskets? And when I went up to the balcony to get the light for Stan, I opened the women's restroom up there, and it smelled to high heaven. Three of the toilets had been used—one of them for serious business, if you know what I mean." She looked at those of us eating and muttered, "Sorry," and then continued. "Who *does* that? Who doesn't even have the common decency to flush? And I've told you before, you are not even supposed to *be* in the balcony area. There's a reason for that red rope across the stairs. It's off limits during rehearsals!"

She was gaining momentum. "And don't leave your props and costumes in the area in front of the fire exit! How many times do I have to tell you? Last night I found a hat with a stuffed rabbit in it." We all looked over at the guy playing Marco the Magnificent, who gave a little shrug and muttered an "Oops." "*Plus* a boa, a bra, three tutus, and a pair of tap shoes. Get your act together, people!" She turned to Caleb. "Let's go. We've got stuff to do."

As she headed for the door, Stan called after her. "You do realize that most people aren't here yet, right? And didn't hear you?"

"Spread the word when they get here," she ordered, and left.

I remember that Caleb grabbed two California rolls, one in each hand, and followed Noreen out of the greenroom. I scraped the sides of the container for the last bit of lasagna. Feleesha relished another package of string cheese, and Joe slurped his shake while we all kept an eye out for Judith.

All of that I remember pretty well. But what I remember most clearly was what we heard next.

A scream.

CHAPTER 3

THE SCREAM CAME from the theater. Feleesha and I jumped up and rushed out, heading toward the stage. The men stayed behind, evidently opting to finish their food and let us investigate. Helena and her friend couldn't be bothered, either. They must have been at a critical point layering on blusher.

We ran out onto the stage and looked out into the auditorium. Noreen was standing in an aisle just under the balcony and talking into her cell phone. Caleb was sitting near her, his head between his legs.

"Stay back!" Noreen said to us, but Feleesha and I ignored her and hurried down the steps toward Caleb.

Then we saw her. Judith lay slumped in a seat, but we could barely see her face for all the blood. Her black hair was now almost entirely red, and blood covered her clothes and pooled onto the floor. Feleesha stepped away quickly. I gagged, worrying that the lasagna I had eaten was going to come up and join the mess on the floor.

I took a deep breath, and then stepped forward to see if I could give CPR or take her pulse or something. "Don't," said Caleb, his voice breaking. "She's dead. I checked."

I swallowed hard.

Feleesha stepped forward again and took a closer look, then began trembling. "Oh my god, oh my god, oh my god," she breathed. She turned away and sat down beside Caleb, staring straight ahead.

I took another look at the scene, trying to make sense of it. What the heck had happened?

Then I saw Tillie—or pieces of her. Parts of my accordion lay all around Judith—the keyboard in her lap, the bellows punctured and in an adjacent chair, the section of bass buttons smashed on the floor.

"Tillie!" I moaned.

"It's Judith," Noreen said, off the phone now. "Don't touch anything." Did she think none of us ever watched *NCIS* or *Law and Order*?

"But Tillie . . ." I wanted to cry.

"It's Judith," she said again. "It's clearly Judith."

Caleb sat up and looked over at me. "Who the hell is Tillie?"

Tears came to my eyes. "My accordion." I suppose it doesn't speak well of me that I was as upset about my bloody accordion as I was about Judith.

Judith was most definitely dead. Worse, it looked like my accordion had killed her. I'm no detective, but it appeared that Tillie had been pushed off the balcony onto Judith's head. Tillie certainly wasn't an instrument anyone could swing around like a baseball bat.

Tillie was also unlikely to have made her way to the balcony by herself, perched on the ledge, and accidentally taken a fall. Murder was definitely in the cards here.

"Get away from the scene," ordered Noreen. "We all need to sit down and wait for the police and ambulance." She led us to the light and sound booth at the back of the theater, and we obediently followed.

Caleb's eyes were red, and Feleesha kept muttering "Oh my god, oh my god, oh my god."

"Shut up so I can think," said Noreen.

We all sat quietly for a minute.

"How did you guys get through the stage door tonight?" asked Caleb suddenly. "Noreen and I were both late, and we have the keys. We're the ones who open up."

"It was unlocked when I got here," said Feleesha. "I went into the green room and Helena and her friend were already unpacking their makeup on the counter."

"How the hell did the door get unlocked?" Noreen asked. "I locked it last night as soon as rehearsal began, like always. And it stayed that way the rest of the night, like always." The locked-door policy had been put in place after a drunk high school kid walked in the unlocked stage door and wandered across the stage during a production of "The Foreigner. "If you leave, you can't get back in unless someone lets you in. Everyone knows that."

"I was the last one out of here last night," Caleb added, "and I double-checked the lock when I left."

"So how did Judith get in?" I asked.

Noreen and Caleb looked at each other and hesitated. "Okay, don't tell our boss, but we gave her a key to use during the show," Noreen said. "She likes to get here an hour before everyone else and sit back and quietly go over her notes before the madness starts. You know how she is . . . um, was . . . very, very insistent."

"We just didn't want to come an hour early to accommodate her," said Caleb. "We have enough trouble getting here by 5:00."

"We made her promise not to let anyone else use the

key and to give it back after the show is over," Noreen added. "She also had to promise to lock the door behind her when she comes in early. We don't want unauthorized people waltzing in behind her before we officially unlock the doors."

"Maybe she forgot?" I suggested. It seemed unlikely, knowing Judith.

"Not a chance," said Noreen. "Has there ever been a detail Judith missed about anything? You can be darned sure she locked that door after her."

"Oh, man, are we in trouble," Caleb said.

Feleesha started with her "Oh my god, oh my god, oh my gods" again. Noreen told her to shut up again.

"I've seen Judith sitting back here when I come early," I said, "always in the same seat."

"It's the one she and her husband donated in a fund-raiser a few years ago," Noreen said. "If you go back and look at the plaque on the back of the chair, you can see that it reads, 'Lovers and theater lovers. Judith and Jared."

"They must have donated the plaque a long time ago," Feleesha said. "Like before Jared left her for the woman who played Maria in Sound of Music. Darla Oglesby." She said the name with distaste, but I understood. I had gone to school with Darla Oglesby. "Jared and Judith are separated," she added.

"So why would she sit there if her husband screwed around on her?" I asked. "That seems weird."

"Some people are just stupid," Noreen said. "I guess she still loves him because she keeps going back to him. She probably will again."

I looked at her. "Not this time."

She sighed. "Right. Not this time." She returned the subject of the key. "It's not like Judith is a stranger. She's directed dozens of shows here. We thought it would be okay to give her a key."

"I guess it wasn't," I said. Suddenly, I was crying, and it wasn't just because of Tillie. A human being had just lost her life, and violently, right here in our theater.

Caleb had been carefully looking away from the crime scene, but now he glanced toward it again. He promptly threw up on Feleesha's shoes.

"Arghhhhhhhhh!" she cried.

That's when we heard pounding. Help had arrived, but no one had thought to unlock the front doors. Noreen rushed out with her keys, and in a moment, in walked two EMTs and two police officers, one male and one female.

The female was prettier than I thought a police officer would be, even in her quite unflattering police uniform. I wondered if she hated putting on something like that, day after day. Pleated pants are bad enough, but the gun belt and holster added a lot of unwelcome bulk. Or at least I imagined it would be unwelcome.

I pulled my attention to the EMTs, who were checking for signs of life. In a few minutes, the officers walked back to us. "Are there others here?" the female officer asked.

"Just the one," I answered without thinking.

"Not bodies. People."

We nodded. She turned to the other officer. "Secure the back entrance,"

"It's the stage door," I corrected. She gave me a dirty look.

"Where are the others?"

"In the green room. Up there near the stage." I nodded to the stairs.

She turned to the officer. "After you secure the door, secure the green room."

"It's actually beige," I mentioned helpfully. "It's the one on the other side of the black room next to the stage."

Another dirty look. "And you . . ." She looked at the three of us. "Stay right here."

"Can I go get some paper towels?" Feleesha asked.

"No," said the officer as she left us.

Feleesha had been holding her hands in front of her eyes, head turned to the side. Now she was swaying a bit, and I was afraid she was going to add her own stomach contents to the pile already on her shoes. I sighed, took off my pink hooded sweatshirt, and covered up the vomit. I helped Feleesha carefully slip off the shoes, then used a sleeve of the sweatshirt to wipe off her feet.

Silently, we then watched the action surrounding Judith. There was a lot of it. When we heard one of the EMTs tell the officers to call the coroner, we knew we had been correct. Judith was dead.

The police officers moved Feleesha, Noreen, Caleb, and me to separate parts of the theater for interviews. Another officer joined the two who had arrived first, and he is the one who questioned me.

Detective Dan Sherman had the kindest blue eyes. After we sat down and he wrote down my name, he must have noticed that I had been crying. My eyes were red and puffy, so it didn't really take a detective to notice.

"I'm sorry for your loss," he said. "You must have been close to the deceased."

"No," I said without thinking. "I couldn't stand her, really." I realized what I'd said and added, "Though I'm sorry she died, of course."

"The tears then?"

"Shock, I guess. A person died, even if she wasn't my favorite person in the world, and so did Tillie, my accordion. I don't know how she got involved in this. I left her in the pit last night before I left."

"Tillie? The pit?"

"The orchestra pit. And somehow Tillie got up to the balcony and flung onto Judith. I mean, I guess. I'm no expert, but it sure looks like that's what happened to Judith. And I don't know how someone could fling Tillie. She weighs 29 pounds. They must have propped her up there on the edge and pushed her."

He was looking very confused and had stopped taking notes. I knew I was talking too much.

"You've got to slow down, ma'am. Let's start at the beginning. We've established that your name is Belle Ella Polansky. And I'm guessing you play the accordion."

"Yes." I decided to let him lead and didn't elaborate.

He led. He asked more questions than I thought possible. How long had I been involved with the theater? Why did I keep my accordion in the pit? What reason would I have to want Judith dead? What reasons might others have had? Did I have any enemies? Did Judith have any enemies? Why was Judith in the theater before anyone else? Who had Judith angered recently? . . . and on and on.

When he finally dismissed me, I was drained. I texted my best friend Sammie:

DRINK. NOW.

DONE EARLY?

DRINK. NOW.

I saw no need to elaborate. I left, feeling chilly without my pink sweatshirt (I didn't think I'd be wanting it back) and thankful that Whitney's was only one door away.

Sammie Russo lives downtown above Second Chance, the upscale used clothing store she recently opened. It's only two blocks from the bar and restaurant next to the theater, so it was only a few minutes before she joined me at Whitney's. I'd already drunk half my chardonnay when she sat down.

"A little stressed?" she asked, glancing at my glass. "What's up?"

"Murder!" I said.

"That will do it," she said, clearly not taking me seriously. She ordered a tonic water.

"I'm serious," I said. "Just listen." I told her all that had happened, words tumbling from my mouth in what I knew was probably a jumbled mess. Sammie didn't interrupt once.

"And they kept Tillie as evidence," I said, winding up my story. "I mean, what was left of her. I didn't even get to see if anything was salvageable."

"You said she was in pieces, Ella. I'm sorry, but I seriously doubt if you're going to be playing Tillie anymore." She reached across the table and put her hand on my forearm.

"But part of her is made of something like the stuff bowling balls are made of. It seems awfully tough. Maybe . . ." I hadn't quite let go of hope.

She sighed. "Think about it. The speed of an object makes a big difference. Remember what the back of your car looked like when that guy rear-ended you in line at the car wash? Going, like, five miles an hour?"

I remembered. And I gave up hope. "I know, I know. Tillie's done for." I took another drink. "That detective wasn't real sympathetic about her."

"Maybe he was focusing on solving a murder instead?" Sammie can be a little sarcastic sometimes.

"He wasn't *that* focused. And after he asked me how long I've played the accordion, he sort of smiled and said, 'You don't *look* like an accordion player.'"

She started to smile, then didn't. "That wasn't very professional."

"Exactly. So I said, 'What's an accordion player supposed to look like? You don't look like a detective, either.'"

"Good idea," Sammie said. "Alienate the detective, the guy who knows you are the owner of the murder weapon."

"He just made me uneasy."

"Understandable. You were being interrogated regarding a murder case."

"There was that, but . . ." I hesitated. "Okay, I think it's possible that he meets 'The Profile.'" Sammie and I have a list we made up to assess if a guy is worth dating long-term—and maybe someday even marrying.

Sammie perked right up at that. She began ticking off the items. "No ring?"

"No ring. And no white line on the ring finger."

"Manly shoes?"

Okay, this was really my item, not hers. I had gone out with Stanley twice a few months ago. Then I had confessed to her that I couldn't go out with him again because of his shoes.

"Are you kidding me? What's wrong with his shoes?" she had asked.

"They are delicate with little tassels—not manly at all. I just think a man should have sturdy shoes. Solid shoes. And Stan does not."

"Doesn't this indicate a bit of shallowness on your part? Maybe more than a bit?"

"No. There are other reasons. He doesn't tip well. He doesn't think 'Key and Peale' reruns are funny. And he plays New Age music in his car all the time."

"Okay, I get it. Those could be deal breakers."

"Yes. But it was his shoes that put me over the edge."

I drained my glass and answered her question. "Yes, Detective Dan has manly shoes. Sturdy. Sensible. No tassels."

She nodded. "Nice eyes?"

"Kind, despite my status as a possible murderer."

She nodded again. "Not gorgeous?"

"Not gorgeous but very attractive."

"Good." This was really Sammie's item. I wasn't so sure I bought into her theory that we shouldn't go out with great looking guys. "Gorgeous guys make god-awful lovers," she has explained to me more than once. "They are so used to having women fall over them that they haven't learned to give. They just lay back and expect a woman to do all the work and then be grateful."

I guess I believe her, but, truthfully, I wouldn't mind testing the theory myself.

I decided to elaborate on the detective. "His name is Dan Sherman, and he is pretty much fire fighter quality, but with a more ordinary face."

Sammie nodded. Firefighters are almost always good looking.

"It's not like his face is unattractive. He's a nice-looking guy, just more *ordinary* nice." I pictured him in my mind. "But his body is more than ordinary nice. And so are his eyes."

"Got it," Sammie said. "Let's move on. Tattoos?"

"None visible." Sammie and I are probably the only women our age in America who are not fond of tattoos snaking up arms and legs. Sammie's older brother Jeffrey got a dragon tattooed down his arm when he was in college, and it became infected. To this day, Sammie and I can't look at any tattoos without thinking about his giant, oozing, disgusting arm.

"No ex wife? No kids to share?"

"To be determined."

"He sounds promising."

"I know. That's the problem." I dropped my head to the table and moaned. I tend to get nervous and babble around men I like. If I can't stand them, I'm calm and flirty and possibly even adorable. But with men that I'm attracted to, I become stupidly talkative. I was sure I had been stupidly talkative.

"You probably seemed guilty as hell," Sammie said.

"Thanks for the insight," I said.

"Look on the bright side. If Detective Dan doesn't work out, we could always take manly shoes off the list, and you could reconsider Stanley," she said innocently.

I gave her a look.

"Is he still asking you out?"

"No. After I told him I have other plans about four times, he finally stopped."

She shook her head. "You could have just told him you weren't interested and . . ." She saw my warning look. "But I won't go there." We'd been over this subject before.

I am not a straight shooter.

At least not when it involves telling someone something difficult.

A fiftyish man walked slowly by our table. "Hello, ladies," he said, looking only at Sammie. She said a polite "hello" but accompanied it with a look so devoid of interest that he hurried on without lingering. Sammie is drop-dead gorgeous with long, almost-black hair, dark eyes, and a dancer's lithe body and shapely legs. I'm not exactly chopped liver myself, but no one notices me when she's around.

Not that it bothers me.

Well, not much. Sammie looks at her beauty as just a fact of life, a personal characteristic no different than having a love for cilantro or excelling—as I do—at spelling. She's not at all conceited about her looks.

Neither am I, but that's because I have a lot less to be conceited about. I think of myself as beige—light brown hair, light brown eyes, light brown freckles on my nose. I do get my share of attention from men, but not when Sammie's around.

Sammie said, "I guess you've had a pretty bad day."

"Murder does kind of put a damper on things." I looked at my empty glass and wished for another drink. I knew I'd be driving home, so I reluctantly abstained. "And school wasn't so hot either. Nathan wasn't absent, again."

She stuck out her lower lip and patted my hand. "Poor baby. Nathan is *never* absent, is he?"

I'm a kindergarten teacher, and this year I have the

misfortune of having the principal's son in my class. I know I am supposed to love all my students, and I do, but Nathan is giving that love a severe testing.

"So what did he do today?" Sammie asked. I think she secretly gets a kick out of hearing about Nathan. He probably reminds her of her oldest brother, the one with the infected tattoos.

"While they were in the reading corner, he wanted to sit beside Carlos instead of Emily, so he told Emily to move. When she didn't, he called her a 'poopie head.' When she complained, I confronted him, and he said it was an accident. He *accidentally* called her a poopie head."

Sammie shook her head. "I hate it when that happens."

"His mom said I must have misunderstood, as Nathan doesn't use language like that." I sighed. I sat quietly, wallowing in self-pity for a few more moments. It had been a bad day. I didn't suspect then that even worse days were just ahead.

I finished wallowing and finally remembered my manners. "I'm finished venting now. How was *your* day?"

Sammie picked up her swizzle stick and poked at the ice cubes in her drink. She didn't say anything for a long time. I raised my eyebrows and leaned in. Finally, she blurted, "I'm pregnant."

"Whhhhaaaatttt????"

"Well, maybe. I'm late."

"So immaculate conception, or what?" I didn't take her comment seriously, as I was quite familiar with Sammie's love life. Currently, she didn't have one.

"Donald was in town, and we went dancing."

"So?" She always goes dancing when Donald's in town. By "in town" we mean Denver, an hour and a half away.

Donald Sanders is a hot shot model based in New York City. Seriously. The two met on the dance floor years ago, and they have been meeting up, just to dance, whenever he has work in Denver. The two of them look spectacular together, and they know it, but their relationship is strictly platonic. Donald, of course, is gorgeous.

She sighed. "So Donald suggested I stay in his hotel suite so that I didn't have to drive home and we could go out for some drinks. I mean, it was a *suite.* And I felt like a couple of drinks. *"*

I was starting to get worried. "So?????"

"So I had a few glasses of wine, and I was feeling, you know, restless."

"Uh-oh," I said.

"Yeah, not good. When we got back to the hotel, I decided to see if it was remotely possible that Donald might be the exception to my rule. And have, you know, skills in areas other than dancing. Just that once." She looked embarrassed. "It had been awhile, you know."

"Holy moly," I said. I don't like Donald much. The man's cocky awareness of his good looks is off-putting enough, but I also can't get past his bad grammar. I know that suggests, as with my pickiness about shoes, that I'm shallow, but eight years of old-fashioned Catholic school grammar is hard to shake off.

Luckily, I haven't had to be around Donald much—only when the two of them occasionally decide to dazzle the locals at a country western bar in town and ask Sammie's brother and me to go along.

I sighed. "So should we toss your gorgeous guy rule off our list?

"No." She shuddered. "Definitely not."

I wanted to know more—how bad was he, really?—but decided not to go there. The best I could come up with was a lame "Oh dear."

"You know I want kids. A lot of kids," Sammie said.

"Okay, but do you want kids with *Donald?*"

"No. But think about babies." She smiled. "Wouldn't you just love to be Auntie Bellella?"

My name is actually Belle Ella Polansky, after both my grandmothers. Mom thought "Ella Belle" was just too cutesy and Southern-ish, so she named me Belle Ella. I guess she never noticed how awkward the names are to say together, but my family quickly mashed them into one word that sounds like "Bellella." Wisely, when I started school, I chose to go by my middle name and become Ella to everyone else.

"Of course I would love to be Auntie Bellella," I said.

I actually would not, if Donald was part of the package. The child would grow up saying things like "Alls I want is" and "supposebly."

Another man approached our table, smiling at Sammie. She gave him a polite but dismissive nod, and he turned right around and went back to the bar. I always admire Sammie's ability to pull down what I call her "force field," an invisible, impenetrable wall that men seem afraid to cross. If a man is bothering me, I have a hard time shaking him, even with words. Sammie does it without speaking at all.

"So, if you are pregnant, which I sincerely hope you are not, what are you going to do?" I asked.

She sighed. "I don't know. You know I can't marry him."

"Of course you can't."

"He's not the one, I know. And I know you hate him."

"I don't hate him," I said.

"Okay, you don't like him. I know he's sometimes . . . well, kind of conceited." That was an understatement. "And he can't speak correctly."

I nodded. "Me and him. Irregardless."

"Funner. Pronounciate."

"Misunderestimate. Flustrated." I grimaced.

She smacked the table with her hand. "But Holy Mother of God, can he ever dance!"

I nodded. That was true.

She sighed again and took a sip from her glass. She caught me looking at it. "Just tonic, no gin," she said. "I'll follow the rules on this."

I nodded again. "We'll figure it out, Sammie. It's going to be okay…somehow."

CHAPTER 4

THE NEXT MORNING, I hurried through my shower, threw on a little mascara, and let my hair dry while I ate breakfast. Then I started the tedious process of using a heat protection spray and a flat iron to straighten my long mass of curls. I hated how much time it took, but I had been bowing to fashion for years and wasn't ready to stop. With every hair wash, I found myself thinking, "Maybe someday I'd find the courage to just let my hair do what it wants to do, which is go a little wild. Maybe . . ."

But I am not a trend setter.

I threw on black pants, a blue cashmere sweater, and boots. (I refuse to be one of those kindergarten teachers who wears cutesy vests with pencils and apples and letters of the alphabet appliquéd all over them.) Cobalt blue is a good color for me, adding a little pop to my beige look.

I was in such a hurry that I almost forgot to feed Fluffles, who stood in the kitchen whining loudly. I grabbed the plastic container of dry cat food, dumped some in her dish, and gave her some fresh water. I decided there was no time to open a can and scoop out her usual tablespoon of "wet" food.

Fluffles did not agree.

I sighed, grabbed the can opener, and fed my spoiled little princess her Fancy Feast. Then I put on my leather jacket and headed for school.

In my classroom at Emerson Elementary, I saw that Victoria was wearing the same purple "swirly, twirly" dress she had been wearing for a week. Her mother had already apologized, telling me, "She does have other clothes. Really. She just refuses to wear anything else to school." I sympathized. Victoria refuses to do a lot of things.

I sat down with the kids for sharing time. Claire's grandma was coming to visit. Blake was going to a Rockies baseball game. Henry had a loose tooth.

I wasn't really focusing, though. My mind kept turning to the murder. Who could have done such a thing? Why? Would they find the murderer quickly? Surely no one would *seriously* suspect me, just because it was my accordion that did the deed? Were all the rest of the cast and band members in danger?

I needed to concentrate. I had a packet of 32 required district assessments to give each child by the end of month. It was a challenge to figure out how to give a test to one child while keeping an eye on 23 other children and, at the same time, make sure Nathan didn't poke someone's eye out with a pencil.

After I had all the kids working at various learning centers, I called Macy to my desk. Little lights flashed on her sneakers as she came up to me. "Macy, do you remember what *rhymes* are?" She looked scared. "Remember, they are words that sound alike at the *end*—like pig, big, gig, dig, rig." A light came on in her eyes. "Remember?"

"Yes!"

"Okay, I'm going to say a word, and then you tell me another word that rhymes with it. It can be a real word or a made-up word. Here we go—*cat.*"

She thought. "Cuh . . . cuh . . . caterpillar!"

"That's the first sound. We're doing words that sound the same at the end. *Cat-bat-hat-sat.* Let's do this one—*bug.*"

"Spider?"

I took a deep breath and then went through the eight remaining items quickly, skipping over *bed.* The only rhyme I could think of was *dead,* and I wanted to get my mind off anything to do with last night. I marked a zero in Macy's assessment column for rhymes.

I called up Antonio. He knows almost no English and lives with his cousin Valeria, also in my class. Both families, I suspect, are undocumented, though Valeria has been here all her life and speaks perfect English. Looking at Antonio's frightened face, I cursed silently, angry that I was required to give him this test in a language he couldn't understand.

I hesitated. I am not a rule flouter.

I decided to flout anyway. I skipped the test and put a zero down for his score. Why make him suffer? Instead, decided to use his test time for a little language lesson.

I held up the picture of a cat. "*El gato—cat.*"

He smiled and said, "Cat."

"Si!" I said. I held up a picture of a dog and said, "*El perro—dog.*"

He repeated, "Dog."

And so we went through the stack of cards. When Antonio went back to his seat, he looked happier and more confident.

I got no further. Raymond looked down at his feet and realized he was wearing two left shoes. His twin Carlos had on two right shoes, but Carlos was busy coloring a gorilla for "G" at his table and couldn't be bothered switching shoes, so Raymond pitched a fit. Then Nathan bonked Austin on the head with a copy of *If You Give a Moose a Muffin*, and things went downhill from there. When was I going to get the darned rhyme assessments done? And the initial sound assessments? And the ending sounds assessments? And the....I couldn't bear to think about it all.

"Thinking about the murder might actually be less stressful than dealing with this," I thought as I lined the kids up to take them to recess. I needed the break as much as they did.

When I went to the office to check my mailbox during my lunch break, I took one look at Evelyn, the school secretary, and knew that word of the murder was out. The eager look on her face told me she must have heard about it on the radio she keeps turned on low beside her desk all day. Evelyn likes to be well-informed.

She wanted to talk. I did not. "It was awful, really awful," I said. I arranged my face in a look that I hoped indicated traumatic emotional damage. "I can't talk about it yet," I choked.

"But . . ." She wasn't going to be deterred by a bit of traumatic emotional damage. "Who. . .?"

I forged on. "My mother doesn't know what's going on, and I have to call her." I turned and left quickly.

It was true. I did have to call my mother. I had received

a text reading, CALL ME! BABA TOLD ME ABOUT THE MURDER! Baba, my grandmother, must have learned about it on "News at Noon," the TV show she watches every day. I needed to call them both, but after I left the office, hit the bathroom, and wolfed down a cheese sandwich in my room, there were only two minutes left until my kids came back. I gave Mom a quick call and promised to give her and Baba more details later.

I used my phone to check my email quickly. There was a message from Tess Moreland, the assistant director for *Carnival*. It was brief, saying only "No rehearsal tonight. Show opening delayed. More information soon. Our thoughts and prayers are with Judith's family."

Knowing the show had been delayed relieved me of the need to decide on a replacement accordion—not that it was a problem. I have six of them. First there is my previous "good" accordion, the one I used before I'd saved up the money to buy Tillie. Then there are the four accordions others have given me. When people find out I play, they are thrilled to give me the accordion from their grandpa/cousin/sister/ex-stepdad that is taking up space in their closet/basement/garage/attic. And finally, there is the lightweight accordion I use for my gigs with a polka band, the Streusels.

Yes, I play in a polka band—five men over 70 who have been playing together for years, and me. When Harvey, their accordionist, died two years ago, they were stuck. Otto's step-daughter knew someone who knew my mom, who gave Otto my number.

What could I do? It's not often I get a request for a polka audition, so I went. They loved my rendition of the "Clarinet Polka," and they begged me to join them. An offer of no pay and one or two gigs a month, often at retirement homes? How could I refuse?

It is fun, though. The men in the band treat me like a favorite granddaughter, and I love them. Both my father and my grandfather have passed away, so it's nice to have these adopted older men in my life.

Sammie insists on approving my outfits for performances, especially the more public ones like Octoberfest celebrations. "You need to be careful to counteract all this weird shit you do," she tells me. "No cute little German dirndl dresses for you." I usually wear tight pants, red boots, and low cut blouses—not that anyone can tell with my accordion strapped in front. (And, yes, I know every joke there is about women getting their you-know-whats caught in the bellows. And, no, it doesn't really happen.)

Because I need to stand up for our polka performances, I use a small, very lightweight accordion I call Frankie, named in honor of America's Polka King, Frankie Yankovic—not to be confused with Weird Al Yankovic, the king of hilarious song parodies. I have many books of Frankie Yankovic polkas, and though my dad had once commented, "These all sound kind of alike," I think that was more of a comment on the polka genre in general, rather than on Yankovic's song writing talents specifically.

One of Sammie's favorite party games is to make me drag out my accordion and turn songs into polkas. It's not hard, really, if the song has a distinctive melody. I've played the "Hey, Jude Polka," the "God Bless America Polka," and many more, but Sammie's absolute favorite is the "Oh, Holy Night Polka." That one just cracks her up, so it's a must at every Christmas party.

After school, I called my insurance agent to begin what would probably be the long process of getting money for Tillie. The agent needed evidence, but I had no pictures, and the accordion pieces were in custody.

I called Detective Sherman. He had given me his card after our interview, in case I thought of anything else (just like they do on *Law and Order*).

He answered with, "Sherman here."

"This is Ella Polansky?" I heard my voice rise in a ridiculous uptick. "Oh, sorry. I hate people talking in questions, so ignore that question mark. Or virtual question mark." I mentally smacked my forehead. Why did I say that?

I thought I could feel him rolling his eyes, right through the phone line. Or, rather, through whatever you call the waves going through cell phone towers.

"As I said, this is Detective Sherman?" he question-marked back to me. Was he messing with me?

"As you know, it was my accordion that, um, perpetrated the accident with Judith," I said.

"Accident?" Another question mark.

"The death of Judith. I guess it couldn't have been an accident."

"It's not every day an accordion falls off a balcony onto someone's head," he said.

"No," I plunged on. "The reason I'm calling is that my accordion was an expensive one, and I had it insured. My insurance agent needs to see the damage, or pictures of it . . . and it really is tragic about Judith," I added, thinking I might sound crass to be talking about money.

"Let me see what I can do," he said. "I'll get back to you."

"Let me give you my number."

"I've got it. Cell phone display, you know . . . plus the information I took last night."

"Oh, I forgot."

"Are there other things you've forgotten?" Another question mark, and this one definitely didn't have a smile behind it.

"No. At least I don't think so."

"Okay. Goodbye?"

He was definitely messing with me.

CHAPTER 5

THE NEXT DAY, I pulled up the digital version of the *Juniper Reporter* on my phone before I even got out of bed. The headline read: "Local director killed at Juniper Theater."

The story went on: "Police say a large object was pushed from the balcony of the Juniper Theater onto Judith Pence, who was seated below. Foul play is suspected." The accordion was not mentioned. I figured it would be another day before that 'large object' was made public. Word of mouth would make it common knowledge sooner, but I was relieved it wasn't broadcast to the world yet.

The rest of the day, almost everything reminded me of the murder.

The kids sat "crisscross applesauce" on the rainbow rug while we went through our regular morning routine. We sang the days of the week song and said good morning to Ferdinand, our fish, as I dropped a pellet into his bowl.

Suddenly we heard a commotion at the door. Amelia, the teacher next door, hurried in, followed by all her kindergartners. "Miss Polansky, may we visit today?" she asked sweetly.

Uh-oh. That was our code for "Something bad has

happened and we need to get out of the room. Now." I sighed. I didn't need another something bad.

But I pulled myself together. "Of course," I said. "Please come join us on the rainbow rug. I was just about to read a story."

I hadn't been, but plans had to change. I gave Amelia a questioning look as the kids crammed into the small space on the rug. She pointed to a gray-faced Olivia out in the hall before hurrying off with her toward the nurse's office.

"Who puked?" asked Nathan, and all the kids started talking at once, making gagging sounds, with Amelia's kids giving colorful descriptions of what had just happened. Those colorful descriptions reminded me of Feleesha and my pink hooded sweatshirt and what I had done with it.

But again, I pulled myself together. "If you can hear me, touch your nose," I said, and the kids quieted down, hands on noses. "I want to see good listeners while I read a story." I reached into the bin next to me and grabbed the first book I saw—*Dragons Love Tacos*. I knew that 47 five-year-olds squeezed together on the rainbow rug wouldn't remain calm for long, so I read fast. Luckily the book was short, and by the time I finished, Amelia had returned.

"Guess what!" she announced. "We get to go to the gym to play!"

"Is it because Olivia puked?" Nathan asked helpfully.

"Eww!" The children erupted again—luckily, not literally. We quieted them down and lined them up at the door. Then we all sang, "My hands are hanging by my side. I'm standing nice and tall. My eyes are looking straight ahead. I'm ready for the hall! Catch a bubble!" The kids caught imaginary bubbles in their mouths and held them there while we trooped quietly to the gym.

Amelia filled me in as the kids played. "We had a major explosion all over the giraffe rug. Copious amounts. Amazingly copious, and with leaking diarrhea as an added bonus. I sure hope it's something she ate and not catching."

We knew the custodian would use vomit absorbent quickly, and a follow-up steam clean would leave things wet for a while, but clean.

"Nathan!" I called. He had punched Stewart in the arm, hard. "Over here, now. Both of you . . . Are you okay, Stewart?"

He sniffed and nodded bravely. I sat Nathan down at the wall. "We do not punch people! Two minutes." I didn't ask him to tell Stewart he was sorry because I knew he wasn't.

Our principal, Seraphina Conway, walked in. "Why is Nathan in time-out?" she asked me.

"He punched Stewart."

"I'm sure it was an accident."

"It wasn't." She shook her head, looking unconvinced, and I marveled at her inability to recognize the truth about her son—that he was well on his way to becoming a bully. She switched subjects.

"Mr. Young is out today," she sighed, "and we've got a new guy working. He went in there, took one look, and *he* threw up."

"On the giraffe rug?" asked Amelia.

"I don't know where." She shot Amelia an annoyed look. "So Melissa grabbed some rubber gloves and will have a go at it. Such a trouper!" As our part-time nurse, Melissa is known to be good with bodily fluids. "She's starting with the Smelleze. Evelyn volunteered to try to figure out how to run the steam cleaner."

She may have remembered Evelyn's difficulties with the copy machine and the intercom system. She added, "It may be awhile."

I wondered who would be cleaning up the mess in the theater. Are there police crews assigned to clean-up? Would it be the responsibility of the theater? Who would actually do it? Who would pay for it? Would funds have to come out of the theater budget for cleaning up the vomit and blood?

I pushed away such thoughts and tried to think kind thoughts about the poor woman who had died. But then Seraphina said, "The kids are getting a little wild. Rein them in!" She turned to go.

Her bossy voice sounded way too much like Judith's, and I cringed.

Then Nathan stuck a foot out and tripped Levi.

Of course his mother was already gone.

The day did not improve. At noon I found a voice message on my phone from Detective Sherman. He asked me to stop in after work to answer more questions. I was not looking forward to that.

Okay, maybe I was, just a little.

Then I saw an angry email from Garret's mom, who had evidently emailed me around 9:30 with a "concern" about someone pushing her child and now was concerned that I wasn't taking her concern seriously because she hadn't heard back from me. I sighed. Did she not understand that I was *teaching*, not answering email during the day? Or rather, in this case, dealing with puke and diarrhea?

I quickly emailed her to set up a time to talk and then tried to mark some papers in the two minutes before the kids came back. I couldn't concentrate, though, and found myself thinking more about pushing. I was pretty sure who was probably responsible for the pushing Garret's mom wanted to talk about. But what about another kind of pushing—like pushing my beautiful Tillie off a balcony? Who would do such a thing?

Maybe it was someone like Nathan, all grown up.

On the way to the police station, I stopped at Walgreens to pick up some dental floss. As I got out of the car, I saw Aiden coming out of the office building across the street. I waved and called, "Hi, Aiden." He stopped and looked at me. Then he got on his bike and rode away quickly.

"Holy moly. Am I poison now?" I wondered. Sure, I had been a little bit short with him a couple of times as I tried to teach him "Love Makes the World Go Round," but on the whole, I thought my level of patience with him had been admirable. I shook my head, disappointed that he must not have felt the same.

Inside, I grabbed some dental floss and then spent way too long looking at eye shadow. I finally selected a lavender shade that promised to bring out the gold in my light brown eyes. That didn't make sense to me, but I thought I'd give it a try.

CHAPTER 6

At the police station I met with Detective Sherman and the same pretty officer who had been at the murder scene. She introduced herself as Detective Mildred Kendrick.

Mildred? She looked too young to have one of those old-fashioned names that parents are naming their kids nowadays. Maybe it was a family name. I tried to imagine the detective's parents looking down at their cute little baby and saying, "Here's your binky, Mildred!" I couldn't. I gave silent thanks that my own parents hadn't decided to name me after my great-grandmother Ethel Maude.

Detective Kendrick interrupted my thoughts, telling me that the interview would be recorded. She started the recorder.

She must have drawn the role of Bad Cop, and she played it well. I cleverly deduced that she and Detective Sherman thought the murder must have occurred after rehearsal Sunday night, since she asked, "Where were you after rehearsal on Sunday night?"

I thought back. "I met my best friend Sammie for a glass of wine at Whitney's and then went home. You can ask Eric. He's the bartender."

"He went home with you?"

"No, but he can tell you where I was until about 12:30.

When I saw the time, I freaked out a little. I had to teach the next day, so I said a quick goodbye and drove home."

"You drove after drinking?" Detective Kendrick looked stern.

"It was *one* glass, and I nursed it for an hour and a half—with food," I added. "Popcorn." There hadn't been popcorn.

"Was Eric with you?"

"He's the bartender, as I said." I realized I might have sounded a bit testy.

"Was he with you in the *car*?" She definitely sounded a bit testy.

"No. Why would he be with me in the car?" I was puzzled.

"In other words, you have no real alibi. You might have *said* you were driving home but actually sneaked back into the auditorium."

"For what? Oh. No! I didn't have anything to do with Judith's death."

"It was your accordion, wasn't it?"

"Yes, but I didn't do it." I looked her in the eye. I remembered something about liars always looking up and to the right, so I tried not to let my eyes move that direction.

"You admitted that . . ." She looked at her notes. ". . . that you 'couldn't stand her.' Correct?"

"Yes, but it was a 'can't stand' in the same sense that I can't stand runny poached eggs. I don't like them and avoid even looking at them. The runny yolk makes me sick to my stomach."

I saw Detective Sherman put his hand over his mouth and cough. Was that a hint of a smile? I looked closely.

He looked up and said, "Miss Polansky, how do you think your accordion got up to the balcony?"

"Someone obviously took it there, but it wasn't me. I would never push Tillie off of anything. I loved Tillie."

Detective Kendrick abandoned her professional demeanor for just a second. "Who the . . . Excuse me, Miss Polansky, but who is Tillie?"

"My accordion. I name things that are really important to me. My accordion is Tillie. My car is Penelope. And the really nice bag my friend Sammie gave me is Galoochi—a mash-up of 'Gal' and 'Gucci.'"

"You have a Gucci purse?" Detective Kendrick's eyes opened wide. Clearly, she knew how much they go for.

"Yes. My best friend Sammie's mom got a deal on three of them one time at a sale in New York City. Sammie's mom is the Pickle Queen."

"Pickle Queen?"

"Geraldine Betz." I explained how Geraldine had inherited all the wealth her grandfather made from his pickle factory just east of Juniper. At one point Betz Pickles (Betz are the best!) were quite the rage not only in Colorado but throughout the West, and her grandfather made a killing. After Geraldine inherited the family fortune, she became known in town as the "Pickle Queen," not only because of her heritage, but also because she knows what she wants and doesn't give in. Those who stand in her way usually give up out of sheer exhaustion.

"So anyway," I continued, "The Pickle Queen gave Sammie one purse for herself and another to give to me for Christmas." I held up my Baggallini. "Not this one. I save Galoochi for special."

"What color is it?" Detective Kendrick couldn't help herself.

"I think we can move past the purses now," Detective Sherman interjected.

Detective Kendrick hurried on. "I see here in our paperwork that you would like pictures of your damaged accordion for insurance purposes."

"Yes. When can I get those?" I hoped I didn't sound too impatient, but I really wanted to get the ball rolling on insurance.

She ignored me. "How much is that accordion worth?"

"I paid almost $10,000 for it. It was used and refurbished, or it would have been even more."

"You paid $10,000 for an accordion on a teacher's salary?" Both detectives stared at me.

"I saved for years," I explained. "You should see the ancient Camry I drive—the one I call Penelope. She has over 200,000 miles and a mashed rear end where a guy ran into me at a car wash. Also a dented fender where that deer came out of the ditch and hit me that time. I took the money instead of fixing it, so that helped. Well, it helped me but it didn't do the deer any good, I guess. Or the car."

Detective Kendrick had stopped taking notes while I explained. She focused again. "So this insurance money is pretty important to you?" she asked.

"Of course. Wouldn't it be important to you?"

She didn't answer. "Do you have outstanding debts?"

I shrugged. "Who doesn't?"

"Like . . . ?" This was a *lot* of talking in questions.

I sighed. "Okay, I owe about $900 on my Southwest credit card. I splurged on a shopping trip this summer. I had a wedding to go to, and then I realized my winter coat wasn't going to make it another season. A teacher really needs a warm coat at recess for playground duty. And then I saw some boots I liked. Red ones." I knew I was talking too much again.

"We don't need a shopping list," she interrupted. "How about other debts? Like a mortgage?"

"No, I rent a duplex. I can't afford a house."

Detective Kendrick closed her notebook. She looked stern. "Is there anything else you'd like to tell us, Ms Polansky?"

I took a breath and decided to come clean. "I lied. There was no popcorn."

She looked confused for a moment. "Noted. Anything else?"

I shook my head.

Detective Kendrick folded her hands on top of her notebook. "I think we're done here. You may go, Ms. Polansky."

"What about pictures of my accordion?"

"I'm afraid we can't release them to you until you are ruled out as a suspect."

I gulped. Could they really be considering me as a suspect?

"We would need a request from your lawyer in the discovery process," she added.

"I don't have a lawyer."

"You may want to consider getting one." She gave me a noncommittal look.

Detective Sherman looked down at his paperwork.

I sat stunned.

She said again, "You are dismissed." She stood up, as if to remind me what I was supposed to do.

"I would never kill anyone," I said. "I don't even kill spiders, and I *hate* spiders!"

"And runny eggs," said Detective Sherman, smiling just a tad.

"You may go," said Bad Cop, a little more forcefully.

I went.

CHAPTER 7

My day finally improved in the evening. *Carnival* musicians don't meet on Wednesdays because Becky, the band director, has Bible class then. I'm not sure how she managed to get Judith to agree to such a schedule, but she had, and I was glad. That allowed me time to rehearse with the Streusels at Otto's house.

Otto's wife Moriko always insists that I come to dinner before we meet in the basement to practice. "You should not be eating alone!" she has decreed, at least not on rehearsal nights. She is a great cook, so I don't argue. Her mother, who grew up in Japan, tried to teach her daughter Japanese cooking, but Moriko wanted no part of it. "Too much chopping," she told me. She has, however, learned to make all of Otto's favorite German foods, and he swears she makes them better even than his mother, "God rest her soul."

The two of them married in their fifties after their spouses died. Otto says they met when Moriko drove into his car in a Safeway parking lot. Moriko says they met looking over vegetables at Whole Foods. I tend to doubt Moriko's version only because Otto isn't a huge fan of vegetables.

On this Wednesday, Moriko had invited everyone to come early for dessert, a very American apple pie. I think she knew everyone would want time to talk about the murder before settling down to rehearse.

Moriko cut the pie, and I scooped ice cream on top of each slice. While waiting for their plates, the men all expressed appropriate horror at Tillie's demise. They knew how special she was to me.

"Who could have used Tillie in such a terrible way?" wondered Moriko as she passed out the plates.

"I don't know," I said, "but it's not my job to find out."

"But aren't you a suspect?" Allan always gets right to the point. He's our drummer.

"Maybe. I don't want to think about it, though."

"Maybe Celeste figured out the perfect way to move from understudy to star," said Henry, who plays clarinet. Celeste is the granddaughter of Henry's handball partner, and Henry doesn't like her a bit. He thinks she is not respectful enough to her grandfather. "She's on my shit list," he had told us before. When you get on Henry's shit list, there is no going back. "She sure wouldn't have any trouble lugging Tillie to the balcony," he pointed out. "She lifts weights three times a week."

"Wanting to take over as lead would certainly give her a motive," said Carl, the bass player. He asked for more ice cream on his pie, and Moriko, for once, didn't glance pointedly at his growing pot belly.

"What about the drummer?" offered Moriko, scooping more vanilla on Carl's remaining bit of pie. "What's his name?

"Stanley."

"Right—Stanley. You've always said he is weird. Maybe he crossed over from weird to murderous."

"Maybe." I was getting caught up in the speculation, despite myself. "But why? Why Judith? Why use an accordion?"

"Maybe he's really mad you dumped him and wanted revenge," she said. "He used your accordion so you would be blamed."

I rolled my eyes. "I did not dump him. Two dates do not make a relationship."

"I never thought he was right for you," she said firmly.

"You didn't even *know* him." I couldn't believe I was defending Stanley.

"He was wrong for you," Moriko insisted. "You can tell a man by his shoes."

I looked at her suspiciously. Had I told her about Stanley's shoes? I must have. She's a good listener, and I often talk too much when I help her with the dishes.

I smiled, though, to see five men suddenly looking down at their feet—all in well-padded sneakers. Moriko patted Otto's shoulder and nodded to the others. "See—sensible men, all of you."

"What about the light or sound guys?" Leroy, the saxophonist, asked. He was scraping every flaky bit of crust off his plate with his fork. He started to use his finger but caught Moriko's look and stopped himself.

"Another piece, LeRoy?" Moriko asked. He nodded. Leroy is skinny, and she is always trying to fatten him up. Luckily, she had made two pies.

"It's sound guy and light *gal,*" I corrected him. "They do have keys, and that would certainly explain how they got in. But if it was one of them, they missed their calling and should have been on stage, not backstage. They acted genuinely shocked and upset when they found the body."

"Isn't that the way murderers usually act?" Carl asked.

"Good point. But Caleb also threw up after he saw the body. It would be hard to fake that."

"So who else could have done it?" Allan asked. He doesn't like people to stray too much off the topic.

"It could be anyone. There are probably close to 75 people involved in the show—actors, musicians, stagehands, dancers. I don't even know some of their names."

"Start a list," he said.

"Not my job," I said. "I'm sure the police will figure it out."

"Don't be so sure," he warned. "The police have a lot on their plate, and they might even jump to the wrong conclusion—like that *you* did it."

"Listen, I've had a very bad day. Can't we go downstairs now and play some music?"

Nobody said anything. They clearly wanted to talk some more, but Otto took pity on me. "Okay, we'll play," he said.

"Good." I started collecting plates. Otto went to the printer in the corner of the kitchen and picked up some copies of sheet music. "This is going to cheer you up," he said as he passed out the music. "It's a new song I wrote—the 'Bellella Polka.'" He smiled. "We have to do everything we can to keep you interested in hanging out with us old farts. I thought we'd appeal to your vanity with a song about you."

"What vanity?" I said innocently. I sat down and read the lyrics:

Sweet and kind and caring,
Reserved and rather shy.
Sweet as apple cider
But doesn't have a guy.

By day you might not notice her,
But when the sun goes down,
Then she plays a polka,
And Bellella goes to town!

Bellella. Bellella. My oh, my oh, my.
Bellella. Bellella. Watch her fingers fly!
Bellella. Bellella. No one stands a chance.
Bellella. Bellella. Makes everybody want to dance!

I looked up and smiled at him. "Nice. There are some factual errors here, though. For one thing, I'm not shy."

"I know. I took liberties for the sake of my art. *Easy on the eye* would have rhymed, but that wouldn't have been factual either." He winked.

"Be nice!" Moriko said. She looked at me. "You know you're beautiful, inside and out."

"I'd actually call her cute as a button," said Carl. He knows I hate that.

"And let's just hope there's not a murderer hidden behind all that cuteness or beauty or whatever," added Otto.

Moriko snapped him with a dish towel. "Enough," she

said. "Go on downstairs and get busy. I want to hear the 'Bellella Polka' while I'm cleaning up, so get started."

We went to the basement and took our places with our instruments. Otto had written just a lead sheet, so the first time through I played only chords, and others stuck to the basics while Otto sang. The next time through, we started improvising. We have an "anything goes" rule for the first three or four times we play a new song, letting what feels right eventually emerge. Otto threw in some trumpet when he wasn't singing, and I experimented with a lot of what I call "the diddlies," ornamenting the music with trills and runs and arpeggios. Henry pretty much stuck to melody on the clarinet and Carl and Allan were steady and dependable on the bass and drums. Leroy, though, just sat and listened for three run-throughs. Then, on the fourth, he let loose with one of his signature saxophone solos, and we could hear Moriko applauding from upstairs.

Next we reviewed some of our standards, starting with the "Pennsylvania Polka" and the "Liechtenstein Polka." Then it was my turn to sing. Always, always, no matter where we perform, someone shouts out, "Play the 'Beer Barrel Polka' and/or "Play 'Lady of Spain.'" The truth is, I hate playing both numbers. The request is always my cue to step to the microphone and sing. I begin slowly:

> *I've got a little problem.*
> *It's time that I confessed.*
> *Whenever I take the accordion out,*
> *people have a request.*
> *It never, ever varies.*

It's always the same.
It's "Play the 'Beer Barrel Polka' and
"Play 'Lady of Spain.'"

Then the guys start playing in polka time as I sing with them:

Well, I am tired of the "Beer Barrel Polka.
And I am tired of "Lady of Spain."
Tired of playing the same old thing
whenever I entertain.
Well, I am tired of the "Beer Barrel Polka."
I don't like to complain.
But I am sick of playing the "Beer Barrel Polka"
and I'm sick of playing "Lady of Spain!"

Then we all launch into a lively, foot-stomping instrumental chorus with a bit of an angry sound—but only a bit. It's hard to make a polka sound angry. Finally, in our spectacular finish, Allan stops playing the drums, and I stop playing the accordion as the others continue. I lean into the microphone and begin beat boxing in polka time, providing the percussion while Allan holds his drumsticks frozen in the air. The audience always loves it.

But they still make me play the "Beer Barrel Polka" afterwards.

CHAPTER 8

THURSDAY MORNING, I pulled up the *Juniper Times* on my phone. There I was, pictured with the headline "Local teacher's accordion is murder weapon." Of course they hadn't used this year's staff photo, the flattering one. They had dug up the previous year's photo, taken when I'd had a terrible cold. I'd been miserable but had come to work anyway because I didn't have the energy to make up lesson plans for a substitute teacher, and the craziness of school picture day is nothing I wanted to foist on a substitute anyway. My nose was red and my smile was forced, and I looked, I had to admit, like someone who *might* have pushed an accordion off a balcony and killed someone.

And then I read on. An unnamed source described an "altercation" between the victim and me the evening of the murder.

The discussion with Judith about Aiden and "Love Makes the World Go Round"—that was the "altercation?" Who would have told a reporter such a thing? I was furious.

I fumed as I let the water run over me in the shower, carefully standing so that my hair didn't get wet. It was not hair washing day, and I didn't want to have to straighten my hair again. I knew a shower cap might make it easier, but I didn't have a shower cap and had never once remembered to buy one at Target—if they even sell such a thing.

By the time I had dried off, I was calmer. I chose my clothes carefully and took a little extra care with my make-up. I wanted to look good in case any photographers happened to show up at school wanting another picture.

When I walked into the office to get mail out of my cubby, Evelyn busied herself at the copy machine, even though she wasn't copying anything and the machine didn't appear to have a paper jam. (When there's a paper jam, she mutters and slams things a lot.) Maybe she hadn't heard my "Good morning."

Two teachers huddled in the hallway. They gave a quick nod as I approached, then disappeared into their respective classrooms.

Instead of popping in to tell me the latest cute thing her one-year-old had done, the speech therapist gave a little wave as she passed my room. She avoided my eyes.

That was how the morning went. People looked away. They spoke but didn't linger to talk. They suddenly remembered somewhere else they needed to be whenever I came near.

At recess, Amelia stayed by my side, though the other teacher on duty suddenly felt that she really needed to monitor the activity at the slide more carefully.

"It's like I have a giant 'M' on my chest. Nobody wants me to infect them," I said.

"I'm talking to you," Amelia pointed out. "Great photo in the paper, by the way."

I gave her a dirty look. "Don't people understand that it was my accordion, not me?"

"People love scandal. It will be okay once they figure out who really did it. Just hang in there."

I hung. It was a little easier since three kids were absent that day, including, surprisingly, Nathan.

When I checked my email at noon, I saw an update from Tess, our new director. The show would go on, but the opening would be delayed a week and then continue a second week, as originally planned. Canceling the show would have ruined the Spotlight Players. I knew how much had already been spent on costuming, deposits, posters, and music and script rental. We desperately needed the income from ticket sales to offset the expenditures, so board members had agreed over the phone that canceling the show was not an option. Rehearsals would begin again on Friday, and to help make up for the missed rehearsals after the murder, Tess was adding a Saturday afternoon rehearsal and lengthening Sunday's by an hour and a half.

"There goes my weekend," I thought.

I still needed to catch up with Mom, so I texted her and told her I would be over after school. And then I slunk back to my classroom, feeling as though everyone in school hated me.

Except for Amelia.

And the kids. Luckily, they still loved me.

"Altercation?" I complained to Mom. "Judith told me to do something stupid, and I just walked away. *That's* an altercation?"

"Of course not, honey." She poured me a cup of French

roast she had made in her new single cup Keurig and started a cup of decaf for herself. I had told her not to buy that machine because all those little plastic coffee containers are a blight on the environment, and she had agreed but bought the machine anyway. "Now that Daddy's no longer with us, I only need one cup most of the time. And it makes *such* good coffee." So much for the environment, but I had to agree that the coffee *was* good.

"It was Stan. I know it. Those shoes were an indication of his rotten heart," I said.

"What shoes?" She looked blank.

"It doesn't matter. He just doesn't like me ever since I 'broke up' with him. Two dates do not make a relationship. I know he must have done it."

"Really?" She seemed surprised. "What did Stan have against Judith?"

"I don't mean that he *did* did it. I mean that he's the one who told the police about our 'altercation.'"

"So who do you think *did* do it?"

"I have no idea."

"I think you'd better figure it out." She put three short-bread cookies on a napkin for me as an after school snack, just as she'd done when I was a kid.

"That's the police's job . . . Police's? That sounds funny. Maybe I should say 'the job of the police.' . . . .No, that sounds kind of formal . . . 'The detectives, I believe, are the ones to solve this case.' . . . Or 'The job of solving belongs . . .'"

"You're getting hung up, Bellella." That's what my family calls my little obsessive digressions involving words and grammar—"getting hung up." I admit that I do have a thing about language, largely because of Sister Dalmatia. My mother sent us all to Holy Name, a Catholic school in town that draws students from several cities and towns near us. (It's not because all the parents are staunch Catholics. I think they just want to be able to say their kids go to a private school.) Sister Dalmatia was the only nun on the staff, and I had her for three years—sixth, seventh, and eighth grade English.

She was tough. We had to memorize the nominative, possessive, and objective forms of pronouns and use them correctly, and we were pretty much forbidden to use passive voice in our writing, not because it's always wrong but because she wanted us to learn to use active verbs. She gave any paper with a grammatical or punctuation error back to us for correction, and she forbade the use of "like" as a filler in our speech. If a guy in class said, "I, like, talked to my mom and…," he wouldn't get far. "You *like* talked to your mom or you talked to your mom?" she would ask.

She drove most kids crazy, but I really took to her direct and precise approach to language—maybe too much so, some have suggested.

I took a moment to pick my words carefully, but Mom didn't wait. "It's your obsessive-compulsive disorder," she said, not for the first time. "Just speak. You don't have to be perfect."

"I am not OCD," I said, not for the first time either. She hadn't mentioned OCD in a long time, though, so I felt compelled to add, "Remember—everyone has quirks."

She waited.

"Alexander?" I reminded her. She knew I was referring

to my oldest brother's aversion to peanut butter breath. He refuses to sit anywhere near anyone eating peanut butter. With two young boys, that's not always easy.

Mom waited some more. She knew I wasn't finished. Mom is a very patient woman.

"Christopher? Sevens?" I continued. My other brother eats small items in sets of seven. Seven M&Ms. Seven potato chips. Seven crackers. Since he lives alone and pretty much does nothing but write computer code all day and play video games most of the night, I don't imagine this habit is much of a problem now. When we were kids, it was. My brother Alexander once ate the last black jelly bean in our Easter basket, and it turns out Christopher had just eaten six black ones and was going in for the seventh. Alexander had hell to pay. My father actually had to step in, break up the fight, and confiscate the rest of the jelly beans, which I didn't think was fair at all.

Finally, I added one more. "Feet? Elevators?" Mom can't stand to have her feet touched, and she won't ride in elevators unless there is absolutely no other option. Even when forced to ride, she will stand by the doors, rigid and breathing heavily, until she can burst out the second the doors open.

"Finished?" She said. I nodded. "Is your point that the whole family is nuts?" Mom asked.

"No. My point is that everyone has things about them that others might view as not normal." I bit into a cookie and brushed crumbs off my chin. "I'm not nuts."

"Of course you aren't. And I know you aren't a murderer. That's why you have to figure out who did it."

"As I said, That's the police's . . . that's the job of . . . the police should . . ."

"Forget the police. Who has more of a stake in this, them or you? I'm sure their intentions are very good, but their goal is to get 'solving a murder' off their to-do list."

I polished off my second cookie. "I don't think it's appropriate to put solving a murder on a to-do list . . . Grab a carton of milk. Pick up Sienna at ballet. Solve a murder . . ."

She ignored me. "For you, solving a murder means saving your precious name and reputation, unless of course you actually did do it, in which case solving it would actually hurt you."

"I didn't do it!"

"I know, I know. I was just clarifying my statement for the sake of accuracy." I gave her a look. Baba's observation that we are more alike than we think may have some validity. I decided to move on.

"So how am I supposed to solve it? I'm a teacher. I teach all day. I don't have any murder solving tools at my disposal." I ate my third cookie and picked up the square of paper towel and scrunched it into a ball. Idly, I began playing with it.

"The murderer has to be someone involved in the show," Mom said as she took the paper towel ball from me and put it in the wastebasket under the sink. "How could anyone else have gotten in? Or known about the accordion? Or known that Judith always sat in the same place under the balcony each night to review her notes?"

"How do *you* know that?" I asked, surprised.

"You were complaining about Judith one night after rehearsal. I think it was the night you came over for Baba's birthday. You talked about how ridiculously rigid she was. . . . Hmmm, maybe Judith is a little OCD, too. I mean *was a little OCD.*"

"Mom, stop with the arm chair diagnosis . . . diagnoses? . . . Diagnosis-es?"

"You're getting hung up again."

"Calling everyone OCD minimizes OCD, which is a real disorder."

She ignored me again. "So someone had to find a way to stay in the theater after it was locked. If they left, they couldn't have come back in the locked door."

"Right. They had to already *be* there, along with Judith. But not to Judith's knowledge." I was getting interested, despite myself.

"Or else they came in with her—but surely Judith would have noticed. And she definitely would have noticed someone dragging your accordion out of the pit and lugging it to the balcony."

I sipped my coffee, thinking a moment. "Somehow, during the day or the previous night, someone had to have hauled my accordion up to the balcony and left it right below the ledge so that they could go back up there and pick it up while Judith was working and then tip it over on her while she was writing."

"So who could have done that?"

I grimaced. "In the right circumstances, just about anyone in the show. Except maybe one of the puppeteers, Cecil. He has a bad back."

"So you need to look at motive. Who might have had a reason to kill Judith? Make a list of everyone and their possible motives."

My interest evaporated again. "It's not my job, Mom. Really, it's not my job."

"Ella, making a list will not involve phone calls or favors or asking anyone for anything. It's just a list."

But I am not an asker.

If I made a list, I would want to follow up, and I would need to ask people for things—information, ideas, advice, observations, whatever. I hate asking people for things. What if they say no and I feel bad? Or mad? Or rejected? Or at their mercy? I much prefer that people read my mind and just give me what I want.

Of course, that doesn't usually happen. But asking directly for what I want or need is sometimes more difficult for me than just doing without. Mom knows me entirely too well.

I got up and put my cup in the dishwasher. "I'll think about it," I told Mom.

But I knew I probably wouldn't.

CHAPTER 9

I picked up a pizza and a bottle of wine and went to Second Chance. I had promised to help Sammie steam, hang, and tag a huge stack of clothing someone had brought in.

Sammie's idea to open an upscale consignment clothing store hadn't exactly been met with enthusiasm by her parents or her stepdad. "Who makes any money selling used clothes?" the Pickle Queen had asked. But Sammie had a plan, one that she had been putting together for years.

After three semesters of college, successful only in the sense that she'd had a lot of fun, she had flunked out and supported herself for a while with waitress jobs at high-end establishments in Denver, always careful to save a good portion of her earnings. Then she got a job as a secretary at an insurance company and eventually worked her way up to an assistant to the vice president, arranging for corporate meetings, plane tickets, etc. She had to dress well, so she haunted consignment stores for good buys, saving money and developing a real sense of style on a low budget.

Last year, she unexpectedly quit her job, and no one was more surprised than her mother to find out that Sammie was moving into one of the properties the Pickle Queen owned in downtown Juniper. Through her mother's management company, Sammie had leased a small storefront, the apartment above it, and the very large space next door that had previously housed an oddly successful old-school hardware store. (It had gone belly-up after 40 years when the founder's son took over and sent profits up his nose.) Someday that large space was going to be Sammie's dance studio. With a lifetime of dance lessons in her background, she was ready to start teaching ballet, tap, hip-hop, ballroom, and swing. In the meantime, she hoped the consignment store could be her bread and butter while she had the other space renovated, a bit at a time, to meet her needs.

Geraldine was impressed by how Sammie had done everything on her own, not asking for any special favors, so she decided to give her a special favor. She reduced the rent on the potential dance studio to almost nothing until it was completed.

When I arrived, Sammie pulled down the shades and locked the door. She got out plates from the cabinet in back, and I grabbed the wine opener I knew she kept in the drawer by the sink. We sat down at the storeroom work table.

I hesitated, then said, "Are you still a non-drinker?" I looked at her, hoping that her condition had changed—or rather, never really been there in the first place.

"No change, except that I took a pregnancy test."

I held my breath. "And?"

"And it's real."

"Oh my god." I put the wine opener back in the drawer.

We both looked down at the pizza, at a loss for words. Then Sammie grabbed a slice. "I'm eating for two. You can drink for two."

I opened the wine. "What are you going to…"

She interrupted me. "I don't want to talk about it." She

was using her "Don't argue with me voice," so I knew better than to continue. I took a slice of pizza.

We ate quickly and got to work. I steamed while Sammie put on price tags and hung things in the appropriate areas of the store. Out of respect for her condition, I nursed my one glass of wine all evening.

When we were almost finished, I couldn't help myself. "Any ideas for baby names? I mean, if you keep the baby?"

Choosing a name is such an important task, and I'm always shocked by how casually some parents approach it, often with disastrous results. Witness some of the unfortunate names in my classroom over the years: Stuart (for a girl, named after her father), Winchester (for a boy, named after a gun), and Dickles (for a girl, named after Grandpa with an added little feminine flourish at the end.)

I thought for a moment that I had stepped over a line and she wasn't going to answer. Then she said, "I was thinking 'Nathan' for a boy."

I gave her a horrified look.

"Kidding! 'Benjamin' is at the top of the list right now. I've never met a Benjamin I didn't like."

"Benjamin Feldspar was a nightmare. I had him three years ago in class. A holy terror."

"I didn't know Benjamin Feldspar."

"What about 'David'? I haven't had any difficult Davids."

"I dated a difficult David once. Remember the Doofus?"

"Oh yeah. I forgot he had a real name." I finished steaming the wrinkles out of a prom dress and handed it to her. "What about girls' names?"

"'Katie' is one I like."

"That's a cat's name."

"Just because you had Katie Kitty once does not make it a cat's name."

"Okay, okay. Katie is cute. But she couldn't be president with a cute name. She needs something with more, you know, *gravitas*."

"I'll think about it," she said as she hung the last item in the "large" section.

All the talk of names had made the pregnancy seem more real. Was Sammie really thinking of keeping the baby? If she was thinking of names, I suspected she was.

We cleaned up, and I grabbed my jacket and purse. Sammie unlocked the front door and let me out, then watched as I walked down the block to my car. I thought I heard something and felt unaccountably nervous, as though someone other than Sammie was watching me. I walked a bit faster, got in the car, locked it, and drove home.

As soon as I opened the front door and picked up Fluffles, my cell phone started playing "You've Got a Friend in Me."

I answered. "Did I forget something?" I asked.

"Just wanted to make sure you made it home okay," said Sammie. "I saw a guy lurking behind that statue in front of the theater. He was watching you."

"Weird. I thought something felt off. Probably just a homeless guy."

"Be careful."

"You're the one who lives downtown. You be careful, too."

"I've turned on the alarm system. I wish you had one."

CHAPTER 10

WHEN I GOT TO SCHOOL the next morning and went to the office for my mail, Evelyn saw me coming and escaped to the photocopier again, turning her back and fiddling with the paper feed. This was getting old.

Four more kids were absent, bringing the total to seven. That was unusual. "Is there a flu outbreak I don't know about?" I asked Amelia at recess.

"All my kids are here."

As Amelia and I stood on the playground and watched our kids blow off steam, I told her about my interview with the police.

"You definitely need a lawyer," she said when I was finished. "Jeremy! No pushing!"

"How am I going to afford a lawyer?"

Simon ran up to tell me he hurt his finger. I took a look. "Oh, dear. Give it a kiss, and you'll be fine."

He did, and he was.

"Do you even *know* a lawyer? A criminal lawyer?" I couldn't believe I was having this conversation. "Emily! Feet first down the slide!"

"I don't. Maybe my husband does. I'll have him ask around."

"How can I afford to hire a good lawyer on a teacher's

salary?" I thought about my Southwest credit card bill and frowned.

"Maybe you need to ask your mom for help."

Mom works full-time as a nurse and is still paying off hospital expenses from my dad's long illness before he died five years ago. "No, she's already got enough on her plate. I guess I could ask the Pickle Queen for a loan."

"But how would your mom feel if she found out that you went to the Pickle Queen for help before her?"

She had a point.

So did Nathan. Where the heck had he found that branch? He was running, full speed, with the branch aimed right at Salvadore. I ran, grabbed Salvadore, and pulled him aside at the last moment, before he was impaled. Unfortunately, I fell down with him and he hurt his knee. Now I was going to have to explain to his parents why I had tackled their five-year-old. I hope they didn't read the papers and find out I was a suspected murderer.

After lunch, there was a note in my mail box reading, "Please see me first thing." It was on a note-pad with "Seraphina Conway, Principal" printed at the top. I looked over and saw her in her office.

"You wanted to see me?" I said at the door.

"Yes, Ella. Come in. Can you close the door and sit down?"

This did not bode well. I closed and sat.

Seraphina sighed. "I'm afraid I have some bad news for you. I am getting a lot of calls . . . a *lot* . . . about your picture in the paper."

I knew from previous experience that "a lot" to Seraphina could mean "one." She was sensitive to even the slightest criticism about anything at all when it came from parents, and she tended to exaggerate when she talked to staff members.

"What's 'a lot'?" I pushed. "Two? Twenty? Three hundred?"

"I don't remember exactly, but a lot. The Macafees. The Bacas . . . Sylvia Moore's grandparents. Desmond's step-mom. The Crawfords . . ."

"Okay, I get it. A lot." It was unusual for her to name names, so I figured what she was saying had to be true. "But I could hardly help getting my picture in the paper."

"Because you owned a murder weapon—granted, not the usual kind of murder weapon, but still a murder weapon." She held a pen at one end, between two fingers, and let it swing back and forth in the air. I suddenly thought of "The Pit and the Pendulum" and got nervous.

"I owned it, yes. But that doesn't mean I used it."

"Parents don't know that. *I* don't even know that." She put her pen down and sighed. "The parents are saying that you have been a wonderful teacher, and their kids love you, but what if, what if you really *are* a murderer?"

"I'm not."

"The name Ted Bundy came up. Handsome, wholesome guy who turned out to be a serial killer."

"Geez Louise!" In my brain, I said "Jesus!" But this was school, and she was my principal. "Now I'm being compared to a serial killer?" I held my arms out to my sides in an "Are-you-kidding-me?" gesture.

"No, I'm not saying that. But you *might* be a murderer.

It was your accordion. We know you've been questioned by the police."

She picked up the stupid pen again and started swinging it. I wanted to reach over and smack it to the floor—and then rip off the poster on her wall that read, "You're not here to be average. You're here to be AWESOME." "Awesome" is a word that is seriously over-used in schools.

"*Everyone* in the show was questioned by the police," I pointed out.

She hesitated for just a second. "But Evelyn saw you going into the police station for more questioning."

"For all Evelyn knows, I might have been going to drop off evidence I found against someone else." No wonder Evelyn was avoiding me—a guilty conscience.

Seraphina hesitated again. "Okay, her sister-in-law works there. She told her they were questioning you again."

Of course she did. Evelyn loves knowing everything about everybody. "I have not been charged with anything," I said.

"Yet."

I shook my head. "I can't believe this."

Seraphina looked down at the pen still dangling from her fingers. "So . . . because of parental concerns and erring on the side of caution, I am putting you on leave—with pay—until this matter is cleared up."

I stood up and stared at her. "Are you *kidding* me?"

She finally looked up at me. "Sadly, no. I'm not kidding. If you need some things from your room, go on down and get them now, before the kids come back from lunch. Your sub will be here in a few minutes."

"Gee, you're going to trust me to go down there on my

own?" I'm not generally a sarcastic person, but I couldn't help myself.

"Go."

Shaking my head in disbelief, I left. In my classroom, I picked up my water bottle and my coffee cup and started to pick up a pile of papers to be graded. Then I thought, "Screw it. Let the sub do the grading."

Amelia came in as I was putting my purse and tote bag over one shoulder. "Do you have a couple of red file folders I could have?" Amelia color codes everything.

"Nope. And I couldn't give them to you if I did. Seraphina just suspended me."

She just stood there for a moment, apparently processing what I'd just said. "Suspended you? For *what?*"

"For having my picture in the paper, I guess. And owning a murder weapon that I didn't use as a murder weapon." I walked to the door. "I have to go. Now. It seems we can't run the risk of having the kids poisoned by my presence."

"This is ridiculous. Call the teacher's organization rep. See if they can do something."

"Why? Do I really want to be here with everyone treating me like I might be a murderer? And who knows what the kids have already been told? I'm out of here."

"This is wrong. You need to fight this."

"I don't feel like fighting." I walked to the door.

"Wait!" she said. "What if the sub is Mrs. Markham?"

That did give me pause. We despise Mrs. Markham, and so do the kids.

"Nathan will do her good," I said.

I turned back, hugged Amelia, and left.

I managed to hold back tears until I reached my car.

Putting my head on the steering wheel, I sat and cried for a while. Then I sat up and stared at the corner of the building where my room is located. What were my kids going to be told? What did the rest of the staff think? Did all the parents think I was guilty? How was I going to get my job back?

Finally, I pulled myself together, temporarily, and drove home. Fluffles heard me pull in and leapt to the window sill beside the driveway, watching me. I gave her a dispirited wave as I got out of the car, and she jumped down to greet me at the door. I scratched her ears, then went to the kitchen, climbed up on a stool, and pulled a bag of Lindor dark chocolate truffles out of the hard-to-reach kitchen cabinet above the refrigerator. Taking it to the bedroom with me, I threw off my clothes, put on my softest flannel pajamas, climbed into bed, and pulled my new pink tulip comforter up to my chin. Fluffles hopped onto my chest and kneaded for a bit, then nestled into my shoulder, purring in my ear.

"At least *you* still like me," I said and vowed to give her an extra helping of Fancy Feast when I got up. *If* I ever got up.

I ate half a bag of Lindor dark chocolate truffles and watched a Hallmark movie, not because I especially like Hallmark movies but because I knew everything would turn out fine in the end. Then I ordered a pizza with extra anchovies because I love anchovies and what did it matter if no one I know likes anchovies? Nobody would want to share a pizza with me anyway because no one would want to hang out with a murderer, so I might as well eat chocolate and pizza and maybe later some popcorn with extra butter, and if I got fat and died in bed because of high blood pressure or diabetes or whatever, maybe eventually someone would find me and bury me. Or have me cremated. I preferred cremated.

Nobody had to cremate me. At 6:00 I remembered rehearsal was starting again, and I was supposed to be there by 6:30. I flew out of bed and threw on the clothes I'd worn to school. I was backing out of the driveway when I remembered that I needed an accordion. I hurried back for Frankie, the only accordion I had that wasn't stored in my mom's basement.

CHAPTER 11

A SECURITY GUARD stood at the theater door, with a gun. He made me take my accordion case off the luggage wheels, open up the case, and lift the accordion out, looking for contraband. I wondered if he knew that it was an accordion that had been used as the murder weapon.

He looked through my tote bag and my purse, and I wondered if a pat-down was next, but he finally approved me for entry. I noticed that the three people behind me got much more cursory checks.

I rolled my case to the greenroom and saw Helena and her friend dabbing liquid foundation on their perfect skin with little cosmetic sponges. Paula sat at a table next to them in the nook she had turned into her costume work area with a table, a portable sewing machine, and a small rack for hanging items she was finishing or repairing. She was apparently doing something to a leather vest. Suddenly she looked up with a concerned look and said loudly, "Where's my awl?"

Helena paused her dabbing and said, "All your what?"

"Awl!" Paula said. "A-W-L."

"Not how you spell it," Helena said, shaking her head at her friend and rolling her eyes. She turned back to her make-up and started smoothing the foundation over her cheeks.

Paula patted the layers of fabric strewn over the table and

picked up pattern envelopes, looking under them. "An awl—A-W-L—is a *tool*," she said. "Like an ice pick. I need it to pierce holes in this leather."

"Oh." Helena's friend reached under her chair. "Is this it?" She held up the awl. "It must have rolled off."

Paula snatched it.

Helena watched her start piercing the holes. "Is that for Joe to wear in the show? A vest?"

"Yes, if I ever get it done. That funeral last week really set me back."

Helena layered cream eye shadow on her lids. "I don't get it. A funeral is only an hour or so."

Paula finished poking the holes and took out a long string of leather, something like a shoelace, and began lacing up the vest. "It was in Kansas. I had to drive."

I wondered if Helena would need more clarification but decided not to wait to find out. I rolled my accordion case on through to the stage, where the choreographer was helping Feleesha with an eight-bar bit she kept screwing up. Aiden stood at the side, evidently waiting his turn for some remedial dance instruction.

"Hey, Aiden," I said. "Can you give me a hand?"

He nodded, then picked up the case, still strapped to the luggage wheels, and carried it down the stairs to the auditorium, then down the steps into the orchestra pit, placing it in a small area clear of cords. I followed him and stood right behind him, as there was nowhere else to stand in the close quarters. I must have been closer than he thought because when he stood up and turned, we were face to face, our bodies touching as if about to embrace. Aiden let out a kind of yelp and stepped backward, bumping into my accordion case and losing his balance. Flailing his arms, he fell to the floor, bumping Stanley's drum screen and knocking my music stand sideways. Stanley grabbed the drum screen to steady it, and I grabbed the music stand before it fell. Looking at Aiden with alarm, I asked, "Are you okay?" I reached a hand to help him get up, but he ignored it. His face was scarlet. He managed to get up and then fled.

Feleesha and the choreographer were looking down into the pit. They had probably witnessed both the fall and the accidental hug. Poor Aiden.

As I put my polka accordion on the wooden stand, I had to take a moment to admire him. While Tillie had been a much better quality instrument, Frankie was much flashier in the looks department—red with gold speckles. Too bad no one could appreciate him except me, hidden in the pit as I was.

I was surprised to see a card and a tiny bag on the ledge of my music stand. "Hang in there!" said the card. Inside the bag were four Lindor dark chocolates. I looked over at Stan. Had I ever told him I loved Lindor dark chocolates?

Or maybe Becky, the conductor, was trying to be nice. I thought about that a moment. No, if she had given me a card it would have had scripture on it somewhere, and she wasn't really one for sweet gestures anyway. I'd never even seen her hug Aiden.

It must have been our new director, sugary-sweet Tess. I felt guilty about it, but Tess's unrelenting sweetness made me a little sick sometimes. She was just so, so positive. So, so perky. So, so huggy and chirpy and gushy. Even her voice got on my nerves, the pitch going up and back down again in a sing-songy, almost melodic flow. Sometimes I wished she would shout a "Damn" or a "Hell!" just to break up the musical monotony.

Yes, Tess had probably given everyone a little gift of encouragement, not just me. That would be Tess. I looked around on the other music stands.

No. No cards. No gifts.

I considered Stan again. Could he possibly have feelings for me? Puzzled, I put the card and the chocolates into my bag and got ready to rehearse.

Tess wanted to talk to everyone before rehearsal started, so we all moved into the theater auditorium and sat down.

For once, she toned down her perkiness. "I know how sorry we all are about what happened to Judith." Her voice rose in volume and pitch. "So, so sorry." Then it came back down again. "An awful, awful thing. Our thoughts and prayers are, of course, with Judith's family, and all of us here mourn her passing." She bowed her head and crossed her hands over her chest for a moment in a gesture that was sort of, but not quite, prayer-like. Then she looked up again. "So before we go on, let us all honor Judith with a moment of silence."

We did.

Then Tess continued. "This is a sad and serious time for us, but I know Judith would agree that . . . " She assumed her more natural cheerleader persona ". . . the show must go on!" She smiled a little in her enthusiasm, then caught herself. "In our case, it will go on with caution."

She went on to describe safety measures. The security guard would be in the theater with us at all times, so no one should ever be alone, even if the first to arrive. We were to alert him to anything suspicious, anything at all. "And absolutely do not walk to your car alone, unless you've parked immediately behind the theater in the lighted lot. Walk with a companion, and then drive your companion to wherever their car is parked."

"What if our companion turns out to *be* the murderer?" Helena asked.

It was a good point. Tess seemed stumped for a moment, then rallied. "Use the lighted parking lot next to the theater, and you won't need a companion to walk you out," she said.

Helena's friend raised her hand. "There are never enough parking places there."

Gordon whispered to me, "Let's see what she does with this."

Tess took a deep breath and looked thoughtful, as if searching her mind for a win-win solution. "You can always car pool," she said, looking satisfied.

Helena wasn't letting this go. "What if your *car pool* person turns out to be the murderer?"

People were getting restless. Would this go on forever? Tess thought a moment, then acknowledged defeat. "I don't have all the answers. Just use your best judgment about everything, and be careful." She gathered herself and came back with full-strength motivational speaker enthusiasm. "To save the Spotlight Players, we need to save the show! That's what Judith would have wanted!"

Obediently, we applauded. Then I stood up. "May I say something?"

Tess nodded. "Of course."

"I know that a lot of people suspect me because my accordion was the murder weapon. But I would just like to say, for the record, that I did not kill Judith. I would never do such a thing."

To my amazement, it was Stanley who spoke in my defense. "We all know it wasn't you, even if the police and the school district don't." Word was evidently already out about my suspension. "You loved that accordion like a child and would never intentionally harm it."

I'd rather he had spoken to my character, but, hey, I'd take it. Several people actually applauded, and I smiled gratefully. After the meeting I was surprised at the hugs and words of encouragement I received from band members. It really does seem that musicians understand a fellow musician's bond with her instrument.

"Thanks, Stan," I said, back in the pit. He nodded. That was it.

Rehearsal started but did not proceed smoothly. Although Joe had clearly worked on his lyrics since our ill-fated previous rehearsal, Feleesha, unbelievably, was still scrambling the lyrics to "A Very Nice Man," one of the earliest songs in the show.

Tess was gentler on her than Judith would have been. "You can do this, Feleesha. I know you can. Take a moment to look at your music, and we'll try again."

She looked at her music.

She tried again.

She didn't get it.

Feleesha took Joe's arm, as if for protection, and turned sorrowful puppy-dog eyes on Tess. "I think it's the murder. It has affected me *so* much."

"Of course it has, sweetie. I understand. I really do. But you have to keep working. I know you can do this."

Next to me, Gordon mumbled, "Poor baby. She's so traumatized." Then he took the opportunity to empty his spit valve onto the paper towel next to him. He looked over at me and grinned, fiendishly pleased, as always, to gross me out.

"It's not all spit," he had told me helpfully when I made a face the first time I saw him do it. "It's also condensation from hot, moist air leaving me and coming into contact with the cold metal of the instrument. If I don't empty it, the water collects in the tubes and creates a snapping or clicking noise when I play, kind of like a bubble popping."

I was getting used to the spit valve, so I didn't shoot him a look of disgust this time. He looked disappointed.

We had to play the song over and over again until, finally, Feleesha managed to get through it once correctly—for the most part.

"I feel like emptying my spit valve on Feleesha," Gordon muttered as we at last turned the pages of our music to the next song.

"Nasty, nasty." I said, but I completely understood his sentiment.

"I hope you're not a murderer," I said to Gordon as he walked me to my car after rehearsal.

He took my arm. "Come with me, my sweet," he said in a sinister voice. "I have some etchings in my boudoir that you must see." He laughed in a maniacal way.

I grabbed my arm back. "Very funny."

He dropped the impersonation. "At least *my* musical instrument hasn't killed anyone."

"That could change," I warned, eyeing his trombone case.

He changed the subject. "I will never understand what the heck Judith was thinking when she cast Feleesha instead of Celeste as lead."

"Only Judith knows. Knew, I mean." I unlocked the car. "What I heard is that Feleesha actually did well at her audition."

"And Celeste *didn't?*"

"Of course she did. Or I assume she did because Celeste always does well. What I heard—from someone on the theater board—is that Judith thought Feleesha had that lovable, vulnerable quality the role of Lili needs."

Gordon put his trombone case in the backseat and got in. "She may seem vulnerable, but it's only because we all want to kill her."

"There's that."

"And if she did well, it was probably because the audition was short. Who knew she'd be so challenged learning a whole show?"

"Maybe she'll get her act together," I said hopefully as I drove him to his car.

"Of course she will." He changed to a sing-songy voice, doing what I presumed was a Tess impersonation. "Feleesha will transform into the dazzling performer she was always meant to be—one who knows her lines, despite the challenges presented by memorization. When she waltzes out onto stage at almost the right moment, she will mesmerize the audience with her mediocre charms. She will dazzle us with her slightly better than okay voice. She will sort of remember her dance moves. She can do it. I know she can!"

I smiled as I stopped the car to let him out. I just loved Gordon.

CHAPTER 12

WHEN I GOT HOME, I met my neighbor on our shared front porch. Foster, who lives with his wife and two-year-old in their half of our duplex, was just getting home from his second job, this one running a fork lift in a warehouse.

"Sorry about your troubles," he said. "Funny, but you don't look like a murderer."

"You saw the paper, I take it."

"We did," he said. "Maria and I were shocked. We thought you were just our nice neighbor who watches Skyden when we're in a jam sometimes." He walked over and gave me a hug. "We know you didn't do it. Anyone who knows you knows you didn't do it."

"So will you still let me babysit Skyden sometimes?" I adored Skyden.

"Of course."

I felt better. I went inside, where Fluffles was squirming on her back, asking for some serious tummy rubbing. I complied.

As I got ready for bed, Fluffles batted a gift wrap bow around the house. She loves that bow, which will sometimes disappear for days until I realize it's stuck too far under a chair for her to reach. I'll move the chair for her, of course.

As I brushed my teeth, she climbed onto the ledge

around the tub and waited expectantly for me to turn on a dribble of water for her. I did, of course.

I crawled into bed, so tired that I didn't even try to read. Fluffles settled at my feet, and I turned out the light and hoped for sleep. I thought about how nice it was that the band believed in my innocence. How nice that Foster and Maria did, too. How nice that they trusted me with little Skyden.

Skyden. How on earth had they chosen such a name? It was going to lead to a lifetime of confusion for the boy, as no one reading his name would know if he was male or female. But, on the other hand, why would it matter if no one knew if he was male or female? Maybe it could be an advantage. Or maybe, if there was confusion . . .

Fluffles interrupted my thoughts. She climbed on top of me, kneaded my stomach for a while, and then decided to stay there. I was reluctant to move her, though I wasn't comfortable at all. It took me a while to fall asleep.

Fluffles is a little spoiled.

I woke up suddenly, alarmed. I'd heard something, but I didn't know what. I looked at the red numbers on my digital alarm. It was 2:17 a.m.

My usual approach with strange noises is to blame Fluffles, who likes to roam on top of counters, sometimes tipping things over. She especially loves finding a ballpoint pen and knocking it around on the kitchen floor.

I felt a lump at the end of the bed and realized that Fluffles was curled up at my feet. I thought the noise had come from the front of the house, so—heart pounding—I got out of bed, displacing Fluffles, and crept to the front window in the living room. I pulled the drapes aside, just a little. Nothing. I crept to another window and looked out. The side gate to the back yard was open. Not good.

I returned to the bedroom to look out the window there, but I tripped over the footstool I had left in the wrong place. I fell, hitting my forehead on the bed's foot board, hard. I curled up on the floor in agony, trying not to cry out and alert anyone outside as to my whereabouts. When I could eventually move again, I touched my head and felt blood.

I felt around in the dark for my pillow and pulled off the case. Even in my pain and fear, I didn't want to touch my new pink tulip comforter and get blood on it. I held the case to my head but quickly realized the cotton/polyester fabric wasn't very absorbent. I mopped the blood as best I could, then searched in the dark for something else to use. I crawled to the dresser, reached up, and found a stack of clean cotton panties I hadn't put away yet. I held one pair to my head, pressing hard, and put another pair in the waistband of my pajamas as backup. I managed to pull myself up with one hand and then crept to the bedroom window. Pulling aside the edge of one of the drapes, I peeked out.

The moon was bright, and I could see that the gate to the alley was also open, swinging in the breeze. Something was lying on the back patio, next to the kitchen, but I couldn't quite make it out. An animal? I walked quietly to the kitchen and turned on the outside light.

I gasped. There was Ginger, Skyden's cat, stretched out in a grotesque position on the cement. I didn't need to open the door to see that she was dead.

I stared for a few moments, blood dripping down my

face, trying to take it all in. Ginger? Dead? Sweet Ginger? Why?

I knew what I had to do. I didn't want Skyden to wake up and see the family pet dead on the patio in the morning. What would that do to his impressionable young mind? I pressed "Foster" on my iPhone.

He muttered a hello after about eight rings.

I spoke softly. "It's Ella. You need to get up quietly and come over. It's important. Try not to wake Maria."

"What the…"

"Just do it. Please."

I waited at the door and opened it when I heard him come out. He looked at me and all the blood.

"My God. What happened?" He took my arm.

"I fell. But that's not why I called." I tried to think of a nice way to put it, but there was no nice way. "It's Ginger. She's out back." I gulped. "I'm pretty sure she's dead."

"What???!" He dropped my arm.

"She's on the back patio. Something woke me up, so I was looking out all the windows. That's how I saw her."

He walked to the kitchen door, opened it, and walked out, bending down to look closely at her. Then he stood up and seemed to be composing himself. In a moment he looked again, then came back inside. "Damn," he said. "What could have happened?" He noticed the open gates. "Are you sure you didn't leave the side gate open when you took the trash out?"

"I'm sure. You know I'm paranoid now." Last year a dog in the neighborhood had managed to get out of its fenced yard and come through the gate that I had accidentally left open. I later opened the back door to face a growling pit bull—an experience I never want to repeat. Ever.

"I'm calling the police," Foster said, reaching for his phone.

"For a dead cat?"

"For a dead cat and an intruder."

My head was throbbing, so I sat down at the kitchen table. I replaced one pair of panties with the other pair from my waistband.

"Maybe I need to take you to the emergency room," Foster said. "That's a lot of blood."

"No, I'm okay. I'm sure it looks worse than it is."

He used a paper towel to wipe up some of the blood that had dripped on the table.

Then we saw lights from the police car pulling up in the driveway out front, behind my Camry. We got up and went to the window. One of the officers circled the house, shining a flashlight. The other came to the door and rang the bell. I answered.

"You okay, ma'am?" The officer looked over at Foster. "Did this man harm you?"

"No, no. He's my neighbor. I was creeping in the dark to see what it was that woke me up, and I fell. Then I saw Ginger, and I called him."

"The cat," Foster nodded. "Ginger is my cat."

"So I called him. I didn't want Skyden to find her."

"My son. Skyden is my son."

"It's really Skyden's cat, not his," I explained.

The other officer knocked at the screen door and came in. I sighed. It was Detective Sherman.

"You do night duty, as well as homicide?" I asked.

"Sometimes, yes. We don't have a lot of homicides in Juniper."

The other officer frowned. "You two know each other?"

"Miss Polansky is a person of interest in the Juniper Theater murder," Detective Sherman explained.

The other officer looked at me suspiciously, as though anything I'd said earlier was now suspect. "Are you sure this man didn't harm you?"

"He did not. But someone hurt Ginger." Fluffles rubbed herself against my leg, and I looked down at her, thankful she is an indoor cat. Suddenly, I was crying.

"We need to get that head examined," said Detective Sherman.

"I've been told that more than once," I sniffed.

Detective Sherman smiled, just a little.

"It's just a cut on my head," I said. "Don't call an ambulance." There was no way I was going to the emergency room and risk stitches. I have a severe phobia of needles.

"At least let's clean it up. There's a lot of bleeding. Bathroom?" I pointed the way. He waited. "You coming?"

As I followed, I heard the other officer say to Foster, "Sir, I need to ask you some questions." He was stern.

"No, really!" I called. "He didn't do anything. I called him to come deal with the cat."

Detective Sherman ushered me into my bathroom. "The cat, I'm sorry to say, is dead." He mopped at my face with my panties, then took a good look at them. He quickly put them in the sink and pressed a clean towel to my forehead. He started to rinse out the panties, then thought better of it.

"I know. But what happened to her?"

"It looks like poisoning. There is a small dish of what appears to be yellow antifreeze just inside the back gate."

"A dish of it????"

"Your cat has been poisoned."

"It's not my cat. It's Foster's."

"And Foster is . . .?" I blushed. Maybe he thought Foster was my staying overnight boyfriend. I didn't want him to think that.

"Foster is my neighbor."

Just then I heard Maria come in. "What's going on?" we heard her ask.

I was relieved. "That's his wife."

"I think you're going to need a couple of stitches," Detective Sherman said. "Is there someone who can take you to the emergency room?"

There was no way I was going to go to the emergency room and risk having someone stick any kind of needle in my head. "I'll call my mom," I said. "She's a nurse."

"Okay, I guess. You're sure?" Those kind brown eyes were on me again.

"I'm sure." He and the officer left. I called Mom. Foster, sadly, went to the shed out back for a shovel.

My mother didn't even bother to fight me about going to the emergency room. She knows my history. Ever since I passed out getting a flu shot when I was a teenager, I have been ter-rified of needles. Now I associate that incident with needles, and even the sight of one causes me to sweat, feel nause-ated, and fear that a panic attack is coming on. According to Mom, the nurse, I may be more afraid of my "vasovagel syncope reaction" to the needle, rather than the needle itself, but I don't really care. I just know that even a picture of someone getting a shot is enough to send my blood pressure rising and my stomach lurching.

Mom cleaned the wound thoroughly and used what she calls Steri-strips and I call butterfly bandages to close up the inch long cut at my hairline. She said it wasn't deep and that head wounds bleed a lot. She thought I might be more sore from what she calls a hematoma and I call a goose egg than from the cut.

As she fixed me up, I thought over all that had happened. Someone had murdered Judith, using my accordion. My principal had suspended me because I might be a murderer. Someone had poisoned Ginger with antifreeze in my back yard. And whoever had done so had caused me, in my fear, to fall and gash my head and wind up with stitches—butterfly stitches, but stitches nonetheless.

"I'm finished waiting around," I said angrily. "I'm going to figure out who is responsible for all this and clear my name! Maybe even push a spare accordion onto *their* head!"

"It's about time," Mom said. "For the clearing your name part, I mean."

"Besides, what else am I going to do? I can't go to work."

She patted my arm and handed me two Advil.

CHAPTER 13

When I got up in the morning, my head hurt. After I ate some yogurt, I took another couple of Advil and sat for a moment, making a plan.

I called Geraldine, Sammie, and Mom. Mom, of course, knew what had happened, but I brought the others up to speed quickly on the phone. Then I asked them all to come over at noon for a meeting. We were going to put our heads together and figure out how to solve this case.

At 11:00 a.m. Sammie's younger brother Derek rang the doorbell. I was surprised. He had a gym bag with him, as well as his laptop.

"Mom sent me," he said. He did not look happy.

"I guess I'd better let you in then."

Derek was in hipster mode today—skinny jeans, Buddy Holly glasses, a SpongeBob SquarePants T-shirt, and a hoodie. He took off the hoodie as I led him to the kitchen, invited him to sit down, and poured him a cup of coffee. As I turned around with the coffee, he was carefully arranging his hoodie in his lap, and I caught a glimpse of the quill and feather tattoo on his arm. Derek had been at summer camp during the worst of his brother's tattoo infection, so he hadn't been affected the way Sammie and I had been.

"The Pickle Queen has spoken," he said as I sat down

across from him. "I am to stay with you until the murderer is caught. As your bodyguard." He shrugged. We both knew it was pointless to protest. The Pickle Queen is a force of nature.

"So I guess I have a roommate," I frowned.

"I'm not exactly thrilled about it either," he said.

Derek, the youngest of Geraldine's children, is an aspiring writer working on his first novel, though Sammie and I suspect he spends a lot more time working on physical rather than mental activities. He runs and works out every day. He is also quite an outdoorsman, backpacking in summer and backcountry skiing in winter, using his trips to take spectacular wildlife photos.

He took a deep breath and then lifted the sweatshirt on his lap and pulled up his T-shirt. Around his waist was a holster and a gun.

I gasped and scooted my chair further away from him. "What in the world are you doing with a gun?"

"Just calm down. I have a concealed carry permit, and Mom is demanding that I take advantage of it."

"Holy moly! Are you kidding me? I don't want a gun in my house!" I stood up and stepped back against the kitchen counter.

He put the sweatshirt back over the gun. "I knew you'd say that. So did Mom. So here's the deal—the first few rounds are loaded with birdshot—not enough to kill anyone but enough to get someone's attention and stop them in their tracks."

That was better than blasting someone to oblivion with one pull of the trigger, but I still wasn't happy. "Why do you, of all people, have a gun?" This was a young man known to demonstrate for causes that would make many NRA members cringe. Why would he have not only a gun but a concealed carry permit as well? "Are you driving a truck now with a rifle hanging in the back window, too?" I added.

"Just relax and let me explain. Sit down." I hesitated but stepped carefully forward and sat. He continued. "Remember the mountain lion?"

How could I forget? Derek had kept us on the edge of our seats one evening telling us about the encounter. He had been backcountry skiing near Steamboat Springs, alone, taking wildlife photos. When he saw mountain lion prints, he began tracking the animal, hoping to get a glimpse of it and a photo with his zoom lens. He had climbing skins attached to the underside of his skis, allowing him to go uphill easily as he bushwhacked through the trees, in some spots finding a path with difficulty through fallen beetle-killed pine.

As he skied over the top of one hill, he came within 20 feet of a startled mountain lion that had been nestled in brush on the other side. There was a face-off. Derek used his ski poles to make himself as large as possible and, he started softly repeating, "Hail Mary, full of grace," over and over. The skins on his skis prevented him from sliding backwards, but he didn't want to turn his back on a mountain lion in order to face downhill. He found himself wishing that he had a gun to fire to scare the animal. After what he said seemed like ten minutes but was probably only a minute or two, the mountain lion turned and took off. Derek quickly turned around and skied like crazy in the other direction.

"So you encountered one measly mountain lion and decided to get a gun?" It didn't seem like enough of a reason to me, though of course I hadn't been the one to face the mountain lion.

Fluffles came in and eyed Derek's lap. "No!" I cried and picked her up. I was not going to let her sit anywhere near a gun.

"There's more," Derek continued. "The next weekend I challenged a couple of snowmobilers who were sledding where they weren't supposed to be. Not my smartest move. They turned out to be *drunk* snowmobilers with a macho attitude. Luckily, they couldn't maneuver their machines through the trees the way I could on my skis." A little smile of satisfaction played on his lips as he remembered.

"So if you'd had a gun, you would have shot them?" This was not the Derek I knew.

"No, I wouldn't have shot them!" He put his cup down a little hard, sloshing some coffee on the table. I scooted the napkin holder closer to him, trying not to disturb Fluffles. "But maybe I could have made them *think* I would shoot them."

"Okay, so you got a gun just so you could protect yourself from mountain lions and drunk snowmobilers?" I could tell I was trying his patience, but I didn't care.

"There's still more. Last summer, my friend Al was hiking near Granby and managed to accidentally get between a mama bear and her cubs. Mama was not happy, and she started to charge. He shot into a tree and managed to scare her enough to stop her, at least momentarily. He was able to back away from both her and the cubs. If he hadn't had the gun, he'd have been toast."

"Okay, I get it. Sort of. You want protection in the wilderness. But why the concealed carry permit?"

"God, this is getting to be a long story," he sighed.

"I need to hear it." Fluffles took that opportunity to jump off my lap and stand by her dish, looking at me longingly for an extra helping of Fancy Feast. I ignored her.

He continued. "After I got a 9mm, I carried it to the mountains in my backpack for a while. Then Al told me it's illegal to have a gun that isn't visible. Just driving with it in my pack would be breaking the law, and so would hiking or skiing with it in my pack. So I bit the bullet and took a concealed carry permit class so that I'm legal."

"And now Geraldine wants you to actually wear the gun around so that you can protect me," I said. "Even if I don't want a roomie with a gun."

"I don't like it any more than you do, but the gun is legal, and it is protection."

"Great," I sighed. I was quiet for a moment. Then another problem occurred to me—privacy. "So what if I want a gentleman caller to stay the night?"

"You currently do not have any gentlemen callers."

"But I might get one."

"In that case, I'll act 'flaming' so they know I'm not competition." Derek is gay, though most people would never know it, except when he puts on an act, usually to amuse or embarrass Sammie and me.

With elbows bent, I rested my head in my hands and faced reality. "So I guess I don't have a choice."

"Do *you* want to tangle with her?" He raised an eyebrow and gave me a look. It was a look that always distracted me. Derek has one brown eye and one green eye, which is disconcerting enough, but I thought I remembered that he always raised the eyebrow over his brown eye. This time he raised the one over his green eye. I wondered if he used different brows for different purposes. Could we call him "ambi-browed"?

Derek must have noticed that I hadn't answered. "I ask again, do you want to tangle with her?"

I shook my head vigorously. No one wants to tangle with the Pickle Queen, a study in contradictions. Geraldine had given her four children a strict, clean-your-plate, no-playing-with-your-toys   until-you-write-thank-you-notes kind of upbringing, with Holy Name Catholic school for all through eighth grade. She was a strict mother, yet when she caught Sammie and me smoking a joint in the back-yard when we were 13, she didn't freak out, as most par-ents would have. She just looked at us, shook her head, and said, "Really?" Then she walked back inside. When we cautiously came in later with a serious case of the munchies, there was not a snack to be found anywhere in the house.

Though she is reportedly rich beyond belief, she raised her children in a rather ordinary 1970s-era split level in a rather ordinary subdivision, and she still lives there with her second husband Jake, and Derek. Derek has set up a lower floor room for his novel writing and is living there rent-free—for one year only, according to Geraldine. In return for free rent, he takes care of the yard work and cooks dinner three times a week. I wondered if he would now cook dinner for me three times a week.

Geraldine is careful with her money, but she is far from cheap. One indulgence is her little purple Miata convertible. She gives generously to causes she believes in, such as the Humane Society, the ACLU, and Doctors without Borders.

She still attends mass each week, never mind that she is divorced and also freely admits to being an agnostic as well as a supporter of Planned Parenthood. Sammie and I have a theory that the priest is afraid to excommunicate her. For one thing, her endowment pretty much keeps Holy Name in business.

I heard a car in the driveway and looked out. It was Geraldine in the Miata, with Sammie beside her. They came in carrying a bag of sandwiches from the King Soopers deli.

"Mom should be here in a minute," I said, but Geraldine wasn't listening. She was examining the bump on my head. Sammie was, too.

"Beige bandages? Surely you could find some cooler ones than that," Sammie said. "Glitter strips. My Little Pony. Care Bear."

"I prefer understated," I said, taking the sandwiches and going to the kitchen. I got out paper plates. "Where's Jake?" I'd just assumed Sammie and Derek's stepfather would come along.

"He's in West Papua, New Guinea, working for a couple of weeks. We'll have to do without him," said Geraldine. Jake is a construction manager who is often involved in large, international projects.

Geraldine sat down at the kitchen table and got down to business. "I'm glad we're taking this meeting," she said.

"We're not taking it. We're *having* it," I said.

"It's another one of her pet peeves," Sammie explained to her mom. "*Taking* a meeting."

"Okay, I'm glad we're taking or having or whatever. Judith's murder was bad enough, but now *you* are in danger. And Fluffles, too."

"Fluffles is an indoor cat," I said.

"And Derek is going to keep your indoor cat and you safe. As I hope he has already explained, he will work on his novel here during the day. He will drop you off and pick you up from rehearsals at night. Anywhere else you go, he will go with you. And wherever he goes, you will go."

"Great," I sighed. "What about my privacy?"

"Not important. There is a murderer on the loose. Derek can move into your den. You can use your laptop anywhere. Besides, you're going to be too busy to worry about privacy."

"Too busy doing what?" It was Mom, who had come in without knocking. She said hello to everyone, then opened the cupboard where I keep napkins and passed them out. My home was evidently no longer my own.

"What's Ella going to be busy doing?" Mom repeated. "I mean, besides trying to solve a murder?" She got out mugs and started pouring. Of course she gave me "Rocky," the raccoon cup my father had given me many years ago. Dad was quite a Beatles fan, and "Rocky Raccoon" was the song I always wanted him to play for me on his guitar.

Geraldine answered. "She's going to be busy catching this heinous criminal. Anyone who would poison a *cat* deserves a special place in hell."

"Killing a human probably deserves a special place, too," Mom said mildly.

"Well, yes. But, really, a *cat?*" Geraldine really, really loved cats.

I looked for a ham and cheese in the pile of sandwiches on the table, but Geraldine said, "They're all turkey."

I took turkey. I decided to officially begin the meeting, since I was the one who had called it. "Does everyone have what they need?" They all nodded, so I began. "Clearly it behooves us . . . " I winced. "I hate that word, but nothing else is ever quite right...It 'necessitates'...We are 'impelled' to....'obliged' to...It is 'incumbent' upon us to..."

"You're hung up," said Derek. He had spent a lot of time around my family.

Sammie helped. "I think what you are trying to say is that we've got to do something to help solve this murder."

"Which is what I told her a couple of days ago," Mom said. "She said to leave it to the police."

I shot her a dirty look. "As you know, Mom, my thinking has evolved on that."

"That cliché is beneath you. How about a simple, 'I changed my mind?'"

And she wonders where I get my language fixations.

"Okay, it behooves me to say I changed my mind." I took a bite of my sandwich.

"Good. So let's start listing suspects and their possible motives," said Geraldine, taking over. "We've got about half an hour before Sammie has to be back at the store." She looked at me. "Quick, without thinking, name the first couple of suspects who come to mind."

"Stanley," I started.

"The guy you dumped?" Geraldine knows way too much about my personal life.

"I did not dump him," I said.

"Irrelevant. Why him?" Geraldine asked. "Why did he come to mind first?"

"She thinks he's mad at her for dumping him," said Mom.

"Is he?"

"I think maybe she thinks she had more of an effect on him than she did," said Sammie carefully.

"*Someone* put a card and Lindor chocolates on my music stand last night," I said. "Unsigned. And then Stan defended me at our cast meeting. He said no one who loved her instrument would use it to kill someone."

"That's a fact, not a declaration of love," Mom said.

"And that's not evidence for him killing Judith," added Derek. "It's evidence for him—supposedly—still having the hots for you."

"Let's suppose he is mad at Ella for dumping him," said Geraldine. "Is he mad enough to use Tillie to frame her for murder?" She looked around.

Everyone looked skeptical. "And if he was the murderer and was trying to frame Ella, why would he switch to trying to win her back by putting chocolates on her music stand?" Derek asked.

"Especially when the first step to winning her heart would clearly be to get a decent pair of shoes," commented Geraldine.

"Is there *nothing* that stays private around here?" I couldn't believe she knew about the shoes. Mom hadn't.

She ignored me. "And why would Stanley kill Judith if he is in love with Ella? Any ideas for a motive there?"

Everyone was silent, including me.

"Okay then. Who else comes to mind as a suspect, Ella?" Geraldine asked.

I was stumped.

"Aiden, the concertina-playing guy," suggested Sammie.

"He doesn't play the concertina," I said. "He can't even fake-play the concertina. He has no musical ability whatsoever."

"That doesn't make him a murderer," Mom said. "What makes you suspicious of him?"

"He's so strange," I said. "Acts like I'm poison, and I don't know what I ever did to him."

"You highlighted his lack of musical ability?" Sammie suggested.

"It seems more personal than that. He barely said a word to me the whole time I was trying to teach him. Then last night we accidentally bumped into each other in the pit, full frontal, and he jumped back like I'd hit him or something." I took a sip of coffee. "And he won't say anything to me. I saw him when I stopped at Walgreens the other day. He was coming out of that fourplex across the street, so I yelled, 'Hi, Aiden.' He just looked at me, turned, and ran."

"Interesting," said Sammie. "That's the fourplex with all the shrink offices."

"Psychologists, please," I said. I looked at Mom and was afraid for a second that she was going to suggest that Aiden was OCD.

"Maybe he had an appointment and doesn't want you to know he's crazy," said Sammie.

"Seeing a psychologist doesn't make you crazy," said Derek. He'd had issues with coming out when he was younger, and Geraldine had insisted that he talk to someone.

I continued. "I don't know what it is, but something is off about Aiden—in addition to him having something against me."

"Who could have anything against you?" asked my mother.

"Spoken like a true mom," said Geraldine. "And maybe

what Aiden needs is a true mom." She knows Becky, his mother. She knows pretty much everyone in town. "He needs a mom who loves her kid as much as she loves Jesus."

"I think she loves him," I said. "She did insist he have a part in the show before she agreed to being musical director. At least that's what I heard," I added.

"That's maybe so she can keep an eye on him," said Geraldine.

"Because he's crazy," said Sammie. Derek shot her a dirty look.

"Has he been in trouble?" Mom asked. "Is that why she wants to keep an eye on him—*if* it's true that she wants to keep an eye on him?"

Geraldine looked up from the notes she was taking. "Let's investigate that."

"I can do it," said Derek. " I know a guy who teaches biology at the high school."

"Oh? How do you know him?" I asked sweetly. I had a feeling he was quite happy to find a reason to meet up with this teacher.

Sammie's cell phone alarm interrupted us. " I need to get back to the store," she said.

"We've got a decent start," said Geraldine.

I interrupted before she could go further. I wanted to be the one in charge of this meeting. "I suggest that we work on two goals. One, we'll investigate Aiden's background. Derek will do that. And two, we know Stan has something against me. Let's work on seeing if he had anything against Judith."

"How do we do that?" Sammie asked reasonably.

I wasn't sure. "Ask around. Lots of people probably know something about Stan. See what you can come up with."

Geraldine got up. "I'll take Sammie back to work. Derek, you can get busy on the novel."

"I'd like to go work out first. Maybe I can do that while Jeanie is here so that Ella has someone with her. Do you mind staying with Ella a while?" he asked my mother.

"Does Jeanie have a gun?" interrupted Geraldine, looking pointedly at Derek.

He sighed. There was no need to answer.

"Ella will work out when you do."

"He stays a *lot* longer at the gym than I do," I pointed out.

"Take a book."

She and Sammie left. While Derek settled into "his" room, Mom and I tossed around other ideas. In the end, we decided the best thing would be for me to establish an alibi.

If I was figuring the time of the murder correctly, I had one. The detectives had asked about my whereabouts the night before the murder was discovered, but I was pretty sure that wasn't when the murder had taken place.

Derek appeared in shorts, a T-shirt, and sneakers—his jock look. "Time for the fitness center, Ella."

I looked at Mom helplessly. She smiled and shrugged. "Your bodyguard is calling." She got her purse and gave me a quick kiss goodbye.

I went to the bedroom for workout clothes.

And a book.

CHAPTER 14

WHILE I WAS SITTING in the cafe area of the gym reading, Detective Sherman called. (I had already done half an hour on the treadmill. I deemed that enough for someone with a head injury.)

"How's your head?" he asked. "Did you need stitches?"

"No. Butterfly bandages."

"I'm glad it wasn't worse. Do you have a minute, or are you in class?"

I closed my book. "It's Saturday. And besides, I've been suspended with pay."

Silence.

No one was sitting anywhere close to me, but I kept my voice down anyway. "It seems that the parents don't want to take a chance that their kids' teacher is a crazed accordion-tossing maniac." I heard him clear his throat. "Which I am not," I added.

"I'm sorry to hear that," he said.

"That I'm not a crazed accordion-tossing maniac?"

"That you're suspended."

Silence again.

"So who did it?" I demanded.

"That, actually, is why I'm calling. I need to know your exact whereabouts on Monday, between 4:00 and 5:15."

"That's pretty specific. But I've already thought about it, in case you asked that question, which I'm surprised you haven't asked before." I put my feet up on the rung of the chair across from me and leaned back a little.

"And why would you wonder about those specific times?"

"Because she didn't look that dead."

"What?"

I decided that it would be wiser to continue the conversation elsewhere. "Hang on a sec." I walked out to the parking lot, away from any cars or people, then continued. "I'm guessing that someone who had been dead all night would look more dead than Judith did. I mean, I don't *know,* but I assume that rigor mortis would have set in, or she'd look gray. She was really, really bloody but not gray."

"Did you touch her?" He sounded alarmed.

"No. But she looked like she'd just walked in off the street and, bam, a flying accordion took her out. Like recently. Like it had just happened."

"Got it."

"And since she always let herself in at 4:00 to go over her notes, the murder had to have taken place between 4:00 and when the rest of us started arriving at 5:15. So all those questions you asked me the other night about where I was after rehearsal on Sunday—completely irrelevant."

I'm pretty sure he would have glared at me at that point, if we had been face to face. "All right," he said, "since you've thought about it, where were you during that time?"

Someone pulled up near me with open windows and loud hip-hop music thumping. "Hang on. I'm waiting for this guy to turn off his car and leave . . . here we go. Now—my alibi. Are you still there?"

"I'm listening," he said.

"I left school at 4:00. I know that because Leonard, the P.E. teacher, held the door open for me as I was leaving, and he *always* leaves at 4:00 because he has to pick up his daughter at day care, and they charge him if he is late. He can be talking to one of us in the hall when his phone alarm goes off, and zoom, he is out of there. He was late one time last spring because his tire had a flat, and they charged him a fortune and we heard about it for weeks. Then another time, he got stopped for speeding in a school zone and . . ."

"Okay, could we get back on track here?"

"I'm just saying that he held the door for me, so I know it was 4:00. I'm sure he would back me up on that."

"And then?"

"Are you taking notes?" I asked.

"Of course I'm taking notes." His voice sounded just a tad chilly.

"Okay. Then I drove home, fed Fluffles, checked the mail, and took a quick shower."

"In the afternoon?"

I didn't like the touch of "That seems odd" that I heard in his voice. "You'd want a shower, too, if you'd been dealing with 23 kindergartners all day," I explained. "They're always sneezing and coughing on you and hugging you. Then you have to stand on the playground with them during recess while they're running around and stirring up dust all around you. Or mud. Or snow. Depends on the time of year. Oh, and then there is the Spitter."

"The Spitter . . . ?"

"This one kid spits all the time. Or he used to."

"And now he doesn't?"

"The last time he did it, he was sitting in the reading corner looking at a book, and he lobbed one on the floor. Disgusting."

"Why was that the last time?" Oh, Mr. Cop was getting interested. I smiled.

"He had one shoe half on and was dangling it on his foot. So I pulled it off the rest of the way. Then I pulled off his sock, used it to wipe up the spit, and handed it back to him. He wasn't happy to put on a wet sock."

"But he never spit again?"

"He never spit again. But I could tell he thought about it."

Detective Sherman paused a moment, then got back on track. "So you showered."

"Yes." I was finding it much easier to talk to him on the phone than in person. I didn't have to look at him. I sat down on the cement ledge bordering the parking lot. "Then I looked to see what I could grab for supper, and all I had was some expired eggs and some tortillas. I might have fried an egg—the expiration dates are just a guideline, not a sign that the eggs immediately rot the second the sun rises on the expiration date. But the tortillas had a little mold on them, and I wasn't going to eat an egg without a tortilla or toast or something. I don't like naked eggs."

"Or poached eggs," he added. "Your memories are very specific."

"If you were suspected of murder, you'd be digging deep, too."

"True. So then?"

"So then I decided to go to Whole Foods to get some of their lasagna. When I went out on the front porch, my neighbor Maria was there playing with Skyden, her two-year-old. I gave Skyden a hug and a kiss and then set off for Whole Foods."

"You drove all the way to Harper Falls just to get lasagna?" The town of Juniper doesn't have a Whole Foods, but Harper Falls does.

"I really like their lasagna," I explained. "And it's only fifteen minutes away. That's not far if you really, really want lasagna. Anyway, I picked up lasagna, Caesar salad, and some garlic bread. And then I hurried back to town and got to the theater just when it always opens—at 5:15. I warmed the lasagna a bit in the greenroom microwave and then ate."

"Got it. With who?"

I silently corrected that to "whom," in honor of Sister Dalmatia, then continued. "I sat down with Feleesha, to start with. I remember that because I felt kind of piggish next to her, with her nibbling on her gluten-free, vegan, organic, non-GMO carrot sticks."

"All carrot sticks are gluten-free and vegan," he said.

"I *know* that. I was exaggerating."

"Oh. Who else was there?"

"I remember several people eating normal things. Stanley. Joe. Caleb. Helena, the hot eighteen-year-old dancer and her poor friend."

"Poor?" He seemed to be having trouble keeping up.

"No one ever knows her name because she's always with Helena, and Helena pretty much sucks up all the attention. I'm really starting to feel sorry for the girl. The friend, not Helena."

"Have *you* ever asked her name?"

I paused. "Good point."

He didn't say anything for a bit, and I watched a young mother rolling a stroller toward her car and looking at her phone at the same time. Then he continued. "Okay, I've written down your alibi: Left school at 4:00, drove home and showered."

"And fed Fluffles."

"And fed Fluffles. Then drove to Whole Foods, picked up supper, and arrived at approximately 5:15."

"Correct."

"Got it. And can you prove any of this? A receipt from Whole Foods maybe?"

I sighed. "I paid cash, and I'm sure I probably left the receipt in the bag and threw it away. That's what I usually do for inexpensive cash purchases . . . not that purchases at Whole Foods are ever inexpensive."

"Some verification would be necessary for us to completely accept your alibi."

At that point, I really wished I could see his face. "Do *you* believe me?"

He hesitated. "That's not relevant. Thank you for your time . . . and I'm really sorry about your suspension."

"Me, too. And I found out that my sub is that awful Mrs. Markham. The kids don't like her, and I don't blame them."

"Maybe the Spitter will find a way to get back at her."

I smiled. The guy had a sense of humor. "I hope so . . . not that I'm the kind of person who exacts revenge on anyone."

"Of course not. Spitting is a different thing altogether."

CHAPTER 15

T ESS WAS IN A SNIT when I arrived Saturday night and cleared the security guard hurdle. (I'd put a big box of Tampax in my bag, just to embarrass him.) It seems that our musical had been mentioned on a Denver TV station morning news show, one that Baba and I like to watch together sometimes so that we can add to the elaborate story we have been constructing about the three talkers. (We refuse to call them reporters.)

Two of the talkers are men, around 55, with the flat, pasted-on look of lots of foundation and powder. Of course they are always well-covered in the obligatory jacket and tie. Next to them sits News Babe, around 24, with long, carefully blown-dry hair, a tight sleeveless dress cut just a tad low, perfect teeth, and false eyelashes—artfully applied, but I always wonder if the weight of them doesn't give her a headache. Her only apparent talent is an ability to laugh at the men's lame jokes.

However, Baba and I like to imagine that News Babe is really a Harvard graduate who does her giggling Barbie routine by day but at night updates her dossier with reports of infractions, sexual and otherwise, made by station management, a dossier that will someday result in her moving into position as head of the news department. I want the dossier to result in the firing of the two male talkers, but Baba does not. She wants, instead, to have them joined on camera by a 55-year-old woman. "This daddy and pretty young thing nonsense on all the stations has gone on long enough," she insists.

We both agree that one of News Babe's first changes, as head of the department, will be to stop having on-camera staff dress up like chickens or zombies on Halloween, and no meteorologist will be forced to stand in a snowstorm every time one blows through, just to report that it is snowing.

They also will be required to use traditional articles and prepositions. There will be no, "He was in hospital for three days" or "She graduated high school this May." "The" and "from" will be required. We aren't British. (I know I'm echoing Sister Dalmatia on this, but Sister Dalmatia is hard to shake off, even after more than fifteen years. "In America, we say *the* hospital and *from* high school," she insisted.)

Tess's snit was about what the TV talkers had said on the morning news. News Babe had evidently reported, "The show must go on in Juniper. Despite the murder of the director earlier in the week at the Juniper Theater, the Spotlight Players' production of *Carousel* will open next weekend, only one week late."

Wrong. Spotlight Players will be presenting *Carnival*, not *Carousel*. Hardly anyone has ever heard of *Carnival*, so people often get the two shows mixed up.

Our perky new director lost some of her perk over this mistake. She worried that people would remember that *Carousel* involves some wife beating on the part of Billy Bigelow, and she definitely didn't want to be associated with that kind of show. She had called the station, and someone promised a correction would air the next morning, but Tess worried that no one would be watching on Sunday morning because they wouldn't be up early.

"They could be up early to go to church," offered Becky.

Tess, for once, did not look optimistic.

Secretly, I was pleased to hear that News Babe had also mentioned in her chit-chat that "Real Nice Clambake" is not one of her favorite songs from *Carousel*, but the inspirational "You'll Never Walk Alone" helps make up for it—thus showing that she might really be as smart as Baba and I imagine. "Real Nice Clambake" really is a dumb song.

Rehearsal was not a rousing success. Feleesha actually got through "Mira" without muffing the lyrics, but that improvement was offset by her making a mess of "Yes, My Heart."

"Maybe if we really were doing *Carousel* she would know the songs," Gordon mumbled as he emptied the spit valve. "Everybody knows *Carousel* songs."

"Opening night is going to be a disaster," I mumbled back. "A complete disaster."

We struggled through the rest of the show, and I could tell Becky was calling on all her spiritual resources in order not to blow up. She touched the cross around her neck a lot and kept bowing her head and taking deep breaths. Tess, certainly not a person prone to yelling, lost it at one point, shouting, "No!!!! No!!!! Don't turn your back to the audience!" Cast members were forgetting even the most fundamental rules of theater. (Tess, of course, apologized immediately for raising her voice and added, "We do need to remember our audience, though. People need to see your lovely faces.")

In the greenroom after the rehearsal, complaints flew. Feleesha blamed Joe for confusing her in one scene by not giving his line *"exactly* as it is in the script!" Joe blamed her for not having "the common sense to recognize a mistake when you hear one and adapt." The choreographer pulled all the dancers together and lectured them about reviewing their steps in the opening number because "That number sets the tone for the whole show, and sloppiness doesn't cut it!" Cecil, one of the puppeteers, grumbled about the band not playing loudly enough in one of his numbers, and that's when Becky's deep breathing finally failed her. "Get a hearing aid!" she snapped, and he stomped off as well as someone with a bad back can stomp.

Helena groused to her friend that their dance costumes still didn't fit right. She looked at Paula's nearby table strewn with fabric, Velcro, thread, and plastic baggies of beads, sequins, and buttons. "Where is she anyway? Our costumes need to be fixed." She turned back and spoke to the room in general. "She measured us, like, twice. I don't know why she can't get it right." She showed no sympathy for the task of molding fabric to highlight her body in the way I suspected she wanted it highlighted. She turned back to the mirror. "This should fit *tight* on top," she said. It already looked pretty tight to me, but who am I to judge?

Paula walked out of the dressing area holding a costume, and Marco the Magnificent stopped her. We always call him Marco the Magnificent, his character's name, because he wears his long magician's cape all the time, even in rehearsal. "It helps me find my motivation," he says.

He held up his cape and said, "Can you fix the broken clasp on this thing?"

"Fix it yourself," she said and handed him a safety pin. The added stress of coaching Feleesha was probably getting to Paula.

I texted Derek to let him know he could pick me up and then, while I waited, walked over to Helena's friend and said, "I don't think I've ever caught your name. I'm Ella." I held out my hand, and she shook it.

"Reagan," she said.

I tried not to wince. Were people also naming little girls Bush, Clinton, Obama and Trump? I fervently hoped not.

I went to the stage door to wait for Derek.

"We're going to Sammie's," Derek said when I got in the car. He was wearing his "regular guy" clothes—jeans, sneakers, and a Colorado State University sweatshirt. Everyone can change clothes, but Derek has an ability to completely transform his appearance based on what he's wearing.

"Great. Did you bring wine or beer?"

"She'll have some."

"Maybe not . . ." I doubted if he knew her condition yet.

Luckily, we found that Sammie still had liquor. She poured me a glass of wine and gave Derek a beer. He noticed her pouring herself a club soda and raised an eyebrow, the one over the brown eye again.

"Upset stomach," she said.

"*You????*" Sammie was known for being able to eat jalapeno nachos without any problem, and she always wanted her curry and her green chili extra spicy.

"Me." She changed the subject abruptly. "Let's talk murder. Did you find out anything about Aiden? "

"I did talk to his biology teacher, a guy I know from the

gym," Derek said. "He said he's had Aiden in class, and he's a loner, gets hassled by some of the cool kids. And he's very shy. Maybe that's why he doesn't talk to you much, Ella."

"Is this teacher someone you're interested in?" I couldn't help myself.

"Not relevant, Ella. The relevant part is that he says Aiden is shy, and that's probably why he doesn't talk to you."

"Maybe. Or maybe he doesn't talk to me because he doesn't like me and wants to kill me. And my cat." I was not in a generous mood.

"Okay, even though I'm not buying it for a second, let's say that he does want to kill you and your cat because he doesn't like you," said Sammie, putting her feet up on the edge of the coffee table. "Why would he kill Judith?"

"Because she was making him do that stupid role that he has no talent for, and he's embarrassed and mad." I grabbed a sofa pillow and held it across my chest defensively.

"A little extreme, but let's go with it," she continued. "Why use your accordion to do it?"

"I'm the one who tried to teach him 'Love Makes the World Go Round.' He suffered. He thinks it would be poetic justice to make me suffer." I tightened my grip on the pillow.

Sammie and Derek didn't seem to be buying it. Sammie said, "And he killed your neighbor's cat because . . . ?"

"Because he thought it was mine and . . . he's just mean . . . and . . . Well, maybe it's not the same person."

"Bingo," said Derek.

At that, Sammie ran to the bathroom and threw up. At least that's what it most definitely sounded like she was doing.

"What the . . . " Derek was shocked. Sammie was never sick to her stomach.

"You okay?" I asked when she came out of the bathroom.

"Yeah. I guess my body has it backwards." She looked at Derek and shrugged. "Morning sickness, but at night."

It took him a beat. "Morning sickness?" Another several beats, and then understanding dawned. "What? You're *pregnant?*"

"I'm pregnant. You're going to be Uncle Derek."

"What? How?....Who?"

"Donald."

"Donald?" He was having trouble processing this information. "I thought you just went dancing with Donald."

"One lapse of judgment is evidently enough."

"But Donald? Surely you're not going to *have* it...?"

"I don't know what I'm going to do yet," she snapped. "Don't tell Mom."

CHAPTER 16

OF COURSE HE TOLD MOM. When Sammie wasn't at our meeting the next morning, Geraldine knew something was up.

"She's a little under the weather," I said, busying myself with trying to slice my bagel without slicing my hand.

"Sammie?" Sammie had not missed one single day of school in her entire eight years at Holy Name. (In public high school, that changed. She missed school all right, but not because of illness.)

Geraldine fixed her Mom eyes on Derek. "What's wrong?"

"Not sure," he said. "Hand me the jelly, Ella." It was a weak attempt to change the subject.

"She's just not feeling well," I said. I got the bagel sliced and became *really* absorbed in the cream cheese application. By this time Mom started to look suspicious, too.

"Why?" Geraldine's eyes were drilling down on Derek, but he was strong—years of practice, perhaps.

"Who knows why?" he said. "Why do people get colds? Why does one person get the flu and another does not? Why does one person get cancer and another is healthy as a horse?"

"Does she have *cancer?*" Geraldine's voice rose and

she stood up, putting her hands on the edge of the table and leaning towards us. "Both of you, look at me now. Does Sammie have cancer?"

Derek sighed. There is no escaping the Pickle Queen, and we knew it. "No, Mom, I promise you. She does not have cancer. She's pregnant."

"Oh, thank God!" She sat back down again.

"Not the reaction I would have expected," Mom commented.

"It's not cancer. It's a baby." She sighed with relief. "But who? Who's the father? She's not dating anyone."

"Donald."

"*Donald????* I thought she just went dancing with him."

I jumped in. "That's true, except for the one time when they hooked up . . . I hate that term–hooked up. I mean, where is the 'hooking'? I guess if you try to visualize the actual act and the two bodies, you can kind of see it, but it just seems crass. Then there's the whole thing about prostitutes and hooking, and . . . "

"Ella, you're getting hung up again," Geraldine said. "And please remember that this is Sammie's mother you are talking to, and I certainly don't want to visualize any 'hooking.'"

My mind was still on the linguistics. "There's always 'getting some' and 'one nighter' and..."

She slammed down her coffee cup, and I worried for a second that she might throw her bagel at me. "Stop! For whatever reason, Donald did the deed, and I am not having that doofus . . . "

"David. David was the doofus," I said before I could help myself.

"Ella, focus. I cannot bear having Donald at Thanksgiving dinner for the next 18 years. We have to get rid of him." Geraldine looked determined.

"I doubt another murder is wise," said Mom, calmly chewing her bagel.

Geraldine was tapping her foot loudly against the table leg. "I'm not talking murder."

"Well, what are you talking?" Derek asked.

"I don't know. A modeling job in Brazil with an 18-year contract…and somehow he has his passport pulled."

"Very realistic, Mom."

She got up, grabbed the bag with the remaining bagels and headed out the door. "Come on, Jeanie. I'll drop you off on the way to Sammie's. My daughter and I are overdue for a good long talk."

I shuddered. So did Mom and Derek. Good long talks with Geraldine were not always pleasant.

So much for the meeting. Mom sighed and folded the remainder of her bagel into a napkin. Then she looked at me. "Work on your alibi," she said. She followed Geraldine out the door.

"Will you protect *me* now," Derek sighed. "From Sammie?"

Judith's memorial service was that afternoon, and I felt it would be bad form not to attend, despite the cloud of suspicion hanging over me. Besides, maybe I would learn something that would help me figure out who did it.

Derek, of course, went with me. I put on the most dignified outfit I had, a dark navy dress with tights and black boots, something I wear when Baba insists I go to mass with her. She requires "real" clothes—no jeans or slacks or leggings, no matter what others wear, because "Proper clothes show proper respect. People who step into a church wearing torn jeans and T-shirts don't have the sense God gave a goose."

I did want to show proper respect for Judith. Even if I had found her picky and petty and annoying, I was sad about her death and felt pain for her family and friends. Tears came to my eyes during her daughter's loving eulogy. Obviously, there had been a lot more to Judith than what we saw at the theater.

After the service, cake and coffee followed in the fellowship hall, and I searched my mind for a sweet memory of Judith to share with her daughter and son. I couldn't think of anything except, "She was so devoted to doing a good job. All of us in *Carnival* appreciated her commitment so much." Her daughter thanked me for coming, and Derek and I headed toward the cake.

We were deciding between chocolate sheet cake and dump cake when I looked up and saw Detective Sherman standing next to a wall and eating cake off a paper plate. I guess it's true that police go to funerals to check out the attendees.

It looked like he had chosen the dump cake, which I knew was made with cherry pie filling and crushed pineapple, so I chose the same. Derek chose the chocolate, and I led him over to the detective, who was looking at Derek carefully.

I felt it important to explain our relationship as Derek was looking particularly handsome in his well-fitting suit and skinny tie. "This is my best friend's little brother Derek," I said. "Their mom is making him be my bodyguard."

"Not a fun job," Derek said, shaking Detective Sherman's hand.

"I can imagine."

At my suggestion, we took our paper plates and sat down on folding chairs. Gazing around the room, I noticed that one man sat by himself near the door. Tears rolled down his face, and he was making no effort to disguise them. Feleesha Farnsworth walked over to him and put a comforting arm on his shoulder, but he squirmed away. She hesitated, then left the room.

He looked familiar. "Do you know that guy?" I asked Derek.

"It's Judith's ex-husband," Detective Sherman answered. "Jared."

"Not ex yet," I said. "Estranged. I wonder if he's been drinking." I had never met Jared, but I'd certainly heard a lot about him.

"He drinks?"

"A lot. Reportedly. At least he's not here with Darla."

"Who's Darla?"

"Shhhhh," said Derek. "Talk about this somewhere else."

I nodded. Gossip is interesting, but there is a time and a place.

It turns out the place was the parking lot. Detective Sherman followed us out when we had finished our cake. As we walked toward Derek's Outback, he asked again, "So who is Darla?"

I adjusted my shoulder bag, which kept falling off my shoulder. "That's the woman Jared ran off with. Darla Oglesby."

"When?"

I stopped and thought. "I don't know. A year or so ago."

"Is he still with her?"

"No. Now this is gossip, of course, but the word on the street is that . . ." I paused and continued, more to myself than to Derek and Detective Sherman. " . . . I guess I should say 'Word on the theater,' not 'Word on the street. But of course 'on' is the wrong preposition with 'theater.'"

Derek unlocked the Subaru. "Ella! Just tell him."

I sighed and chose my words carefully. "People in the theater world, or at least the microcosm of the theater world represented by the Spotlight Players, say that . . ."

Derek and the detective were both giving me very dark looks, so I forged ahead quickly.

" . . . that he broke up with Darla two months later because she wasn't nearly as much fun full-time as when she was a side treat. And he realized, belatedly, how much he loved Judith and that he wanted her back." I shook my head. "That happens so often. You don't know what you have until you've lost it."

"Joni Mitchell said it better," Detective Sherman said. "'Big Yellow Taxi.'"

I smiled and started singing the chorus of the song. He joined me at the "paved paradise" line, and we broke into harmony at "parking lot."

Derek rolled his eyes.

I couldn't help but smile. "Not a bad voice there."

"You're looking at a guy who played Curly in *Oklahoma.* High school."

"I played Ado Annie!" I started singing, again. This time it was "I Cain't Say No."

Derek sighed. "Since you 'cain't say no,' can we go get something to eat? I'm hungry."

"You just had cake."

"I want dinner."

"I didn't finish with what I know . . . heard . . . about Judith's ex." I turned to Detective Sherman. "I mean estranged husband."

Derek leaned against the car and waited, arms crossed over his chest. He didn't look happy.

I continued. "Jared was supposedly working hard to win Judith back, but his daughter and son were furious with him and wanted nothing to do with him. Judith still loved him, but she had been hurt badly and was reluctant to welcome him back, even though she had welcomed him back before when he screwed around. Numerous times. But the two of them had gone out to dinner a couple of times recently, and Jared was hopeful . . . I heard."

Detective Sherman looked very interested. "Anything else you *heard?*"

"Her friends really had it in for him, but it was more because he represented a lot of middle-aged men who think the grass is greener on the other side of the fence—if you'll forgive the cliché—and they kind of wanted revenge in honor of some of *their* husbands, who had done the same thing. This is not theater gossip now, by the way. This comes from circles the Pickle Queen runs in, which is a lot of them."

"The Pickle Queen?"

"My mom," said Derek. "Long story." He stood up straight and told me, "If you don't get through this in two more minutes, I'm going for burgers without you."

"You can't go without me. You're my bodyguard." I opened the door and tossed my purse inside. (Not the Galoochi. I would have been more careful with the Galoochi.) "I thought you were going to cook for me tonight."

"I never said that."

"You're not cooking for your mom now, so why not me?" I thought it was worth a try.

Detective Sherman interrupted. "Could we get back to Judith here?"

I pointedly turned away from Derek. "Okay. Judith was torn. She loved Jared, and maybe she was inclined to forgive and forget, to use another cliche, but her kids and her friends were not so inclined . . . Or so I heard, from the Pickle Queen. And her circles."

Derek got in the car. I decided maybe I'd better join him.

"Thank you for the information," said Detective Sherman.

I shut the door and rolled down the window. (It was an old Subaru. The windows still rolled.) "Gossip," I said.

"Thank you for the gossip then."

As we drove off, Derek began singing another song from *Oklahoma,* "People Will Say We're in Love." Derek is no stranger to musical theater, either.

"What's that supposed to mean?" I asked.

"You clearly have the hots for this guy."

"Well, he sings!"

"He may be trying to put you in prison, for God's sake.

Cool it." He gunned the car—or as much as you can gun a fifteen-year-old Outback.

I sighed. I would work on cooling it.

Rehearsal started early that evening, as planned, so that we could make up for the time we had missed after the murder. It turned out to be quite an eventful evening.

First thing, Tess gathered us together for a little speech. "I'm sorry to have to tell you that Feleesha has strained her vocal cords, and to continue singing before they heal would likely have lasting consequences, poor thing. I'm afraid she and I have decided she must step aside as Lili. Of course, we still want Feleesha in the show—we need her talent in any capacity! So I'm moving her to the chorus, where she can concentrate on dancing. It's just too dangerous for her otherwise. Luckily, Celeste, our very responsible understudy, has been studying all along and paying close attention to rehearsals. She's going to step into the role of Lili tonight and take over."

Feleesha, strangely, did not seem all that upset. She whispered, "I'm sorry."

Tess continued, "Let's all work together to *make this work*!" I thought she was going to pump a fist into the air, but she didn't. "If all of you can help both of them out and adapt as necessary, that will be super. Feleesha will be a harem girl in the chorus, same as Celeste was, so it shouldn't be too hard on her." She turned to Erin, our stage manager. "Celeste may need some prompting with lines here and there, so stay on top of the book." She turned back to all of us. "We're all pros here, so I know we can do it!"

Actually we weren't all pros, and I wasn't at all sure we could do it, but I kept my opinion to myself.

It turns out I was wrong. Celeste really is a pro, or at least behaved like one. She was terrific as Lili, performing in her first run-through as though she'd been doing the role all along. Clearly, she had just been waiting for her chance to shine.

We were all relieved. Out of respect for Feleesha's feelings, no one gossiped that night at rehearsal about what was really going on, though there were a lot of raised eyebrows and "Call me later" gestures. While I waited at the stage door for Derek to arrive from the gym, where he had been working out—thankfully—when I didn't need to be with him, I turned to Gordon and asked softly, "It's a bogus story, right?"

He kept his voice low, too. "Of course it's bogus. Tess is annoying but not stupid. She knew there was no way Feleesha was going to pull this off."

I agreed. "The fake strained vocal cords are a perfect solution."

Gordon gave a little snort. "They actually *might* be strained, as many times as she's had to repeat every song to get it right. Or sort of right." He saw Derek pull in. "There's your bodyguard. Stay safe, sport."

He left and I climbed into Derek's car. Derek and I watched him until he was safely in his Kia at the other end of the parking lot. No murderer was lurking.

CHAPTER 17

Suddenly I sat up in bed and looked at the clock. It was 2:20 a.m., and the front door had just slammed. I was groggy, but I realized that I couldn't blame the cat. Someone was in the house.

Terrified, I didn't move for a moment. Then I realized I had to act and act fast. The cut in my forehead throbbed as I slipped out of bed and slid open the bedroom window as quietly and quickly as possible. I said a mental prayer of thanks that the landlord hadn't yet replaced the screen he had taken for repairs. I climbed up on the sill and then started out the window. The string on the waist of my pajamas caught in the window track, pulling one side of the pants up around my armpits as I eased to the ground, but I yanked it loose and slid the window shut. I was barefoot and cold, but I figured that with an intruder in the house, I'd rather be barefoot and cold outside than barefoot and in danger inside.

I crept to the fake rock where I hide extra keys to my house and car, opened it carefully, and grabbed the car key. I would leave quickly and then call the police.

But I didn't have my cell phone. Thinking quickly, I decided I could drive to the Seven-Eleven on the next block and call from there.

I flattened myself against the side of the house and

side-stepped around the corner toward the driveway, hoping I'd still have enough feeling left in my feet to drive. As I rounded the corner, getting my key ready, I saw the front of my car. Both tires were flat. I wasn't going anywhere.

I moved back around the corner quickly and froze, panicked. Should I knock on Foster's window? Risk going across the driveway to the neighbors next door? Cut through the alley and knock on a random neighbor's back door? As I tried to think what to do, another body edged around the corner and ran right into me. I screamed.

"Ella! It's me!" Derek grabbed me and held me.

"There's someone in the house!" I was shaking, from both cold and fear. "We have to get out of here."

"No one's in there. Let's get back in the house." He kept one arm around me and tried to move me around the corner and toward the front door.

I followed reluctantly. "But I heard the front door slam."

"I know. That was me."

"What?" I stopped. I had forgotten entirely that I now had a roommate. What was wrong with me?

"I heard something and looked out the window," Derek said. "Someone was letting the air out of your tires, so I went out after him. He took off when he heard me, but he got three of the tires first."

We were moving again, almost to the front steps. Derek still had his arm around me, trying to calm me, but I was shaking even more. "What did he look like?" I asked.

Before he could answer, a police car pulled in behind my car, and two officers jumped out. "Let the woman go," one of them ordered.

He let me go.

"He's my friend! This is all a mistake," I said, wondering who had called the police. "I don't have any shoes on. Could we please go in my house and sort this out?" I asked.

They agreed. By then the McConnells from next door had appeared on their front steps, and Foster was on our front porch. I mouthed a "sorry" to Foster as we went in.

As soon as I was wrapped in a blanket and had the afghan from the back of the sofa over my feet, I started explaining. It took a while. When the officers were finally convinced of Derek's innocence, one of them went outside and had a look around.

"Three flat tires," he said when he came back.

"We know," I said.

"Did you get a look at the guy?" the other officer asked.

Derek shook his head. "Dark clothes. Not a real big guy. That's about all I could tell, and he was around the corner and out of sight pretty fast. I did go after him, but once I got to the corner, I couldn't see where he went."

"You left the person you were supposed to be protecting behind," one of the policemen commented.

Derek looked a little sheepish but said nothing.

"This guy could have gone around to the alley, circled back, and gone in the back yard," the officer continued.

"I did think of that. Eventually," Derek said. "That's why I was edging around the side of the house and managed to run into Ella."

At that point the doorbell rang. It was Mr. McConnell, this time fully dressed and looking pretty mad. "I'm her neighbor. Can someone tell me what the hell is going on?"

"We had a report of an incident, sir."

"I know. I'm the one who heard the scream and called 9-1-1."

"It was a misunderstanding, Mr. McConnell," I said.

"Another misunderstanding? Like the dead cat?"

The policemen looked confused. "Sir, we must ask you to return to your home."

Mr. McConnell said, "I don't know what you've got going on here, Missy, but I'm calling your landlord to complain and get you out of here—if they don't lock you up soon for that other matter."

"Other matter?" one officer asked.

"The accordion murder," I explained. "I didn't do it."

Of course they knew about the murder. Everyone knew about the murder. The two of them looked at each other, and one of them took out a note pad. They ushered Mr. McConnell out the door, and then Derek and I had to explain, again, what had happened.

Eventually, the police finished with us and left.

We weren't going to calm down enough to sleep any time soon, so Derek started to open a bottle of malbec. Then he changed his mind. "Hold on," he said, going into the den and rummaging in his duffel bag.

I knew what he was getting. We do live in Colorado, after all. Sure enough, he came back with some edible marijuana, in brownie form. He gave me a small piece, and he broke off the same for himself.

"This will definitely help us relax," he said.

I knew he was right. It wasn't the first time I'd used it as an adult. Sammie had given me some a time or two to help me sleep, but I never bought any myself. I didn't want parents of my students to see me going into a marijuana dispensary.

We ate our bits of brownie. Warm now, I had taken off the blanket and curled up in only the afghan. Derek was sitting across from me. "Someone definitely has it in for you," he said. "Who?"

"Stanley? Aiden? I know I've said it before, but they are the only people I can think of who might have a problem with me."

"Sorry, but it's not them."

"Like you know," I said sarcastically.

"Just think outside the box."

"Okay. Could it be someone who thinks I really *did* kill Judith? Someone who loved her?"

"Her daughter, maybe," he suggested.

"She lives in Phoenix."

"She might still be here because of the funeral."

"Maybe. But women don't kill cats." I petted Fluffles, who was curled up on an edge of the afghan.

He gave me what I thought was a very judgmental look. "That is a sexist view. Women are perfectly capable of killing cats."

"Capable, maybe, but highly unlikely. I don't buy Judith's daughter as a cat poisoner or a tire flattener."

He moved on. "How about Judith's son then?"

"He's a minister. I doubt it."

"Her husband? Could he have it in for you because he thinks you killed her?"

I brightened. "He *is* in love with her, and he did want her back. Reportedly. *And* he has an alcohol problem. Maybe he thinks I killed her. You know, because it was my accordion."

Derek looked interested.

I threw the afghan off, disturbing Fluffles, who hopped down and went to the bedroom. "Both 'visits' here came at around 2:15—right after the bars close! I'm calling Detective Dan tomorrow."

"Detective Dan?" He raised the brow over his brown eye.

"It's my private name for him. I don't use it to his face. " I folded up the afghan and put it on the back of the sofa. "And by the way, where was your gun tonight?"

"I forgot to grab it."

This time it was me raising my eyebrows—both of them. (I can't do one at a time.) "Maybe the Pickle Queen ought to re-evaluate this situation."

"Fine with me."

We yawned at the same time and decided it was definitely time for bed.

CHAPTER 18

I CALLED DETECTIVE DAN the next morning, or, rather, the same morning but much later, and told him my suspicions about Jared.

"You do know that many, many people leave bars at closing time?" he said.

"Of course. But they don't then go to somebody's house and kill a perfectly sweet cat. Or flatten tires."

He sighed. "Ella, you don't even know that Jared actually hangs out at bars at all."

"I know he drinks."

"You've *heard* he drinks. I'm afraid this theory of yours is just conjecture."

I really didn't like the way he said "conjecture." "It's pretty good conjecture, though," I insisted. "Will you at least keep my theory in mind?"

He sighed again. "Okay. I'll keep it in mind."

I wasn't sure I believed him. My voice was chilly as I said goodbye.

Then Derek and I examined the flat tires on my Camry. "It looks like they used a side cutter to destroy the valve stems," Derek said.

"What's a side cutter?"

"A kind of wire cutter."

"So why didn't you just call it a wire cutter?"

"Because it had to have been a side cutter. All side cutters are wire cutters, but not all wire cutters are side cutters. I know how you like specific language." The look he gave me challenged me to continue this mode of inquiry at my own risk. I decided to move on.

"So how do we fix this?"

"We could call a tow truck," he said.

I winced, thinking of the price.

"Or 'we' could take them off one at a time and take them in to be fixed," he added.

I have no idea how to take a tire off. I gave him what I hoped was a winning look and said, "I'll make you cookies."

He shrugged, knowing very well that he was in a good bargaining position.

"Or as soon as I have a free night, I'll make you a huge pile of my famous barbecued ribs."

He looked thoughtful. He was bending but not there yet.

I went all out. "And a chocolate macadamia nut cheesecake."

"Done."

He took off the first flat tire, put on the spare, and then took off the second flat. He left the car on the jack and put the two tires into the back of his Outback. He knows he's not supposed to leave me by myself, and thanks to his earlier errors, he wasn't about to give me a break now. I had to go along.

We waited an hour and a half in the lobby of Big Tire. Uncomfortable plastic chairs. Three-year-old *Sports Illustrated* magazines on the table. Fox News on the overhead television. Coffee that tasted vaguely like burned dirt. Finally, the tires were fixed, and we went home.

The process wasn't over. Derek put one repaired tire on the jacked up side, then jacked up the other side, took off the spare, and replaced it with the other good tire. Then he jacked up the back and took off that tire. We spent another hour and a half in Big Tire hell, hoping our cell phone batteries didn't die. Candy Crush and Words with Friends were all that tethered us to sanity.

Finally, the last tire was fixed, and we drove home again. Derek put it on the car.

It was not an enjoyable day.

Driving me to rehearsal, Derek pointed out that annoying the security guard by putting embarrassing items in my bag was not going to make my life easier, so I decided to be nicer. The man's name, it turns out, is Herb, and I discovered that his granddaughter had been in my kindergarten class two years before. I told him how I'd found little Riley to be adorable and smart, which is true, and he seemed to thaw towards me considerably. He even told me that Riley always referred to me as her "pretty teacher." Awwww . . .

Feleesha made a point of emphasizing her supposed vocal problems all evening, sipping hot tea when she wasn't on stage and speaking to everyone in whispers. Paula sat at her table in the greenroom, sewing extra sequins on the harem girl costume. Marco the Magnificent, I noticed, still had a safety pin holding his cape together.

Rehearsal went well, though. It went so well that I found myself thinking that the show was actually going to be good. Afterward, I texted Derek immediately, and we went right home. We hadn't slept much, and we were exhausted—him from changing tires all day and me from watching him change tires all day. We went straight to bed.

I had trouble sleeping though. The song "Yum Ticky" from the show kept looping in my brain, and I'd find my fingers playing the accordion part on the sheets. This happens to me a lot—not playing "Yum Ticky" on the sheets but having songs loop through my brain. It's usually a song I hate, rather than one I am fond of, though I didn't mind "Yum Ticky" as a song. I just didn't like it on continuous replay.

I tried to get the song out of my mind by thinking about suspects. Maybe Jared was the one out to get me, but who had been out to get Judith first, and succeeded? I needed to consider everyone. Could Helena have had a motive? Reagan? Anyone in the orchestra? The techs, Caleb or Noreen? Tess? Paula? Cecil or one of the other puppeteers? Marco the Magnificent? Any of the other bazillion people in the cast?

I went back to "Yum Ticky." All in all, it was less frustrating than trying to figure out who was the murderer in our midst.

It was well after 1:00 a.m. before I finally fell asleep.

CHAPTER 19

Tuesday morning I had a text from my mother at 6:30 a.m.:
BABA IS WORRIED ABOUT YOU.

I try to see Baba once a week or so, but with all the hullaballoo about the murder, I hadn't even thought of visiting, and I hadn't thought to invite her to our "solve the murder" meeting, either. What was wrong with me? I immediately called her, as I knew she would already be up, and asked if I could come over and bring a friend.

"That would be hunky-dory!" she said. "Come around noon and I'll make lunch." She must have heard from Mom that I was out of a job and would be available.

Before breakfast, Derek made me go for a run with him.

I thoroughly hated it.

He kept telling me to speed up, while I just wanted to sit down. He ran circles around me, literally, looping his route so that he would move a couple of blocks ahead of me, then turn around and circle behind me, then move ahead again. As he passed me, he'd say, "This is a run, not a walk!" or "*How* old are you again?" I'd say nothing back because I was having enough trouble breathing. This went on for half an hour, and by the end I was ready to kill him.

After breakfast, even though I was exhausted, I had to go along with him to the gym. I took a yoga class from an instructor I usually avoid because she talks too much. The stretching felt good on my sore muscles, and I enjoyed the class, despite her long tale about some retreat where she had learned about cultivating a non-dual awareness by seeing past separateness. Or something.

Afterward I went to the café area and, feeling virtuous after my workouts, ordered a smoothie with kale in it. Not my best idea. As soon as I tasted it, I had it replaced with a caramel latte. Then, while Derek spent extra time sculpting his already perfect body, I sat down at a corner table to make notes about solving the murder.

I stared at the page for a while, then wrote down, "Suspects: Everyone involved in the show." I stared a while longer, then gave up and pulled a novel out of my bag. I was soon lost in the story. It was nice to worry about the problems of fictional people instead of my own.

An hour later, Derek approached just as I was shaking my head." Another *padder*," I said, shutting the book.

"Huh?"

"Haven't you ever noticed that when a character in a book goes to the kitchen at night, they always 'pad' to the kitchen. No one walks, scuffs, hurries, creeps. They're always *padding* to the kitchen."

"And that's a problem because . . .?"

"It shows a singular lack of imagination on the part of the author. And it's unrealistic."

"Singular *and* unrealistic." He sat down. He knew he'd have to hear me out.

"Have you ever once in real life heard anyone anywhere say that someone padded to the kitchen?"

"I can't say that I have."

"And have you ever once in your whole life described yourself as padding to the kitchen?"

"No, I have not." He stretched out in the chair, legs out in front of him.

"Of course not. No one pads in real life. And what is it about kitchens that invites padding? Why don't the characters ever pad to the bathroom or the living room or the den? It's always, *always* the kitchen that they pad to. It's ridiculous." I crossed my legs and looked at him accusingly, as if he had done the offensive padding.

"I promise you, Ella, that my novel will have no one, ever, padding to the kitchen. If anyone at all pads, I will have them pad to the living room or the front porch and avoid the kitchen altogether."

"Thank you." I uncrossed my legs, reached for my yoga mat, and started to get up. "Will you also avoid 'me and him" and 'accrost'?"

"No. I've already used them."

"And you call yourself a real writer." I put my book into the tote bag, knowing that my yoga clothes hadn't gotten sweaty enough to damage it.

"Characters are using them, not me," he explained.

"Then I hope they are loser kinds of characters."

"Of course."

I was placated. "Now we're off to Baba's. We have a lot to talk about."

Baba opened the door and smiled. "Bellella!" she said, hugging me. She wore her bowling shirt and a cardigan sweater, her ever-present folded Kleenex peeping out at the wrist. Derek smiled at the logo on the front of the shirt: "Three Gals and a Chick." The team was made up of three women over 60, including Baba, at 80, and the granddaughter of one of the women. (I think they include her because she can still drive at night.) Baba's bowling bag sat beside the door, ready to go, though her bowling league doesn't meet until 6:00 p.m. Baba likes to be ready.

She gave Derek the once over. "And your friend is…?"

"Baba, don't you remember Sammie's little brother?"

She looked him over carefully. "Derek! Oh, my. I didn't recognize you. You're all grown up!"

"He's my bodyguard right now, so I have to take him everywhere with me."

"Have to?"

"The Pickle Queen says," I answered.

"Enough said. Come on in, and I'll pour you some Pepsi." We hung our coats on the clothes tree just inside the door while Baba studied Derek a bit longer. Then she turned to me. "I'm very glad you have a bodyguard, honey, but he looks too darned handsome to scare anyone."

I decided not to add to her worries by mentioning his lapses of judgment. Derek just gave her a sweet smile.

We sat down at the kitchen table as she carefully divided a can of Pepsi between Derek and me, using two old jelly glasses."Let's catch up a little before we eat," she said. She put six Triscuits—two for each of us—on a saucer and handed us napkins. "This will tide you over and shouldn't ruin your appetite."

Derek ate his two quickly and eyed mine. I put them on a napkin and scooted them closer to me. "You can take your laptop and work in the living room while Baba and I catch up," I said.

"Finish your Pepsi first," Baba said. I stifled a smile. Drinks were not allowed in the living room.

Mom had kept Baba up-to-date about the accordion murder, as we now called it, but Baba still had questions. She also had ideas, lots of ideas. She had even drawn up a list of suspects, and first on the list was Stanley. "He probably still likes you and is mad you wouldn't go out with him any more and decided to frame you," she said. She didn't use the word "dumped." There was a reason I loved this woman.

"At last someone agrees with me."

"He is *not* in love with Ella," Derek called from the living room.

"I didn't say *love*. I said *like*," she called back and moved on. "What about the assistant director? What's her name?"

"Tess."

"Maybe she wanted to be the head director. Main director. Whatever you call the head honcho in a show. So she killed Judith so she could take her place."

I shook my head. "I can't imagine her doing such a thing. She's way, way too sweet for murder."

"Bellella, don't be naive. Sweet people turn out to be murderers all the time."

"Maybe, but my gut says it can't be her."

She wasn't convinced. "We'll come back to that another time. For now, let's look at the actors. Who did Judith make mad?"

"Everyone."

"Okay, who did she make the *maddest*?" She broke a Triscuit into thirds and nibbled it.

"She probably gave Feleesha Farnsworth the worst time."

Baba paused, a piece of Triscuit in mid-air. She leaned forward, frowning. "Feleesha Farnsworth? Are you sure?"

"Of course I'm sure. She played the lead, but she couldn't remember her lines. Judith sometimes had the understudy step in so that Feleesha could go review. That had to have embarrassed Feleesha," I explained. "And pissed her off."

Baba frowned. "Watch your language, please."

"Okay, that had to have embarrassed Feleesha and made her mad."

"Why didn't she just learn her lines?" Baba doesn't have a lot of sympathy for slackers.

"She *tried,* Baba. She just couldn't do it."

"Not a real sharp cookie then?" Baba broke her second Triscuit into thirds.

"I think she's just not good at memorizing. Tess—who is now the director—finally did have to replace her."

Baba nodded her head knowingly. "So maybe Tess isn't as sweet as you think."

"She let Feleesha save face by telling us she had damaged vocal cords. That was pretty sweet."

I had eaten my Triscuits, and without thinking licked a finger to pick up some remaining salt on my napkin. Baba gave me a disapproving look, so I stopped. Baba adores me, but manners are manners.

"So tell me more about this Feleesha," she said.

"People say she loves acting so much she went to New York to become a big star and changed her name to

F-E-L-E-E-S-H-A. She thought that spelling would make a more memorable stage name."

Baba winced.

"Awful, I know." I went on. "Anyway, I heard that everybody at her high school was sure she would make it big in New York, but she didn't."

"What high school?" Baba asked.

"What difference does it make?" She was not focusing. "I'm pretty sure it was Foothills High in Harper Falls, not that it matters."

"Is she about your age?"

"Around that. I heard she didn't get a single role in New York, so after a while she came back to town. And now local theater productions are her life. I think she lives to be a star, even if it's just a local star."

Baba got up, as if to do something but then didn't remember what. Then she went to the sink and poured herself a glass of water. "Salty," she said by way of explanation, nodding at the Triscuit box. How could she be getting an excess of salt with just two Triscuits?

She sat back down again. "I might as well say it. No."

That took me aback. "What do you mean, 'No'?"

"No, she doesn't live to be a star."

"What? No disrespect intended, Baba, but how would you know?" Was Baba losing it?

She got up and poured herself a cup of coffee. She always has a pot going, and she sips on it all day. I don't know how she sleeps at night. She sat back down and said, "Listen, honey, I just put all the pieces together and figured out who Feleesha is."

"What are you talking about?"

"Let me tell you a little story." She looked thoughtful, staring up at the window where little glass statues of birds on the sill caught the light. "It all started with a girl named Betty. I went to school with Betty in Harper Falls—many years ago, of course. Back then it still had a Catholic school, all the way up through high school. All the kids called her Princess Betty. Not around the nuns, of course. Back then schools still had lots of nuns." She ate her last third of Triscuit and chewed slowly—way too slowly for me.

"And?????"

"Betty always had to be the best. Best singer, best dancer, best at algebra." Baba said "algebra" as though it is a dirty word. "Best girls' basketball player, best at selling Girl Scout cookies, best at collecting money for pagan babies, best . . ."

"Hold on there," I interrupted. "Pagan babies?"

She looked puzzled for a second. "Oh, I forget that you went to Catholic school when it wasn't so Catholic." She put a heaping teaspoon of sugar in her coffee and stirred, looking thoughtful.

"Pagan babies?" I prompted.

"During Lent, the nuns always wanted us to save money to pay for baptizing pagan babies in Africa. If you saved enough to donate five dollars, you got to name a pagan baby." She smiled, reminiscing. "We even got special containers for collecting the money."

"Jesus," Derek said from the other room.

Baba frowned but ignored him. "It was a big deal. Most of us could never manage to donate more than fifty cents or so, but Princess Betty managed to save $5.00, and she got to name a pagan baby."

I couldn't help myself. "What did she name it?"

"Joanne."

"Jesus," Derek repeated.

"Who put a nickel in you?" Baba called. "If you're going to talk, do not take our Lord's name in vain."

"Sorry," he said.

Baba went on. "Every time I see a picture of a woman in Africa, I find myself wondering if she could be Joanne." Baba smiled and winked. "You never know."

"So what does this have to do with Feleesha?" I asked.

"I'm getting there. You need the back story," she said firmly. Then she reached up to her right ear. "Oh, my. There's my ringa-dingy."

Her ringa-dingy is what she calls the warning her hearing aid battery gives when it is about to die. I tried to be patient as she went to an end table in the living room, where she keeps her batteries. I heard her rummage in a drawer as she talked to Derek.

"How is the writing coming?" she asked.

"Not so well," he said.

"That's good," she answered. The old battery must have died completely.

She came back into the kitchen, fumbled a bit with the new battery, and finally got it in her ear. She smiled. "There we go. Much better. Now where were we?"

"The back story," I prompted.

"Right. So I was jealous of Betty. We all were. We thought she would marry the richest, most popular guy in the school—Spencer was his name." She smiled, remembering. "So handsome…"

Her attention floated off somewhere else. Then she

jerked a little and came back to the present. "But instead Spencer got someone else pregnant and ran off with her. Betty was so upset she married this guy who'd always been in love with her. Harold Farnsworth. Not the kind of guy Betty should have married. He was dull as dishwater. Dull looking. Dull talking. Dull at every job he ever tried."

I was trying to be patient. "So???????"

"So they had a daughter, and she was dull, too. At least that's what Betty seemed to think. Paula was what they named her."

"Who became Paula, our costume person, I presume."
She nodded.

"Are we going to have to go through Betty's whole family tree?" I asked. I was really getting hungry.

"Just be patient. Betty was good at everything, so she wanted her daughter Paula to be so good at everything, too. But Paula just wasn't. She couldn't sing, couldn't dance, couldn't do sports. She was a huge disappointment to her mother, and everyone knew it." She shook her head. "What kind of mother is that? Doesn't appreciate what her daughter *is*, just focuses on what she wants her to be?"

"A rotten mother," I said, thinking of how my own mom and dad had paid for all those years of accordion lessons that Jaja had started. Mom would have preferred I play the piano or violin. Dad would have preferred electric guitar. But I loved the accordion, and they respected that love.

Baba continued. "Finally, Paula couldn't take all the criticism anymore and ran away with a guy when she was only 18. He dumped her eventually but left her pregnant."

"And I'll bet the baby was Feleesha!" Derek said. He

had given up any pretense of writing, pulled up a chair, and joined us.

"Bingo! How did you guess?"

"I just figured Feleesha had to be entering the story soon."

Baba smiled. "Smart boy. Yes, Paula had Feleesha and had to raise her on her own. Betty was too humiliated about having an illegitimate child in the family to help out." She glanced at each of us. "They still called them illegitimate back then. Not now. All children are legitimate."

"We *know*, Baba," I said.

"Good. I'm glad you know that." She continued. "Paula decided that even though Feleesha was illegitimate, Feleesha would be the one to make Betty proud. She became the mother of all stage moms. It was ridiculous."

"How the heck do you know this?" I asked.

"I've kept up with Betty over the years."

"I thought you hated her."

Baba folded her hands in her lap and looked heavenward, putting an exaggerated look of innocence on her face. "I don't hate anyone. That wouldn't be Christian."

I rolled my eyes and Derek laughed.

Baba dropped her act and continued. "I don't keep up *personally*, for heaven's sake. I just talk to people, you know. I'm Catholic. Betty, Paula, and Feleesha are Catholic. Our paths cross. Church committees, you know. Stuff."

"Gossip, you mean," I said.

"That, too." She nodded to the coffee pot. "Coffee, either of you? It's not that fancy stuff—just Folgers."

"Yes, please," said Derek.

"Me, too," I said. Maybe it would stave off my growing hunger, if I added cream and sugar.

Baba got up and saw that there wasn't enough coffee for both of us. She topped off her mug, then opened the cupboard for more filters. She took out the filters and had trouble separating one from the stack.

"I'll make the coffee, Baba. Sit down and tell us about Betty."

"You don't need to do that, sweetie."

"I *want* to." I took the filters from her and started on the coffee. "So fill us in on the gossip."

She thought a moment. "I heard how Paula groomed Feleesha. She started her with dance lessons at about two, then piano lessons and singing lessons. She made her compete in kiddie beauty pageants to learn poise. You know, like that poor JonBenet Ramsey. Where on earth did her parents come up with a name like JonBenet?"

"Baba, the back story?"

She plowed on. "The dresses for those pageants cost a fortune, and she was just working as a receptionist, for heavens' sake! No education, you know." She turned to Derek. "I hope you have continued your schooling?"

"Bachelor's degree in English," he said.

"Good for you." She beamed at him. "Ella was always very good at English, too."

"Back to Feleesha," I demanded, sitting down as the coffee gurgled its way through the filter.

She wasn't pleased with my demanding tone. "Back to Feleesha, *please*," she said.

"Please," I said.

She nodded. "I have a friend whose granddaughter was in school with Feleesha, and she said the girl was really shy and not at all what you'd think after all that training.

She seemed afraid of her own shadow. But then, her senior year, her mom sent her to an exclusive school for budding actresses, back east somewhere. Connecticut, I think. Only . . ." She hesitated.

"Only?"

"Only some people say that she didn't really go to school. She really went to live with Paula's great aunt and had a baby."

"Really?" That was a very interesting piece of gossip.

"Really. And Paula made her give it up. It was so hard on Feleesha that she had some kind of nervous breakdown and was in a hospital for a year. Or so I heard."

"Mental hospital?" Derek asked. Baba gave him an eighty-year-old's version of a "Duh!" look, and he said, "Oh, of course."

"Paula went back east a lot, supposedly to see Feleesha's shows, but probably just to see her in the hospital. Eventually, she brought her home and told everyone that Feleesha just missed Colorado too dang much to stay in the big city."

"Was Feleesha okay then, after the hospitalization?" I asked.

"Who knows? But I doubt it. Paula decided if Feleesha wasn't going to make it big in New York, she was going to make it big here. She was still going to be the person Paula wanted her to be. Or, actually, the person that Betty wanted both of them to be."

The coffee was finished. I got up before Baba could, filled mugs for Derek and me, and topped off Baba's. "I've seen Paula sometimes sitting in the auditorium and taking notes. I've always thought they were notes about costumes, but maybe they're notes for Feleesha." I thought a minute. "Maybe she's really trying to help her."

Baba rejected that idea with a snort. "She's trying to control her, not help her. She's heartless. If half of what they say about how she treated that child is true, there's a reason Feleesha had a nervous breakdown."

"*If* she really had a nervous breakdown," I said. "Could you maybe be biased against the whole family? You know, because of Princess Betty and the algebra and the pagan babies and all?"

"Of course I'm biased! But my sources are reliable." She got up and put her cup in the sink, took out the used coffee filter, and dumped it in the trash.

"Is Princess Betty still around?" Derek asked, changing the subject.

"Of course. Aging perfectly. Looking great. She even wins swimming medals in the Senior Olympics." She picked up our empty coffee cups. "I still can't stand her. And she still treats Paula like…well, you know what. Feleesha, too."

"Wow," I said. "This is a lot to take in."

She got out a skillet. "Enough of that. I'm hungry, and you must be, too. Jaja burgers okay?" She got out a skillet.

"Burgers sound good," said Derek.

"Jaja burgers aren't really burgers," I told him. "We just call them that because that's what my brothers and I started calling them when we were little. Our grandfather loved them."

He looked a bit alarmed when Baba started slicing up a can of Spam. She fried it, then took thick slices of sourdough bread, added sharp cheddar cheese and the Spam, and made grilled sandwiches.

Derek practically drooled as he wolfed down his Jaja burger. Then he hesitated.

"You'd like another?" Baba asked.

"Yes, please."

We smiled. Jaja burgers are always a hit.

CHAPTER 20

TECHNICAL REHEARSAL two nights before opening was, pre-dictably, awful. Tech rehearsals are usually awful. Actors and musicians get cranky at the tediousness of waiting around as the tech crew adjusts levels on microphones, fixes feedback problems, and resets lights to frame the action correctly. Scenes are started, stopped, restarted, and often started and stopped again. People lose patience and snap at one another, and those in minor roles sometimes start to nod off as they wait to go onstage.

When rehearsal finally ended around 12:30 a.m., I texted Derek, who was working at his home instead of mine. I'd warned him it would be late, so he was printing out a new draft of some chapters, using "a decent printer" instead of my "piece of crap."

Gordon decided to flout the walk-with-someone-to-the-car rule. "If someone wants to murder me on the way to my car, I'll beat them with my trombone," he told me. "I've got two sick kids at home and a cranky wife. I don't have time to wait around here and make her even crankier."

I knew it would be a while before Derek pulled up out back, so I sat down in the first row of the auditorium beside Becky, who slouched in her seat, frowning, arms across her chest. "How long are we going to have to vamp before that person playing Rosalie gets her entrance right?" she asked.

"If tonight is any indication, a long time," I said.

"And can Joe *ever* sing anything without increasing the tempo?"

"If tonight is any indication, evidently not."

Stan joined us. He *could* have sat down on the other side of Becky, but he sat beside me. I wished Derek could have seen his choice.

"Brutal night," Stan said.

Tess sank down beside him. "It's going to be a disaster," she said, shocking us all. Where was optimistic Tess?

I surprised myself then by taking on her cheerleader role. "We'll pull it together," I said, actually believing what I said. "Things will be better Thursday night at dress. And not having rehearsal tomorrow will give everyone a chance to rest and regroup." Becky had insisted that she still needed Wednesday for her Bible study class, even on the week of the opening. That was her agreement with Judith, and Tess had to honor it. With no band, Tess realized she might as well give everyone the night off.

Tess smiled at me, perking up a bit.

We sat quietly for a few moments, exhausted. Then we watched Feleesha walk onto the stage and stand there as Paula came down the side steps to the auditorium. Tess said casually, "Paula, could you remember to fix that clasp on Marco the Magnificent's cape?" He had been fussing with the cape all evening, as the safety pin wasn't strong enough to hold the thick material, and it kept coming loose.

"I'll get to it when I get to it," she said curtly and went to stand in the center of the auditorium, about twenty rows back.

Becky and I exchanged glances. Tess looked shocked.

"Stand in the light," Paula called to Feleesha.

Feleesha did.

"Now turn."

Feleesha did. She modeled the harem girl chorus outfit we had seen Celeste model a couple of weeks earlier when Paula was fitting costumes. But now the pants were cut lower so that more midriff was exposed, and the top now featured a plunging neckline. Paula had sewn what had to be hundreds of green and gold sequins all over the chiffon pants, and the outfit had been transformed into quite an eye-catching costume that showed off Feleesha's toned, trim body perfectly.

"That's a lot of glitz," commented Stan.

Tess still seemed to be recovering from Paula's sharp words. She frowned and seemed genuinely puzzled when she commented, "She doesn't have time to fix a lead character's costume, but she has time to sew a million sequins on pants for her daughter?"

We said nothing.

I could almost see the positivity bubble to the surface as Tess rallied. "Maybe Paula is having a rough night, just like the rest of us. I'm sure she just wants her daughter to look her best and will get to Marco's cape soon."

Again, we said nothing.

Aiden came out onto the stage then and looked down at the front row. "I'm ready, Mom," he said.

Feleesha smiled to see him and walked over and gave him a hug. "Great job tonight, Aiden," she said, evidently forgetting about her damaged vocal cords.

Aiden pulled away sharply, and Becky jumped up, looking angry. "Meet me at the door, Aiden. Now. I'm ready."

What was that all about? Was Aiden now acting like someone besides me was poison? And why Becky's sharpness? All Feleesha had done was compliment Aiden. I was puzzled.

I followed Becky up the steps and walked to the stage door with her and Aiden. Aiden looked glum, even though he really had done a great job tonight, relatively speaking. It had been by far his best attempt at fake concertina playing.

As Herb opened the door for us, Aiden started out, then suddenly put his arm in front of me, blocking my way. "Stay back."

I looked around. "What? Why?" And was he actually speaking to me?

"Wait inside until your bodyguard gets here."

"What did you see, Aiden?" His mother was alarmed. He didn't answer but stepped out and peered down the alley, then stepped back.

"I saw this guy who's been hanging around. There's something creepy about him. I think he went down the alley and around the corner." Just then Derek pulled up.

"Where's your car?" I asked Becky. "We'll wait for you."

She pointed. "It's in the lot." She turned to her son. "Leave your bike and go home with me. I'll drive you to school tomorrow." They live only a few blocks away, so Aiden often rides his bike to rehearsal.

"Derek and I will wait until you're in the car, doors locked." Becky looked worried as they walked away. Aiden kept looking back at us. He looked worried, too.

Were we all starting to imagine things? Or was some dangerous guy really hanging around? And could the dangerous guy be Jared?

CHAPTER 21

DEREK INSISTED ON WRITING in my den all day Wednesday—after a morning run, which I again hated. While he worked, I did some sleuthing on my laptop to see what I could find out about Jared Pence. According to Google, he was born in Rock Springs, Wyoming, and now worked as an electrician in Harper Springs. He was fairly active in theater, having played roles in Denver, Harper Springs, Laramie, Cheyenne, and Juniper. A drunk driving arrest came up, though it was from a couple of years ago.

I found myself staring out the window a lot, worrying, my thoughts bouncing every which way. What was Mrs. Markham doing with my kids? What was Sammie going to do about the baby? Why would anyone ever think of using an accordion to kill somebody? Was Jared Pence really dangerous?

A phone call from Sammie interrupted me. "I need serious stress relief now that I can't drink." She begged me to go dancing with her and Derek at the Yellow Rose.

"You know Wednesdays are my rehearsal night with the Streusels," I said.

"You're not working. Couldn't you ask them to meet this afternoon? Then we could go dancing after you rehearse."

I thought they might agree.

And they did.

When I arrived at Otto's at 4:00, everyone wanted an update about the murder investigation. I told them what I knew, and then Henry spoke up.

"I've been thinking about the murder, and your music director is on my radar."

"Becky? Do you know her?" I asked.

"She goes to my church. I'm suspicious because she runs a Bible study group and has a 'Jesus is our lord and savior' bumper sticker on her car. And then there's that jeweled cross she wears."

"Pretty suspicious," I said.

"We're Unitarians." He seemed to think that was explanation enough. "What the heck is someone like her doing in a Unitarian church?"

"Do Unitarians even *have* Bible study?" Carl wondered. He was taking full advantage of the snacks Moriko had provided—Doritos and guacamole as well as tortillas rolled up with cream cheese and olives, then sliced to make little tortilla bites.

Henry didn't wait for a reply. "I had a racquetball match yesterday with a guy from our church. Desmond. I took him out for coffee afterward and asked him what he knew about Becky."

"Subtle," Carl said.

Henry ignored him. "Desmond said Becky's had 'issues' with pretty much all the other churches in town. So now she's a Unitarian."

I wondered if one of the issues could have involved her son. "What kind of issues?"

"According to Desmond, Becky left the Methodist

church because she had a problem with Judith. She and Judith disagreed about all kinds of stuff."

"Like?"

"Oh, dumb stuff. Something about what to include in the newsletters . . . How many greeters to have at the door . . . the kind of donuts to serve at meetings. Or whether to have donuts at all. That kind of thing."

"Who could have a problem with donuts at meetings?" asked Carl, eating the last of the tortilla bites.

"I think maybe Becky isn't sympathetic toward gluten-free folks," I said. "She probably had a problem with Judith being a vegetarian, too. Becky is from Texas, you know."

They all nodded, understanding. Texans like their beef.

"How would Desmond know all this about Judith and Becky?" I asked, piling so much guacamole onto a chip that it fell on the table before I got it to my mouth. "Sorry!" I quickly wiped it off the table with my finger and ate it. There was no chance a table top of Moriko's would harbor any germs.

"His wife's friend is a Methodist, so it's coming from her," Henry explained.

Otto had been thinking things over. "What I don't get is why Becky would agree to be music director in a show directed by Judith. That doesn't make sense if she disliked her enough to leave her church because of her."

Henry had all the answers. "Desmond thought it maybe had to do with problems with Becky's kid."

"Aiden?" I asked. Maybe we were getting somewhere at last.

"That's him," Henry said. "She was trying to get him more involved with people. Maybe she thought being in the show would help, so she decided to try and get along with Judith."

"I have another thought," said Otto. "Maybe she agreed to do it because she thought it would be a good opportunity to get rid of Judith permanently."

We all thought that over. It was a good point. "And of course we should rely on the friend of the wife of the guy you play racquetball with who goes to your church for our information," said Carl.

Henry looked miffed. "Okay, so it's not exactly first-hand."

"I think maybe Becky took the job for another reason," I said. "She's not stupid. She complains, but I can tell she loves being a musical director. I see it in her eyes when we get things right. It's like she sends out a hug to us all by just looking at us. She would be stupid to turn down a chance to do something she loves so much."

"But why would Judith want *her*, if they'd had issues?" Allan asked. He was tapping out a rhythm on the table with his hands. He can never keep his hands still.

"Judith isn't stupid either."

"Wasn't."

"Wasn't. Judith was crabby, but she loved theater. She was known for doing a great job—though lots of people refused to work with her again after they had worked with her once. I'll bet she wanted Becky for the good of the show and was willing to look past their disagreements."

"That sounds pretty altruistic," said Otto.

"Hoo-boy. Big word there," said Carl. "Get me a dictionary."

"Ella might be right," said Otto. He looked at Carl.

"Think about it. We put up with you, just because you play a mean bass. We overlook your flaws for the good of the group."

"What flaws?" asked Carl. Moriko gave him a pointed look and scooted the remaining Doritos and guacamole away from him.

Leroy had been quiet, listening, but now spoke up. "I don't think Methodist problems with newsletters and greeters and donuts would give Becky enough of a motive to murder Judith," he said firmly.

"Probably not," I agreed.

"But the information is worth noting," he added.

"Noted. But I don't think I'll call Detective Dan about it," I said.

"You're on a first name basis now?" Moriko spoke up for the first time, looking a bit too eager. She takes way too much interest in my love life, or lack thereof.

"No, I just call him that in my head. Now let's get some practicing in before I have to leave."

We went downstairs to our instruments and began. Derek sat in the living room with headphones, trying to work. He's not a fan of polka music.

Derek and I went home to put on our costumes. That's what we call the outfits we wear when we go to the Yellow Rose a couple of times a month. For Sammie, it's a tank top, a short—very short—skirt, and cowboy boots. She also wears a cowboy hat, her long, dark hair flowing loose below it. I am more modest (I don't have her legs) in a not-quite-so-short denim skirt, a red shirt, boots, but no cowboy hat. With my thick hair, my head just gets too sweaty. Derek, when he comes with us, wears tight jeans, a black cowboy shirt, a black hat, and, of course, cowboy boots. He gets a lot of attention from the ladies—and undoubtedly from some guys as well.

The Rose was pretty crowded for a Wednesday night. Because it was a week night, there was no band. Instead, country-western music blared a little too loudly over the sound system, with videos playing on large-screen TVs hung around the room. Couples two-stepped in a clockwise circle around the large dance floor while others sat at scattered tables.

Sammie and I approached the railing along one edge of the dance floor, and Derek went to buy a Fat Tire. (He usually has one beer over the course of the evening, while Sammie and I drink only club soda and water. We don't want liquor interfering with our dancing.) In about two seconds, someone held out a hand for Sammie. In a minute, someone asked me to dance, too. Rodney.

When I have children, I will use Rodney as an example to my sons and give them this invaluable advice: If you are a guy, learn to dance. If you are a heavy, unattractive, or uninteresting guy, learn to dance well. And if you are really kind of a loser, learn to be an expert dancer. Rodney is not heavy, unattractive, uninteresting, or a loser—just a pretty ordinary guy with a pot belly—but he is in demand on the dance floor because he can really move. He's popular even with women who would never look at him twice anywhere else. His gracefulness and expert leading make anyone who dances with him look good.

I did a couple of two-steps and a waltz with Rodney.

Then music for "Cotton Eye Joe" blared over the speaker, and couples and singles rushed to the floor. Even people who don't normally dance get up for Cotton Eye Joe, but many serious dancers leave the floor. It gets so rowdy with all the kicking involved that it's easy to get nailed. Rodney and I left the floor, and I used the break as an opportunity to look for Sammie.

I found her out on the floor dancing the Cotton Eye Joe. That was interesting. I nudged Derek, standing next to me at the railing. "Look at that. Who is she with?"

"I've never seen him before." The man was tall and blond, balding a bit but nice looking. He was a good dancer, too—not as good as Sammie, but way better than average.

I kept an eye on Sammie the rest of the evening. Something odd was definitely going on. She usually spreads her charms around, dancing only one or two numbers with any one man. But tonight this blond guy was monopolizing her attention, and she didn't seem to mind a bit. Sammie danced with him the whole evening. The most I got from her was a smile or a nod whenever I danced by.

Derek and I had a hard time getting her attention when we were ready to go. We have a rule that when one of us is ready to go, we all go. Sammie didn't look happy about leaving, but she followed us.

Her new friend came, too. She introduced him as Sam.

"Sam/Sammie. Should be easy to remember," he said. He had a nice handshake, looked me in the eye, and said my name. I liked that. He shook hands with Derek, too, then turned to Sammie and said, "How about dinner Friday night?"

"Sure," she said. Derek and I gave each other a look.

Sammie smiled and called him on her cell phone so that they would have each other's numbers.

As we drove out of the crowded parking lot, I said, "Interesting development—Sammie going out with someone from the Yellow Rose."

We don't generally date the men at the Rose—not that there is anything wrong with them. It's just that we go there to dance, not to look for dates, and the regulars—meaning regular dancers—are there for the same thing. Romances pop up now and then, but the hard core dancers generally stay uncoupled. Sammie and Derek and I are definitely part of that group. We aren't even all that fond of country music.

"Um, yeah . . ." Sammie said vaguely. She doesn't usually sound vague when it comes to men. "He's new in town. Works for that company that cuts metal with water-jets."

That didn't explain her interest in him. I twisted in the front seat to get a look at her. She was gazing out the window at Sam getting in his car. I followed her gaze and was glad to see he wasn't getting into a Ford truck with naked ladies on the mud flap.

"Sam and Sammie. That's a little too cute," I said. She didn't respond.

Derek made his way out of the parking lot and pulled onto the street. He glanced in the rearview mirror at Sammie and then yelled at her. "You're being stupid!"

She didn't yell back. That was unusual. "I know," she sighed.

"Well, stop being stupid!"

"But I like him. I like him *and* he can really dance."

"And you really are pregnant. How's that going to work out?"

She sighed. "I'll cross that bridge when I come to it. I'll probably find out he's divorced with five snotty teenage kids. That will do it."

"You've got a bigger immediate problem," I said. "My show opens Friday night, and you just agreed to go to dinner with him then."

"Oops." She took off her cowboy hat and shook out her hair. "I guess we'll see what kind of guy he really is. Early dinner and then your show—if he says yes, that's a gold star for him. If not, I'll be there without him."

I smiled. I knew she wouldn't let me down.

"If you two are finished discussing Sammie's love life, I have some information," Derek said. "I did some chit-chatting with the ladies."

"Lucky them. Did they know their chit-chatting wasn't going to get them anywhere with you?"

He ignored me. "So I sat down with this gal I know, Chardonnay."

"You're kidding," I said. "About her name, I mean."

"Nope. She drank beer instead of wine, by the way. I knew you'd appreciate that little detail."

"What is wrong with people? I've had kids in class named Merlot and McAdams—that's a Canadian whiskey," I added before anyone could ask. "And Burgundy and Margarita. I'm surprised I don't have kids named Trojan, to memorialize when the condom broke."

"Do you want to hear what Chardonnay said, or not?" Derek asked, an edge to his voice.

"Yes, please," I said politely.

"She saw you wave at me when you danced by, and she asked me if you were the accordion lady. I said yes, and she asked if you really did it. I told her the jury was out on that." He glanced at me and saw me glaring at him. "Okay, I told her you didn't, and she said, 'Boy, there's a guy in town who thinks she did, and he's pissed.'"

This was interesting. "Really? Who????"

"She didn't know his name. Her sister was in town visiting on Sunday, so they stayed out late talking at the Rusty Nail. They heard this guy sitting at the bar, drunk, carrying on about how this accordion lady killed his wife and was still walking around and why don't the police arrest her. He was still there when they left a little before 2:00."

"Evidence! He was at the Rusty Nail drinking 15 minutes before someone was letting air out of my tires. What's her last name, so I can tell Detective Dan?"

"Don't know."

"Maybe you can find out?"

"I might know someone who knows her. I'll ask."

This was information Detective Dan would need. It was 11:30, but I decided to call. This was my life, and I needed to clear my name.

He didn't answer, so I left a voice message: "A woman named Chardonnay heard Jared Pence ranting about me on Sunday night at the Rusty Nail, and he was still there when she left at close to 2:00…This is Ella Polansky."

He called back before we dropped off Sammie. "What kind of name is Chardonnay" he asked.

"A ridiculous one."

"So what's her last name?"

"I don't know. Derek talked to her when we were dancing at the Yellow Rose. He doesn't know her last name."

I heard him sigh. "Can he find out?"

"He's working on it. In the meantime, maybe you could hang out at the Rusty Nail a bit."

There was a long silence. Was he still there? Finally, he spoke. "My top priority at work is not finding who flattened your tires, Ella."

"But it's related to a murder."

"Maybe." He sighed again. He seemed to do that a lot. "Let me know if you find out her name."

"The rest of her name," I corrected him.

"The rest of her name," he repeated.

He sighed yet again and hung up.

CHAPTER 22

I WAS TIRED OF NOT BEING ABLE TO GO TO WORK. I was tired of Derek's toiletry bag flopping on the back of the bathroom door and his towel crowding mine on the rack and his stray hairs curling in the tub. I was tired of that look of recognition on people's faces when they realized I was the accordion lady from the newspaper. I was tired of using my laptop on the kitchen table instead of the desk in my den. I was tired of having Derek go with me everywhere.

One thing I was not tired of was having a full pot of coffee, already made, when I got up. I grabbed my Rocky coffee cup, poured a cup, and sat down beside Derek. "I want my life back," I sighed.

"Join the club." He was sipping his power breakfast of some God-awful looking green drink he makes himself—fruits, vegetables, and some kind of powder. He'd offered me some once, but I wasn't about to try it.

I held Rocky in my hands, feeling the warmth. "I need to do something more about solving this murder. And the intruder problem."

"Which are probably related." Derek poured some granola into a mixing bowl.

"Let's set a trap here," I said.

"For who?" He grabbed a banana and started slicing it into the bowl.

"Whom. For Jared."

"We don't know that he's the murderer," he said. He added dried blueberries, sunflower seeds, and a carton of Greek yogurt to the creation in his bowl.

"We do know he's our vandalizer," I said. "And our cat killer."

"True. At least we're pretty sure. But what would be the point of setting a trap? We don't know that he's coming back." He took a large spoon and started stirring.

"He's a drunk. He hasn't been caught. He thinks I killed his wife. I think the chances are pretty good that he's not giving up on me."

He took a bite and chewed thoughtfully. He took a swig of the green stuff. Then he said, "Okay, so what do you want to do?"

I explained.

When he was finished eating—finally—we got busy. We took out all my pots and pans, as well as metal baking trays, cake pans, and two pizza pans. I found a stack of sixteen metal pie pans from ready-made frozen pie crusts. I don't know why I save them, except that they just seem too nice to go into the trash. From the backyard shed, we dragged out some metal stakes that had been used to prop up a two new trees the landlord had planted in the backyard a couple of years ago.

Using everything we had found, we rigged a pile of metal inside the gate to the backyard from the alley, as well as inside the side gate to the backyard. If anyone opened either gate, everything would come crashing down. The noise was bound to awaken us and probably scare off any intruder as well.

Then Derek took the game camera he uses for backcountry wildlife photography and strapped it unobtrusively to the tree on the other side of my car, aiming it toward the side gate. With the motion sensor and infrared flash, it would, we hoped, snap a picture of any intruder.

Then we decided to go to Walmart for some motion sensor solar lights.

We were rolling past automotive when I saw Paula Farnsworth, her basket filled to overflowing. She was standing at a display of electric fans on sale. "Hey, Paula," I said, walking up to her. Derek hesitated, then followed with our basket. "How's Feleesha doing?"

"She's in a lot of pain," she said, trying to take the display fan off the top shelf. It was anchored in place.

"What's her prognosis?" I was surreptitiously looking into her basket and eyeing the contents the way my students do when they see me out shopping. They'll say things like, "You're buying Oreos! Mommy won't let us get them. She says they're bad for you." Or they'll say in a shocked voice, "You buy toilet paper!" For this reason, I always hide items like Gas-X and condoms under Cheerios boxes, and I choose my check-out lines carefully, picking the longest ones, rather than the shortest. If I'm in the longest line, my hope is that parents are not as likely to get behind me and see my personal life spread out on the conveyor belt. If they do wind up behind me, I'm a master at distracting them with small talk.

"I'm sure she'll recover with enough rest," Paula said. She picked up a box and compared the picture to the fan on the shelf.

"By the way, this is my friend Derek," I said. I wasn't sure why, but I felt I ought to try to talk to her a bit more.

"Your bodyguard, you mean. I heard about that. I wish *I* had a rich friend who could pay to protect Feleesha and me."

"Not that it's anyone's business, but I'm not getting paid," said Derek stiffly. "Ella is my friend."

"Whatever. I think we all need more protection than that lame security guard is giving us." She looked for the price on the box, then put it back.

"He seems quite thorough to me—goes through everything in my bag and purse, every time I enter," I said.

"It's no wonder he would do that for *your* stuff." She really was impossible.

Derek took my arm. "I think we're done here, Ella. On to hardware."

Paula wheeled off. "Nice talking to you," I muttered sarcastically under my breath.

"What a bitch," Derek said, taking the cart and turning into the hardware section.

"Did you notice the antifreeze in her cart?"

"No, but winter is coming up, you know. Not exactly incriminating."

"What woman buys antifreeze? There's something suspicious there."

He stopped in front of a shelf of solar lights. "Women do buy antifreeze. And caulking and chain saws and weed wackers, too. *You* just don't."

"Maybe she was *out* of antifreeze because she used hers to poison Ginger," I said.

He was reading the description on a package and didn't answer. "Well?" I asked, tapping his arm.

"A cupful of antifreeze is not going to make her destitute in the antifreeze department," he said. "Besides, it was Jared who poisoned the cat."

"We *think* it was. But do we know?"

"I think we pretty much do," he said.

"But we don't *know* know. Maybe it was her. She sure behaved suspiciously."

"You were obviously fishing for information about Feleesha." He put three packages of lights in our cart.

"I was being subtle."

He looked at me.

"Okay, not that subtle."

"Let's go check out," he said. "I'll be billing Mom for this. Bodyguard expenses."

Dress rehearsal got off to a bad start, although I did find another card on my music stand, as well as a package of peanut butter crackers. The card read, "We know you're not a murderer." I smiled.

When the circus tent was supposed to rise slowly during "Cirque de Paris," it stuck two feet off the ground. The violinist was gone because of food poisoning. Joe completely forgot to limp, as his character is supposed to do. The cast members left out a section of one scene and skipped an entire song, causing some rapid page turning in the pit as we tried to figure out where they were.

On the plus side, I saw that Helena was bound to distract audiences from any mistakes in the show. She had evidently taken costume tightening into her own hands.

"Did you hear we sold out already?" Gordon asked as he emptied his spit valve one last time for the evening. "All it takes is a murder to get a lot of free media attention."

"It's not the kind of attention all of us appreciate," I said as I pulled the accordion straps off my shoulders. I had replaced Frankie with another accordion from Mom's basement so that Frankie would be free for polka rehearsals and gigs. This accordion did not have a name. I was fond of it, but not *that* fond.

"I thought that picture in the paper gave you a mysterious look," he said, as we made our way out of the pit. "Not in a good way."

"Thanks. You're always so comforting."

As we walked into the greenroom so that Gordon could fill his water bottle, we heard Tess saying, "Has anyone seen my water bottle? The green metal one?"

We knew the one. She was always misplacing it. She swore the Gatorade in it kept her going, but sometimes we wondered if she didn't add a little something extra.

"I know I set it on the counter there when I went to the bathroom," she said, sounding a little frantic and giving credence, at least in my mind, to the little-something-extra theory. "Look around, people, please. I would *really* appreciate it."

"And has anyone seen my pink hair scrunchie?" Reagan asked. "I left it on the counter, too, and it's gone!" I knew she had to tie her hair back for the ballet sequence, but she looked a little more panicked than I thought someone should be about a hair scrunchie.

"While you're looking for stuff, keep an eye out for my wand," Marco the Magnificent said. He had moved from a safety pin to a large metal clamp to hold his cape together. Paula still hadn't fixed the cape clasp.

When Feleesha came out of the dressing area, I half expected her to announce a missing something or other, too, since that seemed the order of the day—or, rather, night. Instead, she was smiling and looking pretty happy for someone suffering from damaged vocal cords. She made a beeline to Aiden, who was eating a granola bar at the table, and sat down next to him. "This is a good luck piece," she said, taking his hand and putting something in it. "Keep it in your pocket for the show, and you'll be perfect."

Aiden took whatever it was, jumped up, and fled. I saw him look around and drop the object in the wastebasket as he joined his mother at the stage door.

"What's the deal with those two?" I asked Gordon as we left. "Feleesha and Aiden," I mean.

"I don't know, but she is always in Aiden's face. He doesn't seem to like it."

"Neither does his mom. I wonder why." I wanted to fish through the wastebasket to see what he had dropped, but it was full of sticky-looking bags and what appeared to be half a tuna sandwich someone had put in the wrong wastebasket and left to rot. I knew Noreen would not be pleased.

At 2:10 a.m., the pans outside came crashing down. Derek leapt out of bed and ran out into the yard. I dialed 9-1-1 and reported a prowler. Then I followed Derek out, throwing the afghan from the couch over my shoulders and grabbing the baseball bat Geraldine had dropped off to help with my protection. Derek brandished a huge metal flashlight as a weapon. No gun again, I noticed.

No one was there.

Headlights shone into the yard as a police car pulled into the driveway behind my car. "That was fast!" I said to Derek

"What's the problem here?" one of the officers said, getting out of the car.

"We heard a prowler," I said. I saw him looking at all the pans. "We've had some trouble here before," I explained.

"That's for sure." It was Mr. McConnell on his front porch again. "I don't know what the hell a person has to do to get some sleep around here."

"Sir, please go back inside," the officer said.

"But I need to tell you that these people should be locked up. It's out of control here!"

"Sir, back inside."

He shook his head at the folly of the police. We all heard him say to his wife, "Why aren't they arresting that accordion girl?"

Then the other officer opened his door. I heard him say, "Later," to someone as he put his cell phone in a pocket. It was Detective Dan.

"You again," I said. My feelings were distinctly mixed. On one hand, I was glad to see him. On the other hand, I was wearing Marge Simpson sleep pants with an *NSYNC T-shirt Sammie had given me. (We had adored *NSYNC as kids, especially Justin Timberlake.) I pulled my afghan closer around my shoulders, hoping to at least hide the photo of the five boy band members on my chest.

I saw Detective Dan glance at my outfit and start to

smile, before catching himself. "So what's the disturbance this time?"

I explained about the pans and the racket. Then Derek spoke up. "We set up a game camera over there. Maybe I got a picture of the intruder."

Detective Sherman nodded at his partner, and we all walked to the camera. Derek took it down, looked at the view screen, and then held it up, looking sheepish. It was a picture of a raccoon. "It must have climbed the fence and jumped down on the pans," he said.

"I think we're done here," said Detective Dan. "May I suggest that maybe the pots and pans aren't the best idea, if you have raccoons around?"

"Thanks for the tip," I said.

We watched them leave, and I started picking up pans. Derek called me over to the camera. "Look at this," he said.

"A shoe," I said, looking at the corner. "Why didn't the police see that?"

"Because I put my thumb over it on purpose. I recognize that shoe."

"Whose?"

"That kid in the show. The one who won't talk to you."

"Aiden?"

"Yes. I happened to notice his Steph Curry basketball shoes the other night—bright red with rainbow stripes along the sole."

I remembered them. "Why the heck didn't you tell the cops?"

"I didn't want to get him in trouble." He put the camera back in place. "I don't think he was up to anything bad."

"A cat died. My tires were flattened. Both are bad."

"I don't think he is the one responsible. The kid just has a mad crush on you."

"Don't be ridiculous. He hates me." We began picking up pans, trying to be as quiet as possible.

"Nope. He likes you. I think he was hanging out for some other reason. I just don't know what."

"Why haven't you told me about this alleged crush before?" I accidentally dropped a lid onto a cookie sheet and looked nervously toward Mr. McConnell's window.

"I wasn't sure. I suspected it, from the way you described him, but the first time I ever actually saw him was the other night when he thought he saw someone in the alley back of the theater. I didn't know who he was until then."

"Was he wearing a sign saying he had a crush on me, or what?"

"I just watched him watching you. That was a face in love. You need to talk to him, find out what he was doing here tonight."

"You're sure about this? I mean the crush part?"

"Yep. It's a guy thing. I know."

"You aren't a regular guy. I mean, you know."

He didn't take offense. "I know. But I recognize that puppy dog look. Trust me. He's the one leaving you gifts. He's not flattening your tires."

I thought about it. Sometimes crushes do leave a person tongue-tied or acting weird.

CHAPTER 23

Amelia called me from school the next morning during her free period. I was still in bed, sipping coffee. "Hurry up and solve that murder," she said. "Mrs. Markham is driving us all nuts."

"Not surprising. How are the kids?" I really was worried about them. Mrs. Markham runs a tight ship, but it's at the expense of squashing any enthusiasm or sense of fun about learning.

"They keep asking, 'When is Miss Polansky coming back?' I just tell them that it will be soon."

"Let's hope so, but I'm not optimistic." I put the phone on speaker and took an emery board to one of my nails.

"Not the reason I called. I found out something you might be interested in. I saw that kid Aiden you told me about at the psychiatrists' fourplex yesterday."

"How do you know who Aiden is?" I grabbed the pump-top hand lotion to squirt some lotion onto a cracked area on my thumb. An annoying little hard ball of lotion was stuck in the spout, so I grabbed a tissue and pinched it off.

"I don't. But my husband was with me, and he recognized him from the soccer team he coached. Aiden was terrible, so he kind of stood out."

That didn't surprise me at all. But what was she doing at

the psychiatrists' fourplex with her husband? I didn't want to ask. I was quiet, slathering my hands, arms, and elbows with lotion.

She must have read my mind. "We were there for some marriage counseling. We want to have a baby soon, and we need help figuring out how to deal with Frank's parents better."

From what Amelia had told me about Frank's parents, they were going to need all the help they could get.

"We saw Aiden come out of Dr. Tooley's office," she explained. "Maybe the kid is getting counseling for some serious problems. Maybe he's even a killer. Or at least a cat killer."

I started to take a sip of coffee, but my hand was too slippery from the hand lotion, and the cup slipped. Drops of coffee fell on my pink tulip comforter. "Darn it! Hold on," I said. I ran to the bathroom for a wet paper towel. "I'm back," I said. "Aiden is not a cat killer." I explained Derek's theory as I dabbed at the coffee stains.

Amelia listened attentively, then said, "Oh. Like he's in love with you and that's making him crazy?"

"I don't think he's crazy. He just has a crush on me. Maybe." I folded the comforter carefully away from me, then picked up my coffee again. Then I realized that I'd wiped my hands on the paper towel, so now there was no lotion on the painful crack in my thumb. I took a sip of coffee, then put it down and picked up the lotion again.

"What are you going to do?"

"Derek and I came up with a plan. I'm going to talk to Aiden tonight and see what I can find out." I said.

"Good luck. By the way, I heard that Tess Moreland took over as director of your show. Is that awkward?"

I was puzzled. "Why would it be awkward?"

She sounded surprised that I didn't understand. "Because you got the job she wanted, of course."

"What are you talking about?"

"You didn't know? She interviewed for the kindergarten position when you did six years ago. You were the one chosen, thankfully, but she never has found a teaching job. She's a receptionist at the city center, so my husband knows her. The job has to pay even less than teaching, and she's a single mom with third grade twins."

"Interesting," I said, turning this bit of information over in my mind. Maybe she needed that little bit of extra money that would come from being director instead of assistant director. Was it enough to risk murder, though? And did she actually harbor any resentment about my getting the job she wanted? I would have to look at sweet Tess a lot more closely.

It was opening night, and—just as I'd hoped—Aiden arrived at the theater early, too. I saw him ride up on his bike just as I was going in the stage door. I waited for him inside.

"I need to talk to you," I said.

He froze.

"It's okay," I smiled. "Nothing bad. I just need to understand something." I asked him to run to the Mocha Bean next door with me for a quick cup of coffee or a Coke before the show started. It was early.

He went along reluctantly, and I paid for our drinks. When we sat down, he pulled his chair as far as possible from mine. I felt sorry for the kid. His face held the stoic terror of someone awaiting a life or death jury decision.

I had thought seriously about thanking him for his gifts and then being direct about how I was flattered at his interest but really too old for him. Then I remembered some of my own crushes at his age. How would I have felt if Mr. Ortiz, my high school chemistry teacher, had addressed me directly about the way I looked at him with adoring eyes? How would I have felt if he'd told me he was too old for me?

It would have been humiliating. Derek had agreed, and we decided it would be best to leave Aiden his dignity and play dumb. Still, I needed information.

I decided to get straight to the point and maybe end his suffering quickly. "Here's what I need to understand—why you were at my house at 2:10 in the morning. I know you're a good kid, so you must have had a good reason." I didn't know that, but I was pretty sure he wasn't up to anything criminal.

"Why would I be at your house at 2:10 in the morning?" His eyes slid around the room, avoiding my face. His pale skin somehow seemed even paler under his freckles, and his red hair stuck out every which way. Unfortunately, it wasn't the purposeful kind of every which way that involves a bit of styling gel and a nod toward fashion.

"I don't know, but you were. I have a picture of you, taken with a game camera. Just tell me, Aiden."

He waited for a very long time, but I waited, too. In murder mysteries, long silences make people talk, so I decided now was the time to give the theory a try. Even though I don't generally use sugar, I opened a packet and stirred some into my coffee. I thought he might relax more if I wasn't looking directly at him.

Finally, he spoke. "Okay, there's this guy I've seen

hanging around. I think he's, like, kind of a drunk. I heard him yelling at someone coming out of the theater last night." He picked up a packet of sugar and fiddled with it.

"What did he say?"

He fiddled so hard he ripped the packet and spilled the contents onto the table. He started running his fingers around in the sugar, making Etch- A-Sketch-like designs. "The guy said, 'Have they arrested that accordion girl yet? You know, the murderer!!!'"

"Really?"

"Yeah." He looked at the sugar, rather than me. "I've seen him out in the alley a couple of times. I think he's, like, dangerous. I waited on my bike outside for you to leave, to make sure you were okay. He was, like, hanging out by the dumpster, and after you left he got in his SUV."

"What kind of SUV?"

"A RAV4, I think. I decided to follow him on my bike."

"Really? How could you keep up with an SUV?"

"He drove pretty slow—you know, like one of those guys who knows he's too drunk to drive so he over compensates and drives like a little old lady."

I knew exactly what he meant. But how did he know? Before I could ask, he continued. "My dad . . . He does that."

"I see." No wonder the boy had problems.

"The creepy guy went to the Rusty Nail, and I hung out there in the parking lot because I was worried he was going to go to your house and, like, do something bad, since he was probably getting even more drunk." He had abandoned the sugar and picked up a napkin, which he was tearing to shreds as he talked.

"Your mom must have been worried sick."

"Yeah, turns out she was. But anyways . . ."

"Anyway," I corrected, without thinking.

"Huh?" He looked puzzled but plowed on, shredding some more. "So I waited until he left and followed him."

"Did you see where he went, or did he lose you?"

He gave me a look. "The little old lady driving, remember?"

I was duly chastened. "Right. What did you think you'd do if he came to my house?"

"Make a lot of noise. Yell. Do anything to wake you up. Everyone else in the neighborhood, too."

"That was pretty nice of you."

He actually looked pleased. "I had pepper spray, too."

"Where'd you get that?"

"It's my mom's." He hesitated. "We've, like, had problems with my dad."

Poor kid. "So you followed him."

He was loosening up. "He drove for awhile and then parked and, like, just sat in the car for awhile. Then he got out and walked around the corner and went to your house. Or I figured it was your house because your car was, like, in the driveway. I got off my bike and followed him. I had the pepper spray out and was, like, ready to yell." He had no more napkin left to shred, so I shoved my open sugar packet over to him.

"What happened?"

"Like, there was a big crash, and he took off. I ran up to the gate and saw a pile of pans. I didn't get why they were there. Then I turned around and ran after him. I yelled at him when he got in his car, but he pulled out and hit some trash cans at the curb and then drove away, like, way too fast. I got on my bike and rode back to your house to make sure you were okay." He took a breath. "Then I saw you and this guy outside. He seemed like your friend. Or whatever. So I decided to get out of there."

"Wow. You did all that to protect me?"

He shrugged. "I think that guy is creepy."

I nodded. "I think you're right. Just so you know, I've got a bodyguard now—the guy you saw. You don't need to protect me anymore."

"Good." He pushed the sugar packet back and forth with his fingers, ruining his designs. "I can't anyway because I'm grounded. I didn't get home until close to 3:00 and Mom went, like, a little ballistic. I tried to explain about the guy, but she's pretty sure I must be dealing drugs." He shook his head.

"But you're not."

"Of course not." He gave me a disgusted look. "Anyway, I'm grounded except for school and this show for the next two weeks. No computer. No TV." He smiled, just a little. "I don't think she understands what all I can do on my phone."

I smiled back. "Maybe not. Aiden, thank you so much for trying to protect me."

"No big deal." He reached into his pocket and held out something. "Want an Altoids?"

"Sure. Now we'd better get in there before Tess thinks we've forgotten to come."

CHAPTER 24

OPENING NIGHT WAS A SUCCESS. There were a few glitches, but nothing that would make the audience too uncomfortable. One actress completely forgot an important line and temporarily caught Marco the Magnificent off guard. He covered nicely, though, as those of us in the pit tensed for disaster. One of the Bluebird Girls slipped and fell, but the others tried to make it seem like part of the routine—a bit of slapstick. It didn't work, but it was a nice try. The chorus started off ever-so-slightly flat in the reprise of "Grand Imperial Cirque De Paris," but Becky had us play more loudly until the singers finally caught on and self-corrected. All in all, though, things went well, and I was as pleased as everyone else when the audience gave us a standing ovation.

Mom, Baba, the Pickle Queen, and Derek worked their way down through the crowd to the pit to congratulate me. They thought the band had sounded great, of course, "Especially the accordion," Baba said.

Sammie and Sam soon joined us. Sammie introduced Sam to everyone and then said, "Clearly it was the fabulous accordionist who stole the show, don't you think?"

The group applauded. They know how much grief I get over my instrument of choice.

"Meet us at Whitney's," said Geraldine. "I'm buying

drinks for everyone." She nodded at Sam. "And bring this handsome young man."

But not too handsome, I thought to myself, or he wouldn't fit the Profile.

They left, and I went to search for Tess. She might resent me. She might have framed me. She might even be a murderer. But she *had* managed to pull our show from the brink of disaster. She deserved congratulations.

Derek followed me, responsible bodyguard that he was. Mostly.

"See? We did it!" I said to her. "Congratulations!" She smiled and gave me a big hug. Her hug did not seem either resentful *or* murderous. Her twins were hugging her as we took off to meet the others at Whitney's.

Derek and I found our group at a large table at the back of Whitney's. He pulled up a chair next to Geraldine, and I sat between Sam and my mom.

Sam immediately turned and looked at me. "You really don't look like a murderer at all."

"That's because I'm not," I said. The place was packed, and I was feeling a little paranoid. "Let's keep our voices down, okay?"

Derek pulled his jacket up over his mouth and squinted his eyes suspiciously as he panned the room, spy-like.

"Stop it," I said. The waitress sat down drinks for the others, and Derek and I ordered. When she left, I said, "Just so you all know, I talked to Aiden tonight, and we're ruling him out. He heard someone—undoubtedly Jared—yelling stuff about me outside the theater and followed him on his bike. He was trying to protect me, and I believe him."

Derek said, "He's just a kid who's got a crush on Ella and no good sense."

"You're probably right," said Geraldine. "He sounds a lot like Alexander that time he had a crush on Miss Howard." Alexander is my oldest brother, and pretty much anyone with any connection to Holy Name School knows the story of Alexander and his love for Miss Howard in seventh grade. He had completely lost his mind.

"Let's not revisit that," Mom said, shuddering a little. She was quite familiar with the onset of hormones and irrationality. "It does sound more like a crush than evil intent."

Geraldine sipped her cosmopolitan. Tonight her red hair had a streak of purple, and she wore amethyst and diamond earrings at least two inches long. Sometimes they brushed the top of the purple scarf around her neck. "Are we ruling out Stanley as well?"

"No one but Ella ever put him in the suspect category," Derek explained to Sam. "Ella thinks he's bitter because she dumped him, and he sought revenge by murdering an innocent woman with a murder weapon that would implicate Ella."

Sam looked at me with exaggerated respect. "You must be one heart-breaker of a woman."

"The rest of us are dubious about this theory," said Mom. She patted my arm. "Not that you aren't capable of breaking plenty of hearts, honey."

"So who else is a suspect?" Sam asked. He actually seemed interested.

"The top of my list right now is Feleesha's mom," said Geraldine. "Feleesha is the woman who used to play Lili, until she got kicked out," she explained to Sam.

"She spells her name "F-e-l-e-e-s-h-a," I pointed out.

He paused, obviously visualizing the name in his mind. "That's ridiculous."

"I know! They say it's a theater thing . . . makes a better stage name."

"Crazy. This weird spelling is getting out of hand."

I was liking this guy a lot. "What do you think of the name Chardonnay?"

Derek interrupted. "Ella! Enough! And just so you know, I found out Chardonnay's last name."

"Sonoma?" asked Sam, and I laughed.

So did Derek. "Nope. Gardiner. So you can tell Detective Dan."

"You call him Detective Dan now?" Mom asked.

"No, Mom. Only in my head." Where was my drink? I was going to need it.

"Speaking of Detective Dan . . ." Derek nodded toward the front of the restaurant. There was Detective Dan with a woman who was definitely not his mother. I felt my stomach knot as Sammie tried to change the subject.

"So what about Feleesha herself? I mean, instead of her mother?" Sammie asked quickly. I knew she was trying to distract me.

I pulled my attention back to our table. "I don't know. According to Baba, she's probably kind of a mess, thanks to her mother," I said. "And her grandmother."

"That doesn't make her a murderer," said Derek. "And people do change. I sure remember your verging on plus-size middle school years."

"Thanks so much for that," I said. I looked up, and saw that Detective Dan had just come to the table. I could only hope that he hadn't heard.

"I just came over to congratulate you, Miss Polansky," he said. "I'm Dan Sherman," he said to the others.

"Detective Dan!" said Geraldine. "We were just hearing about you." I could have kicked her.

"It was because we found out Chardonnay's last name," I explained. "I mean Derek did. It's Gardiner."

"Thank you. I will check that out." He looked at me. "Really, it was a great show. And the band sounded terrific."

"Mostly due to the wonderful accordionist," put in Baba.

"Undoubtedly." He turned his warm brown eyes on her and smiled.

"I'm her grandmother," she smiled back.

"It's nice to meet you." He turned those eyes back to me. "Really—I enjoyed the show a lot. Especially the accordion." He winked at Baba.

"Thank you," I said.

"Have a good evening." He gave a little nod to us all and left.

Mom watched him, then muttered "Hmmmmm." She gave Geraldine a knowing look.

"Does he fit the Profile?" Geraldine asked.

"Looks like he'd rank right up there—pretty good but not *too* good," said Mom.

"And I noticed his manly shoes," put in Derek.

"Manly shoes are important in a guy?" Sam held out his foot for Sammie. "These okay?" She nodded. "Good to know."

Where was my wine? I took a sip from Mom's glass.

"I've got more suspect ideas," Mom said. "Have you

considered the sound guy and the woman doing lights? They must have keys to the theater."

"I already ruled them out. They have pretty sound alibis." I took another sip.

"Detective Dan tell you that?" Mom couldn't resist. She moved her wine a bit farther away from me.

"No. I figured it out myself, thank you very much. Caleb was buying sushi and picking up his kid during the time the murder took place. And Noreen had some kind of kid issue and was at her son's school." I reached over for Mom's wine, but she slapped my hand.

"Still, you should check them out. You don't know for *sure*. And what about Marco the Magnificent? He seemed pretty sleazy in the show."

"He's supposed to seem sleazy," I said. "Could we talk about something else now? I'm really sick of this subject."

"Absolutely. It's your night," said Baba.

Finally, the waitress came with drinks for Derek and me. Sammie raised a glass. "To Bellella—the best accordion player in Juniper!"

"Hear! Hear!"

I smiled, but I couldn't help looking over at Detective Dan and that far-too-attractive woman. They were clinking glasses, too.

Saturday afternoon the Streusels had a gig at the Veteran's Club. I dressed in tight jeans and my favorite bright red, low-cut blouse. I had just pulled on the red boots I'd splurged on in my Southwest credit card shopping spree when the doorbell rang.

It was Detective Dan. I tried not to notice that he was noticing what I was wearing. "Got a minute?" he asked.

"I've got a gig in half an hour," I said.

"A gig?"

"The Streusels. It's a polka band."

He laughed. Then he saw I was serious. "Really?"

"Really." I looked at him grimly. "At the Veteran's Club. It's for Octoberfest."

"In September?"

"You take Octoberfest gigs when you can get them." I put on my leather jacket.

"Okay . . . Well, I just wanted to tell you that I contacted Chardonnay Gardiner and verified her story about Jared being at the bar until 2:00 and ranting about you. The bartender also verified the story."

"Great." I took my bag (again, not Galoochi) off the closet doorknob and put it over my shoulder. "Are you arresting Jared then?"

"No, but I'll be questioning him, as soon as we can track him down. I'm off duty now, but Detective Kendrick is on it."

"Okay, thanks for letting me know. See you." I was distant. That far-too-attractive woman he'd been with had me quashing any of those reluctant but persistent thoughts I'd been having about him.

He left, and I went to my gig.

I have to say that the Streusels were on fire, or at least as on fire as a polka band can get. The beer drinkers seemed to like the music, and people were dancing, even the children who had no idea how to polka but were giving it a try. The Bellella Polka was a hit, and when someone shouted the inevitable, "Play the 'Beer Barrel Polka,'" I stepped to the microphone.

"I have a song that I think you'll like just as much as the 'Beer Barrel Polka,'" I said. Then I started singing "I'm Sick of the Beer Barrel Polka." The audience cheered at the end of the chorus, and they cheered even louder when I started beat boxing. The loudest cheers came from the bar.

I looked over. There sat Detective Dan beside Derek. They held up their beers and Derek gave a whistle. I smiled.

And then Detective Dan left.

I tried not to be sad.

Then I had to play the "Beer Barrel Polka."

The gig ended at 5:00, and I hustled directly to the theater. Derek watched me enter safely, then parked and went to the coffee shop next door to work until the show was over.

In the greenroom, I quickly changed into the black clothes required for the band. Then I sat down beside Feleesha and Gordon to wolf down a cheese sandwich. Feleesha was, as usual, eating carrots and hummus.

"How are the vocal chords?" I asked.

"That's not funny," she whispered. If looks could kill, I would have been dead.

"I didn't mean it to be funny," I said. "I was asking out of concern." I wasn't actually asking out of concern, since I knew her vocal chords were fine, but I had not been trying to be funny or mean.

"Yeah, right. You're only concerned about yourself and

getting what you want," she said normally, forgetting about her vocal chords. She got up and went into the restroom and slammed the door.

"What got up her butt?" Gordon asked.

"Holy moly! What did I ever do to her?" Her nastiness seemed completely uncalled for and out of character. Where was quiet, hesitant Feleesha? I threw the rest of my sandwich away and headed for the orchestra pit.

Gordon followed me. "You okay?"

"Yeah." I just sat for a few moments, fuming.

Then I looked around. I was starting to see everyone as a potential murderer, and I didn't much like that feeling. I watched Gordon arrange his music and wondered if he harbored any criminal tendencies. He was irreverent. Did that correlate to homicidal in some way?

What about Chris, who was noodling on his bass guitar, as usual? Was he noodling to distract us from his psychopathic nature? And Lucia, on the violin? We didn't know her at all, really, because she always sat with ear buds listening to something on her phone before rehearsal and staring at the phone whenever there was even the tiniest break. Was she really researching future murder weapons on her phone? Or listening to inspirational murder music, whatever that might be? Maybe numbers from *Sweeney Todd?*

But what about motives? I couldn't possibly know what motives all the people in the show might have for murdering Judith. I decided I had to stick to my theory that the murderer must have had something against me, as well as Judith. After all, whoever it was had gone to a lot of trouble to use my accordion as a murder weapon.

Maybe Feleesha? She'd never been friendly to me, but

tonight she'd been downright hostile. Or Tess? Maybe she used my accordion to kill Judith because she resented me for getting the job she wanted. Or Caleb? Maybe he hated me because I'd made fun of him for buying his son sushi. Or Noreen? Maybe she thought I was one of the people who put leftovers in the non-food wastebasket.

The lights dimmed, ending my speculation. I looked up and saw Aiden in the wings with the concertina, and I smiled at him. He actually smiled back. Then I began playing "Love Makes the World Go Round" as he walked slowly across the stage. Wonder of wonders, he actually managed to look, sort of, like he was really playing the song.

CHAPTER 25

I WAS HAPPY to see all the Streusels and their wives and girlfriends after the show. They insisted that the accordion was the best part of the band and even suggested that "Love Makes the World Go Round" become part of our repertoire. (Polka bands use waltzes to relieve what some people—my brothers, for example—call the "monotony" of all the polkas.) They invited me out for a drink, but Derek and I had made plans to go over to Sammie's after the show.

"I'm so disappointed," Moriko said. "We wanted to buy a great big bottle of expensive champagne to toast you."

"Not *that* expensive," amended Otto.

I smiled. I was disappointed not to go out with them, but commitments are commitments. I hugged everyone good-bye and said a silent thank-you for my polka family.

Derek met me at the stage door holding a big bag of food and a six-pack. I took the six-pack, and we walked to Sammie's and went upstairs to her apartment.

This time, Sam wasn't around. I was surprised.

"So what's up?" I demanded after we had settled up on the cost of the food and were sitting around the coffee table in the living room with drinks and paper plates.

"I spoke to Donald this week," she said.

"He was in town?" I dipped French fries into catsup and ate. I was starving, since I'd thrown away my cheese sandwich earlier.

"No. I called New York."

"And?"

"And he definitely is not dad material."

"There's a surprise," said Derek. He finished one slider and grabbed another.

Sammie hadn't taken a bite of anything yet. "I mean he's not dad material in that he doesn't want kids. And if he did want a kid, he would want it to be a girl and name her 'Blakely" but spell it 'B-L-A-I-K-E-L-E-I-G-H."

"Good lord." I choked on a fry and took a sip of wine. "I'm not surprised that he's spelling challenged, though"

"He's not. Well, maybe he is, but he thinks it would be cute to spell it that way, and he's always loved the name Blakely because, and I am quoting here, 'because that was the first girl I ever did it with.'"

"Jesus," said Derek. He looked at his sister with concern.

She continued. "But he doesn't really want to have a girl and name her that. He's just saying that he's thought about it and if he did, he'd want it to be Blaikeleigh."

"Jesus," I said. Then I stopped eating and looked at Sammie with concern.

"He wants me to have an abortion," she said.

Derek blew out a breath. I swallowed hard. I wasn't very good at my catechism, but I was pretty sure abortion is a mortal sin.

Sammie finally took a bite of her slider. We waited while she chewed and swallowed. "I'm not going to have an abortion," she said. "You know I want to be a mom someday."

"Someday," said Derek.

"Someday with a nice daddy and a house with a picket fence and all that." She shook some fries onto her plate. "But someday has just come sooner than I thought."

"And without a nice daddy and a house with a picket fence," I said.

"Right."

I had no idea what to say then and, apparently, neither did Derek. We resumed eating. Between bites, Sammie kept talking.

"So here's the deal. I want a child, and I'm sure it will be beautiful, with Donald's genes."

"And yours," I pointed out.

"Yes, and mine. I'm sure he's smarter than he seems, too."

"You're sure about that?" I took a swig of wine. I wasn't so sure.

"His mom is a science teacher, and his dad is a lawyer. I think Donald is just handicapped because his looks get in the way of everything." She picked up another slider.

"Like learning?" Derek said.

"Such a handicap. Poor guy," I said. I took another swig of wine. I'd clearly skipped over the "sip" stage.

Derek started to shake more fries onto his plate, but Sammie stopped him. "I get extra fries. I'm eating for two."

"Be my guest," he said, though he looked disappointed.

Sammie finished the rest of the fries and then went on. "So here's what I told Donald: if he signed away all his rights, he would not have to be a dad. Or pay child support, ever. Or have anything to do with the child. His name would go down on the birth certificate, but that would be it. And I'd tell my child, someday, that her father didn't want to be a dad, nothing against him, and it would be up to her to look him up when she was 18 if she wanted to."

"No child support?" I didn't think that seemed like a good idea.

"You forget I'm the daughter of the Pickle Queen. There is money to support this baby, a lot of money." Catsup dripped from the slider onto her shirt, and she wiped it off halfheartedly. She was very focused on eating and talking at the same time. "I talked to Mom. You know how she is—always willing to ignore what people will think. She is thrilled at the idea of being 'Nana.'" She took a break for a moment and drank some water. "I don't take money from her for *me*, but I'm perfectly happy to take it for my child. She'll pay me child support so that I don't have to deal with Donald being a daddy. Ever."

Sammie doesn't mess around. I wasn't sure about the wisdom of the plan, though. "But doesn't a child need a dad?" I asked.

She shook the bag to make sure no fries were left in it. "Yes, but a child also needs a *good* dad. Donald would not be one."

"No argument there," Derek said. He got up and got himself another beer.

"And suppose we got married? We'd probably be divorced in five minutes, and then she would have to fly halfway across the country to live with him every summer while I worried myself sick."

"You keep saying 'she,'" I said. Could she already know the sex?

"I've decided it's going to be a girl, a girl named Isabelle." She patted her stomach. "She just feels like a girl."

"You've decided her name already?" I was disappointed not to have any input.

"I'm sorry, Ella, but I didn't decide. I just recognized what her name already *is*. It's Isabelle."

I wondered if hormones were affecting her. Surely babies don't name themselves in the womb.

"What if he moved here and you shared custody?" Derek asked. "She'd have a dad that way."

"Donald's a model, remember? What kind of work could he get in Juniper?"

"Right." Derek let go of that idea. I suspected he was relieved.

"And if he did live here, Isabelle would have to spend part of her time at my house and part of her time at Daddy's house—just like we had to do," Sammie said, looking at Derek. "Nowhere is ever home, and you never know where your stuff is."

Derek nodded, remembering. He added, "And you worry about making Mommy mad about something Daddy let you do, and making Daddy mad when you tell him something Mommy let you do. Or said."

"And both of them have to be at your softball games and dance recitals, and you have to worry about them making everyone feel awkward. And then if a stepdad comes into the picture, you have to deal with not wanting to love him because you feel disloyal to Dad and…."

"I get it already," I said. I had been around when Sammie and Derek were growing up. Though their parents are Catholic, they divorced anyway on the theory that murder is probably more of a sin than divorce. Sammie, Derek, and their two older brothers had drawn a lucky card when it came to Jake, their stepdad. He is a great guy, and they adore him, but Sammie pushed him away again and again as a teenager, out of loyalty to her dad. Luckily they survived her adolescence, largely because of Jake's patience.

"So, I've got three brothers, two uncles in town, a dad who's a lot of fun, and a stepdad in Denver who's a rock of responsibility and kindness. Little Isabelle will have no end of male influence."

"So do you think Donald will agree to this?" I asked.

"He's already has. I paid Mom's lawyer to draw papers up, had them faxed, and he was thrilled to sign. You know Donald. Responsibility is not his thing."

"Wow. That was fast," I said. Sammie did not always follow the expected paths in life. She did, however, think through her decisions carefully—except for the decision to sleep with Donald without birth control—and followed through. Her decision seemed extreme to me, yet she did have some good arguments, and I knew her family members would enfold the baby in their arms—their many, many arms. So would I. In my heart, I knew that she and Isabelle would be fine.

I would certainly be there beside her. I smiled to think of another child calling me Aunt Ella. Or, heck, even Aunt Bellella.

"You've got guts, Sis," said Derek.

"To Sammie and Isabelle!" I said, raising a glass. "You've got it figured out."

We toasted.

And then tears came to Sammie's eyes. "Not all of it. What do I do about Sam?"

CHAPTER 26

SUNDAY, WITHOUT AN INVITATION, Geraldine, Mom, and Baba showed up after Mass with pecan caramel rolls. I think they thought the rolls would make them welcome.

They were correct.

I kissed Baba. I knew she had baked the rolls before Mass. I got out plates and cups, and we all sat around the table.

"Baba updated us about Princess Betty and Paula on the way over," Mom said. "That's a lot to take in. What else do we need to know?"

"Paula insulted us at Walmart," Derek said.

"With antifreeze in her basket. And to quote my friend Gordon, Feleesha had a 'bug up her butt' toward me the other night." Baba frowned, so I quickly added, "I'm quoting him, Baba. That's the term he used—bug up her butt."

"You could have paraphrased," she said.

"This is a murder case, and frank language is sometimes required in the serious business of investigating."

Baba frowned again but didn't argue.

"Back to the subject," said Geraldine. "I think this new information about Feleesha's family is worth looking into. How do we find out more about these three?"

"I think I can help," said Baba. "I know people."

Was she imitating a mobster now? "What people?" I asked.

"People who know them." She took a last bite of pecan caramel roll and chewed. We all watched her and waited. Finally she swallowed, took a sip of coffee, and said, "Lillian. My friend Lillian knows stuff."

"Who is Lillian?" asked Geraldine.

Baba looked at her. "As I just said, my *friend*." She turned away and addressed us all. "Lillian is a long-time Catholic who ran a dance studio for many years. I know that she had Feleesha in class."

"Will she talk to us?" I asked.

"I'm sure she will." She turned her fork upside down and pulled it through her lips to get all the caramel off it. "She'll tell you Paula doesn't have the sense God gave a goose."

"So can you call her?" I prompted.

Baba pulled out what she called her senior citizen phone with giant letters and numbers and consulted a small notebook in her purse.

"You know you could enter all those numbers in your phone," Derek said.

"Why? This works." She finally found the name in the address book, punched in the numbers on her phone, and chatted with Lillian about her three children, the new water aerobics class she was taking, her bunions, the new man she was dating, and how the term "boyfriend" just seemed inappropriate at their age. We used the interminable phone call to eat the rest of the rolls. Baba was not going to get a second helping, but it served her right for taking so long.

Finally, Baba closed her phone. "You and Derek have an appointment with Lillian for a late lunch in Harper Falls," she said. She eyed the goo on the bottom of the empty dish, then reached over with her fork to scrape up the remaining caramel and pecans.

Derek and I settled into a booth at Applebee's in Harper Springs and waited for Lillian. I recognized her immediately from Baba's description—an aging artist. She was slim with startlingly white hair, beautifully cut, and such dark lashes and eyebrows that I could see she didn't need mascara. She wore leggings, boots, and a tunic-style dress in vivid orange, with a red silk scarf knotted around her neck and no jewelry except for a giant pair of hammered silver earrings. "I want to look like her when I'm older," I thought. "Actually, I want her sense of style *now*."

On the way over, Derek and I had worried about what questions to ask in order to get Lillian talking, but Lillian had no problem at all sharing. As soon as we had ordered, she started the conversation with "Paula is frigging nuts."

I wasn't sure how to reply to that, so I didn't.

She continued. "What she did to that child was a crime."

"What did she do?" Derek asked.

"She tried to warp her into something she was not. Feleesha was a good kid. She was a pretty good dancer, but nothing special. She was a pretty good singer, but nothing special. I don't know about her acting."

"Nothing special," I said.

"Anyway, Paula decided Feleesha was going to be the next Shirley Temple." She looked at us. "Do you even know who that is?"

I nodded, but I wasn't sure about Derek. He nodded, too, but I suspect he was lying just to keep her on track.

"How did Feleesha feel about that?" I asked.

She snorted. "Feleesha didn't get to feel. She got to follow orders. Paula would come watch dance lessons and give her pointers. That lasted about two sessions before I told her to hit the road, Jack. I mean, Feleesha could stay, but not her."

The waitress put our drinks on the table, mixing up my iced tea and Lillian's Coke. I could understand her confusion. Lillian looked like an iced tea drinker, not a Coke drinker. It wasn't even diet Coke.

"Paula wasn't happy, but she lived with it—until she wanted me to choreograph a solo routine for a Little Missy competition. She wanted Feleesha to sing and dance to 'Roxie' from *Chicago!* She was seven! Who thinks a seven-year-old should be singing about murder and boobs?" She started singing the song, full volume.

People twisted in their booths to look at us.

I cringed at the inappropriateness of the lyrics and also, to be honest, at the fact that people were staring at us. Derek suddenly decided to use sugar in his coffee, but I guessed it was because it allowed him to look down and hide his face as he opened the packet, dumped it in, and stirred.

"You got it. Entirely inappropriate," said Lillian. "I told her hell no, that was a crazy idea. But did she care? No. She just pulled Feleesha from my studio. Stupid woman. She knew my place was the best in town, but she had to get her way. The last I saw of Feleesha that year, she was crying on her way to the car. Poor kid."

"She must have continued with dance lessons. Where did she go?" Derek asked.

"Oh, Paula sent her to Harper Falls Dance Academy, where they don't care about having kids act like sluts."

People had gone back to their food, but I saw one group of women turn again. I don't know if it was "Harper Falls Dance Academy" or "sluts" that got their attention.

"Somebody must have knocked a little sense into her head, eventually. A couple of years later, I saw Feleesha in a Stars of Tomorrow competition. She sang and danced to a number designed for a kid—'Born to Entertain' from *Ruthless: the Musical*. She did fine. Nothing particularly memorable, but fine."

Our food came, and we were quiet as the waitress set things down, once again incorrectly remembering who got what. I guess she couldn't wrap her mind around Lillian as triple bacon cheeseburger kind of gal.

After a couple of bites of burger, Lillian continued. "Afterwards, when the kids came out to greet people, I saw Paula pull Feleesha to the side, and, lordy, did she have a lot to say. The part I heard was, 'Why the hell did you only look at one side of the audience? You're supposed to look everywhere. You know better than that!'" Lillian shrugged. "And in case you're wondering, I had moved closer and was blatantly eavesdropping. I have no shame."

"I take it she didn't win," Derek said. He'd had two caramel pecan rolls, same as me, but he was eating a burger and fries while I picked at a salad.

"Smart observation. She did not." She picked up the bottle of catsup, turned it over, and pounded the end. Nothing came out. Derek tried, and so did I, but with no more success. Finally, she stuck a knife into the mouth of the bottle and scraped some catsup onto her plate. The catsup struggle did not slow down her story, though. She talked the whole time.

"The next time I saw her was when I was choreograph-ing *Grease* at East High. Paula had a fit when we wouldn't allow her to watch Feleesha's audition. She was trying out for Sandy, for God's sake.. The lead. Of course she didn't get the part. Well, Paula yelled at the director about how the auditions were rigged. She said we hadn't let anyone watch because we didn't want them to see that Feleesha had really been the best." She shook her head, remembering. Then she dipped a fry into the catsup and ate.

I knew by this time to just keep quiet. The woman needed no prodding at all.

"A couple of years later, I ran into Paula at a fund-raiser for the arts council. I was very polite and asked about Feleesha. She told me she had gone off to an exclusive act-ing school back east for her senior year and now was making her way in New York City. She said Feleesha had won roles in two musicals and call-backs for the lead in two others."

"Really?" I was shocked. Maybe Feleesha had been bet-ter in her younger years.

"Of course not really! I knew she was lying. Feleesha just wasn't good enough to get any call backs for the lead in any musicals on Broadway. Ever. And while her sing-ing might have been adequate for the chorus, her danc-ing was not. She just wasn't good enough, not Broadway good enough. I don't know what she was really up to, but it wasn't performing on Broadway." She stopped and took the top off her burger. She pulled off a piece of bacon and ate it by itself. "Man, I love bacon," she said.

"You're not alone," said Derek.

"Then, a couple of years ago, I went to the community theater production of *Music Man* in town, and there was

Feleesha, playing Mrs. Paroo. Obviously, she hadn't made it in New York."

"Fries?" she asked, scooting her plate towards me. "I have more than I can eat." We both declined, then watched her eat them all. "So is Paula a suspect in this murder?" she asked.

"Everyone is a suspect at this point. I have no idea who did it, but I'm trying to find out. And get my job back."

"I'm so sorry about all of that. Your grandma filled me in."

"She didn't do it, by the way," said Derek.

"Of course not! And what a loyal guy you are to stick up for your woman."

"She's not my woman."

I didn't like the way he said it—as if I was the last woman he'd ever want for his woman, if he actually wanted a woman, which he did not. "He's my bodyguard," I clarified, feeling a little insulted. "My best friend's brother."

"She wants to clear her name," Derek said. "I want to clear out of her den and get back to writing my novel."

"Oh, you're a writer!" She immediately fixed her eyes on him, the rest of her burger, topless now, pushed to the side of her plate and forgotten. She began asking him questions about his book. I watched as he answered cautiously at first, and then more easily. Soon he was describing the characters and how they had taken over in his imagination. "Sometimes I feel like I'm just a human typewriter, recording what the characters tell me to. They are just so *real* to me now." His hands flew out to punctuate his words, and he almost knocked over a glass of water.

I just listened, so surprised at his enthusiasm. Sammie

and I had never really taken Derek's writing seriously. We figured he was just delaying the prospect of trying to find a job with only a degree in English. Maybe we were wrong.

As we stood to leave, I thanked Lillian, but she ignored me and beamed at Derek. "You are going to be such a success. I just know it!" She reached over and gave him a big hug. He beamed.

I got no hug. Or beam.

As we got in my car, I asked Derek, "Why haven't you ever told me about your book?"

"You've never shown the slightest interest."

He was right. I hadn't. "I'm sorry. Sammie and I thought . . ."

"You didn't think. You just assumed I'm mooching off Mom so I don't have to get a real job. But writing *is* my real job. I just don't get paid for it yet."

"Got it," I said as I backed out of the parking place.

"Stop!" he yelled. I'd just missed a Volvo.

I tried again, this time looking more carefully. We drove towards home in silence.

When I stopped at a red light, I turned to him. "Now, please. Tell me more about your book. Where did you get the idea for it?" Lillian hadn't asked that.

"I hate that question."

I'd already blown it. I tried to think of another question, but he continued.

"Where do ideas come from? I don't know, and I don't know how to explain it to anyone. I just know that I was skiing one day, and this character named Kathleen walked into my brain, and she had a problem. And pretty soon I was writing about her problem and trying to help her solve it."

I listened as he talked about how he had been frustrated working as a barista and writing during his breaks and late at night. When the Pickle Queen saw he was serious, they struck a deal, and he quit his job and moved in.

"One year only is the deal," he reminded me.

And it turns out he wasn't just "working on" his novel. He had actually finished his second draft and was working on his third and, he hoped, final.

"Could I maybe read it?" I asked almost timidly.

For a minute I was afraid he was going to say no. Then he said, "You're the first person in my family to ask."

"I'm not in your family."

"Aren't you?" He raised his eyebrows—both of them.

"You're right. I guess I am," I said, smiling. "So can I read it?"

He thought it over. "If you're serious."

"I'm serious."

"And if you'll be honest."

"I will be honest," I said.

"But at the same time kind."

"I will be honest and at the same time kind," I added.

"Okay. Let's go over to Mom's house, and I'll print you a copy."

"I have a printer."

"You don't want to spend the time or the toner on 422 pages. Besides, Mom needs an update about Lillian."

I turned right and headed toward Geraldine's house.

CHAPTER 27

WE WENT IN WITHOUT KNOCKING—Derek did live there, after all. We found Geraldine at the kitchen island with a Trivial Pursuit game open in front of her. She was reading all the cards.

"I think that's called cheating, Mom," he said.

"I'm just boning up for Holy Name's fund-raiser—a trivia bowl. They won't use these cards, but I think they'll give me a feel for the kinds of questions they *might* ask. Father Francis is pretty convinced that his Holy Cows team will win. We can't have that."

"God no," Derek said. The Pickle Queen was known for her competitiveness.

"My team is the Ball Busters," she said.

I gasped.

She smiled. "That's what we call ourselves in private. For the church, we're just the Busters."

Derek shook his head and disappeared into the basement with his laptop, saying only that he would put in a couple of last minute changes that he'd been thinking about and then print the book for me.

I could hear the printer spitting out pages as I spent the next hour telling Geraldine what we had learned from Lillian. She, in turn, filled me in on what she'd found out about one of our leading suspects. Her massage therapist's daughter worked with Stanley and had once gone out with him.

"And?"

"He sounds kind of boring," she said.

"Gee, I'm so surprised."

"She described him as a good worker. Punctual. Well-groomed."

"Punctual and well-groomed—every woman's dream." I shuffled the Trivial Pursuit cards.

"My point is that I didn't discover anything of interest. Or relevant to our case. I'm working on Becky now. I think there's potential there for her as a suspect." She took the cards from me and folded up the board.

"Because?"

"I'm always suspicious of people who wear Jesus on their sleeve," she said.

"You mean around their neck, at least in Becky's case."

"Whatever. I just think that real Jesus-y people are hiding something." She asked me if I wanted some chamomile tea.

"Sure," I said, and she started the electric kettle

I wanted to be sure I understood her point. "And Becky is Jesus-y, so she's hiding something?"

"It's worth exploring. And maybe that's why her kid is weird."

"I didn't say he was weird. I said something seemed off about him."

The kettle must have been warm already as it clicked off quickly. Geraldine talked as she poured. "I think it might be because he is being raised by a real Jesus-y mom."

"I was raised by a Jesus-y mom."

"Not that Jesus-y."

"She sent us all to Catholic school."

"So did I. But we don't think everything from burned tuna casserole to the death of a child is part of God's plan. We don't quote Bible scripture at the drop of a hat."

"There's someone like that in my school . . . my former school . . . the school where I formerly taught . . . the school where I used to teach and may eventually . . . "

"Get on with it, Ella."

I paused and then continued carefully. "My theory is that a teacher at Emerson Elementary makes up Bible quotes to fit whatever she wants, knowing that no one's going to look them up. Sometimes I think about making them up, too—maybe telling her about the Lord smiteth-ing anyone who decides to ask a question when the teachers' meeting is finally about to end. Corinthians 13:87."

Derek was standing at the door. "Smiteth-ing is not a word."

"I *know* that," I said. "I was being humorous."

"More like blasphemous."

Geraldine shrugged. "It's not blasphemous to worry about over-the- top Jesusy-ness."

"Maybe." He held up three thick piles of paper, each bound with a large black metal clip. I've got the book."

"Good," I said. "And I've got a show tonight. Let's go."

CHAPTER 28

MONDAY MORNING, Derek closed himself in the den to work on revisions to his manuscript. I sat down with a list of bills to pay online before I settled down with Derek's book. Then I remembered to check the pile of snail mail to make sure I hadn't missed something.

There, hidden between catalogs from Aerosoles and Wayfair was something from the police department. It was a camera ticket for running a red light in Harper Springs exactly two weeks ago. Included was a photo of me in my Camry.

"I entered that intersection on a yellow," I muttered, thinking of my trip back from Whole Foods. Obviously, the camera didn't agree.

Then I noticed the time stamp on the photo: 5:02 p.m. This was good news! The ticket would verify my alibi.

I made a list that outlined what I was doing at the time of the murder:

4:00: Leonard holds the door for me as I leave school.
4:00-4:10—I drive home from school.
4:10: I say hello to Foster as we're both getting home. (He gets off at 4:00 from UPS, and we often arrive about the same time.)

4:10-4:40—I feed Fluffles and shower.

4:40: As I leave, I give Skyden a hug and a kiss while he's playing on the front porch with Maria.

4:40-4:55: I drive to Whole Foods.

4:55: I pick up my food and check out.

5:02: I run a red light but don't realize I will be getting a ticket.

5:02-5:15: I drive to the theater.

5:15: I get to the theater, walking in with Gordon and sitting down with Feleesha to eat.

I called Detective Dan and made an appointment for ten minutes later. Then I banged on the door of the den and said, "Derek! We have to go. Now!" Derek came out with his laptop, not bothering to expend any energy asking me why. I guess he could tell by my voice that there would be no arguing with me.

"You may be the first person in history to be happy about getting a camera ticket," he said after I told him what I had discovered. When I parked in front of the police station, he opted to sit at Starbucks across the street rather than wait for me in the police lobby.

"Okay, what have you got?" Detective Dan asked when we sat down in an interview room.

I tried not to sound smug. "I made a time chart. I think this will prove that I have a solid alibi and could not possibly have killed Judith between 4:00 and 5:15 p.m."

He looked interested. I went through the chart carefully and showed him my speeding ticket. He nodded, which I took as a sign of encouragement.

"So all you have to do is verify with Leonard that he saw me leave at 4:00 and verify with Foster that he saw me get home when he did and verify with Maria that I left at around 4:40."

"I already have."

I smiled. "So you can see then that my only opportunity to kill Judith would have been between 4:40 and 5:15. It takes at least 10 minutes to drive from my house to the theater, depending on traffic, so I couldn't have gone to the theater, killed Judith, and then driven 15 minutes to Whole Foods, bought a lasagna, run a red light, and driven fifteen minutes back—all in 22 minutes. So I didn't do it!

"I think we can safely say that." He actually smiled at me.

I took a deep breath. Injustice was making me brave. "So can you issue a statement or something to the media?"

"I can and will issue a statement that Miss Ella Polansky, local kindergarten teacher and owner of the accordion that killed Judith Pence, has been absolved of any suspicion and is not a suspect in the case."

I hesitated, but only briefly. "Can you add *unequivocally*?"

He sighed. "I can. Unequivocally absolved."

I left a much happier woman.

"He's going to do it!" I told Derek when I hurried across the street to the Starbucks.

"Do what?"

"He's going to issue a statement saying I'm no longer a suspect."

"Hallelujah. Maybe you can get your job back, and I can at least be free to do what I want while you're at work." As we waited for my latte to go, he asked, "You don't have rehearsals this week do you?"

"No, except for a refresher on Thursday night before this weekend's shows."

"How about if we celebrate tonight with those ribs you owe me?"

"Deal. You can work the rest of the day, and I can read your book."

"Want to invite Sammie? She loves ribs, too."

"Absolutely. But we're not eating before 7:00. I want a long stretch of time to read."

I made the barbecue sauce and set it aside to use later, then sprinkled all the ribs with salt, pepper, and chili powder and wrapped them in foil. I put them in the refrigerator until time to bake them. I'd had plenty of coffee, so I made a cup of chamomile tea and sat down with Derek's book.

Dust hooked me almost immediately. Derek had written a rather dark tale, a mystery, featuring a woman named Kathleen and her teenage son. Kathleen is three days from being married when her fiancé is killed in a freak farm accident while baling hay on his farm. She and her son both come under suspicion and must work hard to clear their names, in the meantime uncovering the sordid history of the farm and the previous owners.

I was about a third of the way through the book and taking a sip of my now cold tea when I suddenly read, "Kathleen woke up at 2:30 a.m. and padded to the kitchen." I laughed and swallowed at the same time and couldn't stop coughing. Derek came out of the den. "You okay?"

"Water!" I coughed.

He brought me some, and I swallowed. "Your fault," I said.

He smiled innocently. He knew exactly what I'd just read. "I put it in just for you."

"Gee, thanks. Next Kathleen is going to say 'Alls I want is…'"

"Nope. Kathleen would never say, "Alls I want.""

"Thank you."

"Another character does say *irregardless*, though. But just once." I tried to smack him, but he was already heading back to the den.

I resumed reading and became so wrapped up in the story that I almost forgot to put the ribs in the oven. I actually had forgotten to invite Sammie. As I turned the oven on, I texted her:

COME FOR DINNER. RIBS. BRING POTATO SALAD. 7:00.

She texted back:

GREAT. BRING SAM?

OKAY.

Derek had come into the kitchen and poured his umpteenth cup of coffee. He says that coffee fuels his muse and is a lot safer than the scotch some writers have been known to favor.

"She's bringing Sam," I told him.

"She's heading for trouble." We both sighed and went back to our reading and editing.

I finished the book at 6:30 and hurried into the kitchen to finish getting dinner ready. "Help in here, please!" Derek came into the kitchen holding an Odell IPA. When had he switched to beer? I'd been so absorbed I hadn't even noticed.

"Set the table, please," I said. He started getting plates out while I whisked up some coleslaw dressing the way my mother had taught me.

"I hate to tell you this and give you a big head," I said to Derek, "but I loved your book.

"Really?" He stopped, holding four plates in mid-air.

"Really."

He set the plates down and actually came over and hugged me.

I pointed out the book's many strengths and gave a couple of minor suggestions. He had questions about my reactions to some of the events in the book, and he wanted my opinion about the believability of one of the characters. We were so immersed in conversation that it wasn't until the doorbell rang that I realized I hadn't finished making the coleslaw.

Sam and Sammie arrived with wine and beer and a bag I presumed would contain potato salad. Derek passed out drinks to everyone, including ginger ale for Sammie, and I raised my glass in a toast. "Here's to Derek. His book is wonderful," I said.

"You read it?" Sammie looked surprised.

"That's pretty much all I did today—read for six hours straight."

"Wow."

"It's hard to put down—kind of grabs you right off the bat. The characters are really quirky and interesting, too. I especially like the sinister minister."

"I never call him a sinister minister," Derek said.

"I know. I just couldn't wait to call him that. You have to admit it fits him." I smiled as he nodded.

Sammie frowned and turned to Derek. "So are you allowing other readers?"

I realized that she was hurt. "I *asked* to read it," I said quickly.

"She was the first to ask," Derek said.

Sammie sat down, sticking out her lower lip in an exaggerated pout. "I'm a terrible sister. I should have asked a long time ago."

"You should have. On the other hand, it wasn't done a long time ago. Not that it's done now, but a good second draft is."

"Okay. Can I read it now?" she asked.

"You can." He took a swig of beer and smiled. He was a happy guy tonight.

"That's settled," I said. I took out a bowl and opened the bag she had placed on the table. "You *made* the potato salad?" I'd expected to find a plastic container from King Soopers. Was she already doing the nesting thing I'd read about?

"I did. And Sam helped. We made the brownies, too." The two of them did a little fist bump, congratulating themselves.

"I'm impressed," I said, though I thought the fist bump was a little over the top.

"Ready for us to grill?" Derek asked.

"Almost," I said. I removed the trays from the oven, took the ribs out of the foil and put them on a big platter. I handed him the platter and the sauce and Sam a brush. They took everything out to the patio.

"Don't say it," Sammie said softly. "I know I'm crazy."

"He seems like a great guy, but no great guy is going to

stick around when he finds out you're pregnant with another man's baby." I was whispering.

"I know. But I really, really like him. He fits the Profile to a T. *And* he dances. Such a bonus." She looked like she was going to cry. "Maybe I just want to enjoy him for as long as I can."

"What . . . two months maybe? And then your heart will be broken?"

"Don't they say it's better to have loved and lost than never to have loved at all?"

"Just be careful, Sammie."

Sam came in with the empty platter. "Why so serious, ladies?" He evidently didn't expect an answer, just went to the sink, washed the platter, and then took it back outside.

Sammie smiled at me. "He even washes dishes without being asked."

I shook my head. She was really smitten.

CHAPTER 29

THE NEXT DAY, I checked the *Juniper Times* on my phone, as usual, before I got out of bed. Detective Dan had kept his word and issued a statement that Ella Polansky had been "unequivocally absolved as a suspect in the murder of Judith Pence." Sadly, the ugly picture of me ran again.

YAY, Sammie texted me.

Then I received a text from Mom: FINALLY!

I got up and told Derek the good news. He was already at his computer working. "Great," he said but without the enthusiasm I would have liked. He seemed too absorbed in his work to pay much attention, so I went to the kitchen for coffee, which I knew would be waiting for me. I poured a cup into Rocky and crawled back in bed with my laptop.

An hour later, my cell phone rang and the name Seraphina Conway popped up. I answered with a curt "Good morning."

"I read the paper this morning," she said. "It looks like we can lift your suspension." She hesitated a little too long for my taste and then added, "I'm sorry this has been a problem for you, but we'll be glad to have you back tomorrow."

I was in no mood to play nice. "I'll see you then," I said shortly and hung up.

I spent some time googling "motives for murder" to

see if I could find any information that would enlighten me. According to one psychologist named Dr. Buss, "The vast majority of murders are committed by people who, until the day they kill, seem perfectly normal." I did not find that at all comforting. I was surrounded all day, every day, by perfectly normal people.

I also learned that the top motives for murder included greed, humiliation, and cheating. Other sites mentioned love, lust, lucre, and loathing. I was interested to find that the Australian Institute of Criminology's table of murders over a certain period of time showed "revenge" as a motive in a number of murders, as well as "no apparent motive." How could there be no apparent motive?

I was soon lost in reading accounts of weird murder cases. The woman who stabbed her husband and cooked him, then fed him to her kids. Another who suffocated her boyfriend under her huge breasts. Another who beat her boyfriend to death with his prosthetic leg. A man, a former premed student, who killed three sex workers and removed their eyeballs. The serial rapist and murderer who had once appeared as a bachelor contestant on "The Dating Game."

"You've Got a Friend" played on my cell phone. "I think you should get over here," Sammie said when I answered. "I have something to show you."

"What?"

"I think you need to see it."

I quickly jumped in the shower, careful—as always—not to get my hair wet and ruin my straightening job. When I was dressed, I interrupted Derek again. "We have to go to Sammie's. She's got something to show us."

Derek and I headed to Sammie's apartment. Sam was sitting at the table drinking coffee. Derek and I said, "Good morning," and then gave each other a look that read, "Is he *living* here now?"

We made ourselves cups of coffee from the Keurig on her counter. She had promised me she would buy only recycled pods, but clearly she had been lying.

"So what did you find, Miss Destroyer of Our Environment?"

She ignored the jab. "Yesterday Judith's daughter came in with a bunch of Judith's clothes. She's spending some time sorting things out before she goes back to Phoenix. She's going to sell the house."

"Do you know her?" I asked.

"No, but I expressed my condolences and invited her to have a donut. She must have been hungry, or maybe just lonely, so she sat down and started talking." She smiled at Sam. "Sam bought the donuts."

Of course he had.

"So what did she have to say?" Derek looked at the open cellophane-topped box with what appeared to be two leftover donuts. He helped himself to one of them, squeezed it a little, then dipped it into his coffee.

"She said her parents' divorce wasn't final, so that will make settling the estate easier. Her dad doesn't want the house, but he does want the money from it, so that's why they are selling. She's pretty mad at him, you know, for leaving her mother, drinking so much, and generally being a jerk. My words, not hers."

I marveled, not for the first time, at Sammie's ability to weasel information from people, just like her mom. "I guess it's not surprising he sat by himself at the funeral reception then," I said.

"But here's the important part. After she left, I was going through everything she brought, and I found this in the pocket of a jacket." Sammie has learned from experience not to put things out for sale without checking the pockets. She's found money, a report card, pacifiers, Hot Wheels cars, a set of hearing aids, a diaphragm, and more.

She handed me a slip of paper. I read it aloud: "Judith, we're taking care of it. Caleb is paying it back, so leave it alone, please. Talk to me after rehearsal. Noreen." I frowned. "What could this mean?"

"I guess it depends on what 'it' is," she said. "Ideas?"

"Caleb has borrowed some money, maybe?" Derek suggested.

"Or embezzled some? This doesn't sound good." I looked at the time. "Let's walk over and talk to Noreen and ask her. I'm pretty sure she works during the day when there isn't a show or a rehearsal in the evening."

Noreen was happy to take a break and walk next door to the Mocha Bean with us. "I never turn down a cup of coffee," she said.

I explained about the late night visits and introduced Derek as my bodyguard.

"That's scary," she said. "And a murderer is still out there somewhere. We should all probably have bodyguards." She took a sip of her coffee. "So what do you want to talk to me about?"

"This is awkward, but my friend Sammie over at

Second Chance called and told me she found a note in a jacket Judith's daughter had dropped by. It's from you." I showed her the note.

She looked at it, then rested her head in her hands and sighed. "I wish you hadn't found that."

"But we did. What's it about?"

"I'll tell you, but I hope we can keep it from Edith." Edith was the theater manager, her boss.

"No promises. I don't know what you're going to tell me."

"I know. Just listen. Remember how Caleb and I admitted to giving Judith a key so we didn't have to get to the theater by 4:00 on rehearsal days?"

I nodded. "And I know that wasn't exactly kosher, as my grandmother would put it."

"Right. I didn't know it then, but it turns out Caleb had been adding that hour a day to his time sheet for three weeks. Edith was looking at finances and found that the technical staff was a little over budget, so she asked me to see where we could cut. That's when I found out about his charges."

"What did you do?"

"I was pretty mad and confronted him, and he admitted it. He knew he was wrong, but he's having trouble paying for the out-of-pocket expenses on his son's asthma—I guess those inhalers aren't cheap, at least with his insurance. He promised to claim five fewer hours than he actually worked each week until he paid everything back, if only I wouldn't turn him in." She stopped.

"And?" I wasn't sure what to think.

"Caleb is a good guy who made a bad mistake for a decent reason. Right or wrong, I decided to give him a break."

"So how did Judith get involved?" Derek asked.

"She was looking over the tech charges for the show and somehow figured things out. She took me aside just before a rehearsal and said, 'So which one of you is doing the padding?' Before I could answer, two people came up with some backstage problem that needed solving, and she left."

I sneezed. I fished in my purse for a tissue but couldn't find one. I blew my nose on a napkin, wincing at the rough feel. "Go on."

"I needed to do something quickly, before she talked to our boss, so I scrawled that note and gave it to her as rehearsal was starting."

"So did she talk to you after rehearsal?"

"Yes, and she was a jerk about it, of course. But I did get her to agree to shut up by telling her I'd take her key back if she told Edith. She really liked her 4:00-5:00 time alone in the theater, so she agreed, reluctantly."

"I don't suppose Caleb was upset enough to kill Judith over this?"

"I seriously doubt it. And I heard his alibi checks out."

"And yours?"

She shook her head. "I've already told the cops this. I was at the middle school meeting with the principal and two teachers over an incident involving my son. I have three witnesses placing me at the school until 5:00. I was late to rehearsal—even later than Caleb."

"I guess that lets you and Caleb off the hook," I said. "I hope Caleb doesn't get caught. I agree that he's a good guy who screwed up."

"I know he is. He's under a lot of pressure since his

wife had her hours cut. He won't do this again. I trust him—really—and he's embarrassed and sorry."

"His secret is safe with us, at least unless something else happens."

"Okay, two more people off our list," I told Derek as we were driving home.

"Let me remind you that the murderer might be someone not on our list at all," he said.

"Maybe. But the ones on our list seem like the most likely suspects."

"To you."

"To me. And my suspicions are as good as anyone's—maybe better." I fiddled with Derek's radio, which only gets a couple of stations clearly. I didn't feel like NPR in the background today.

"Why better?"

"Because I'm nosy, and I have good instincts. I put things together. Like, oh, I knew your brother was going to marry Bianca right after he met her."

"Everybody knew that. Wouldn't you want to marry Bianca if you were a guy?"

"Yes, but wanting to marry someone doesn't mean she's going to want to marry you." I stopped fiddling when I found a station playing Nathaniel Rateliff and The Night Sweats. "Maybe that wasn't the best example of my instincts. Take my kids at school. I can look at one of them and know instantly that he's sick or needs to go to the bathroom or is afraid of something."

"Sort of like parents know? Again, not remarkable,

given that you have dealt with twenty or so children all day for six or seven years now." The light changed, but he waited for a mom with a stroller to finish crossing. The car behind us honked. "Jerk."

"Okay, here's another example. I knew you were gay long before anyone else did."

"You've already told me that. Numerous times." He pulled into his bank and parked. "And may I remind you that Sammie also figured it out when I was about 10."

"Okay, so she's good at figuring things out, too." I gave up and changed the subject. "So where do we go next to figure out who murdered Judith?"

"I think maybe we need to find out a whole lot more about Paula. I'm going in to get some cash. Google her."

I typed in "Paula Farnsworth" on my phone and scrolled through the items. When Derek returned, I said, " I think this is her. Age 58. Lives at 21 Anchors Away Lane . . . Who comes up with street names, anyway? Why all the sea stuff when we are half a continent away from an ocean?" I scrolled around. "Seaview Lane, Gulf Bay, Whaler's Way, Harbor Walk." I looked out the window, thinking. "I would like to have a job naming streets."

"I'm sure you would." He backed out.

"Maybe I'd name some streets after books and mess with people. I'd name a ritzy street Grapes of Wrath Circle, and a poor street Great Gatsby Avenue or Edith Wharton Way. Maybe I could name other sections of town after foods . . . Cannoli Lane . . . Bouillabaisse Avenue . . . Biscuits and Gravy Circle."

Derek ignored me. We were stopped at a light, and he was putting Paula's address into Google Maps.

"I take it we're checking out her place," I said.

"We are." The light changed. "See if you can find Feleesha's address, too."

I googled. "Same place. Isn't that chummy?"

I continued my ideas for naming streets as he drove. "I could have sections of town named for famous women . . . or wines . . . or Oscar-winning movie titles of two words or less."

Derek turned up the radio.

"Authors of children's books . . . famous animals, real or fictional—Dumbo, Rin Tin Tin, Mr. Toad, Eeyore."

We turned onto Anchors Away Street. We found her home and drove by slowly. It was small, at least by today's McMansion standards. It was a pretty run-of-the-mill house in a run-of-the-mill development—lots of similar houses, set close to the street.

"Dumbo would not be a good street name," Derek said, driving slowly past the house.

I guess he had been listening.

"And it's weird that she still lives with her mother," he continued.

"You do remember that you live with your mother?" I said.

"Not the same thing. It's temporary and for a purpose," he said firmly.

"I guess this confirms that Feleesha and her mom are still close," I said. "Paula is still guiding her daughter's life."

Derek drove on."That's a real stretch. All we really know is that they live together." He turned out of the subdivision. "How well do you know Feleesha anyway?"

"Not at all well."

"Maybe it's time to schmooze a little and get to know her."

"Not going to happen. She has been rude to me. Besides, I can't talk to someone with damaged vocal chords."

"*Supposedly* damaged."

I decided to change the subject. "Can you swing by the police station? I want to pick up photos of Tillie. Detective Dan said I can have them now."

"And we don't want to miss an opportunity to see Detective Dan, do we?"

I ignored him.

At the police station, we went to the front desk, and I asked to see Detective Sherman.

"You are?"

"Ella Polansky. He has some photos for me."

"Oh, these. He left this for you." He handed me a large envelope.

"Thank you." I tried not to sound disappointed. Derek had the decency to keep quiet as we headed home.

We decided to give our detecting a rest, or, rather, Derek decided it. He wanted to keep editing *Dust.*

And I needed to plan for work the next day.

CHAPTER 30

I COULDN'T CONCENTRATE on planning for work. I stared at my list of suspects and notes but could think of no new avenue to explore. I hoped the police investigation of the murder was going better than mine. Yes, we had uncovered information, but so far none of it pointed to anyone and screamed "Guilty!" I was out of ideas.

Deciding to give myself a break, I picked up a highly recommended debut novel from one of my "to read" stacks and stretched out on my bedroom chair and ottoman.

It was not the sort of book I needed. I admired the writing, but the gentle pace allowed too many thoughts to wander in and disturb my concentration. I looked over my stack again and picked up the latest Elizabeth George mystery. That didn't work either, as I quickly realized I could not allow my brain to bend around another violent act. I needed all my brain cells firing together to solve my own murder mystery.

Finally, I got up and peeked in the den. Derek was bent over his printed manuscript, reading, stopping now and then to cross out a word or write in the margin. He wore headphones, making me wonder again how he could write and listen to music at the same time. I couldn't even mark simple kindergarten worksheets while listening to music. If I knew the song, my right hand would start tapping out the melody on invisible accordion keys. If I didn't know the song, my left hand would mark the rhythm, thumping the page lightly with every beat. My brain evidently had a music channel and a do-something-else channel and couldn't coordinate the two.

I needed a walk. My indoor/outdoor thermometer read 50 degrees. Why not walk the mile or so over to Mom's and surprise her? It was her day off. The route was well-traveled, and it was broad daylight. Jared would surely be at work on a week day and not a danger to me. I should be perfectly fine without Derek.

Quietly, I put on a jacket and left a note on the kitchen table. "1:15. Walking to Mom's." Then I slipped out, taking care to close the door quietly behind me.

Walking west on the subdivision sidewalk, I felt free for the first time in two weeks. The crisp air cleared my mind. The sunshine made the world seem brighter. And the view—oh, the view. It made me grateful, as always, to live in Colorado. The Rocky Mountains stretched along the horizon, fresh-fallen snow glistening in the sun on the highest peaks.

I hummed as I walked, my feet keeping the rhythm. I imagined how surprised Mom would be when I knocked at her door. We might go get manicures, treat ourselves to an afternoon movie, maybe just talk. It was my last day off, and I didn't have a *Carnival* rehearsal again until Thursday night—a review before the next weekend's shows—so I had lots of time.

I was two blocks from Mom's house when I heard it. "Stop! Accordion lady!" I stopped and turned. It was Jared Pence, walking quickly toward me. Where the heck had he come from? And what the heck could he want? I wasn't going to wait around to find out.

I started running, and so did he. "Wait!" he yelled again. "Stop running!"

I kept running, barely glancing each way as I crossed the street onto Mom's block. His legs were longer than mine, and just as I reached Mom's front door and banged on it, he was behind me, grabbing my arm. "Mom!" I screamed.

"I told you to stop!" he said. Then he grabbed my other arm and turned me towards him, away from the door, just as it flew open. There was Mom, a can of pepper spray raised in the air.

"Let her go!" she said. As he peered around me to look, she zapped him in the face with the spray. Surprised, he let go of me. He didn't cry out in agony, though, as I would have wished.

"I just want to talk to you," he said. "I want to know *why*. Why you killed her."

"Leave me alone!" I said and rushed past Mom into the house. By then the pepper spray was starting to take effect, and he coughed and rubbed his eyes. He turned around to avoid more spray as Mom was trying to get in another shot. Then Baba appeared in the entry, holding a fireplace poker. She stepped forward and whacked him across his shoulders, hard.

"We're calling 9-1-1," Mom said, and she slammed and locked the door. In an instant, she was on her cell phone, reporting the attack. Baba and I watched from the window as Jared walked away, coughing. I was coughing a bit, too.

"Are you okay?" Baba asked.

"I think I got some of it, but I'm okay."

Mom didn't show the same kind concern. As soon as she got off the phone, she yelled at me. "What is wrong with you? Why did you go off by yourself?" She was shaking.

"How were you so *prepared*?" I asked, amazed at the two of them.

"Derek called and told us you had escaped," Baba said. "He figured from the time on your note that you should be almost here by now, so we were watching for you. We saw that guy come out of a house and start following you and yelling. Then you were running, so we got our weapons together real fast."

My usually unflappable mother was about as mad as I've ever seen her—though maybe not as mad as years ago when Alexander let our new kitten Frankie into the bathroom when she was taking a bubble bath and it walked around the ledge looking at the bubbles. Then, thinking the bubbles were a solid surface, it stepped into the tub with my naked mother. Let's just say that neither Frankie nor my mom was at all happy.

"You put us in a position to need *weapon*s!" Mom said. She was still shaking.

"Where did you get pepper spray?" My mind was still trying to take in what had just happened.

Mom sat down and took a breath, clearly trying to calm herself. "Amazon. I keep it by the door in the corner behind the drapes. I have another canister by the bed. And you should carry one with you if you're going to pull stupid stunts like this."

"I'm sorry, Mom, I thought it would be okay. Jared should have been at work on a Tuesday."

We heard sirens and looked out the window. A police

car was pulling up out front, and Derek was pulling up right behind it. Two officers got out, and one stopped Derek from coming into the house. The other came to the door.

I was not pleased to see Detective Kendrick again. I don't think she was pleased to see me, either.

As I answered questions, I kept an eye out the window, where the other officer was walking around. He finally let Derek get out of the car, and they both came inside.

Derek glared at me. "What were you *thinking*?" he shouted.

"And you are?" asked Detective Kendrick.

"Derek Russo, her bodyguard. Friend, *sometimes*." He gave me a dark look. "She snuck away."

Detective Kendrick raised her eyebrows. "Are you her keeper?"

"Of course not. But I'm supposed to be protecting her from the likes of Jared."

She gave him a *What-kind-of-weeny-ass-bodyguard-are-you?* look, but he ignored it.

"Jared should have been at work," I said. "He just appeared out of nowhere."

"Not nowhere," said Baba. "It was a house down the street."

Detective Kendrick looked at her cell phone and found Jared's address only two blocks away.

"He's my *neighbor?*" Mom said, horrified.

"Evidently, yes," said Detective Kendrick. "If all of you are okay, we'll go talk to him."

"We're not okay," said Baba. "My granddaughter has been assaulted. How could we be okay?"

"Go," I said. "We'll be fine."

"We all need to calm down," said Mom, who seemed the least calm of all of us. She herded us into the kitchen and plopped a bag of Oreos on the table. To Mom, Oreos are comfort food.

"Who knew what I was going to get into!" said Baba. She looked at Mom. "I just came over to borrow your cake carrier—that nice one from Tupperware. I've got to bring a dish to the Trivia Bowl at Holy Name tomorrow, so I thought I'd make a banana cake."

"I was going to take my chocolate cherry bundt cake," Mom said. "I'll need the carrier."

"Oh. All right, I'll just make artichoke dip then instead," Baba said. She was being awfully agreeable. "I have that nice new bowl with a place for chips around the side."

I smiled a little. It was comforting to talk of bundt cake and Tupperware and dip.

With that, the conversation moved back to murders and assaults and crime solving. Everyone made me promise never to do "such a lame-brain thing again." Then Derek and I got up to go.

"Where's your gun?" Baba asked suddenly.

He looked mad. "It's at home. I forgot it." I wasn't sure who he was mad at—Baba for asking the question or himself for leaving the gun at home.

"What kind of bodyguard leaves his gun at home?" Baba demanded.

I took pity on him. "One who works out a lot and could probably take down someone like Jared in two seconds flat."

"Just like two old ladies did!" Baba said with satisfaction, smiling.

"I'm not old," said Mom.

The police car was no longer parked in front of Jared's home as we drove past, though we had seen it there earlier, through Mom's window. I was rattled by the whole encounter. Why on earth was Jared so convinced I had killed his wife—even after the police had cleared me?

Or maybe it was all a smokescreen to distract us from the fact that *he* was the one who had killed her. Maybe he hadn't wanted her back at all but didn't want to deal with the financial aspects of divorce.

Or maybe he really had still loved her and was so genuinely distraught that he didn't know how to deal with his grief. Maybe he had to put his anger and frustration somewhere—and I was the lucky recipient. If so, he was going to blame me, no matter what, until the real culprit was found.

Later, Detective Kendrick called me. "Mr. Pence insists that he didn't mean to harm you—quote—'even though you deserved it'—unquote. When he saw you walking by, he thought it would be a good opportunity to find out why you murdered her."

"I didn't murder her."

"I'm just relaying what he said. He seems obsessed with *why* and doesn't understand what you could possibly have had against her. Anyway, I'm calling to see if you want to press charges."

I remembered the fear I'd felt when he grabbed me. I remembered poor Ginger, dead on my patio. I remembered my slashed tires, the cut on my head, my terror in the middle of the night when I thought someone was in my house.

Yes, I wanted to press charges.

CHAPTER 31

Derek and I stayed home to spend a quiet night watching television, but at about 7:30, Maria knocked on my door, holding Skyden and a diaper bag and looking distraught. "Please, Ella, can you watch Skyden for a couple of hours? Foster is at work, and I just got a call from my sister. She's been in an accident. It doesn't sound serious, probably a broken arm, but I need to get to the ER."

"Of course." I looked at Skyden. "Hey, little guy." He smiled shyly.

Maria had no time for niceties. She thrust him at me, along with a key in case I needed anything from their place, and left. "He should be ready to go to sleep soon," were her parting words.

Skyden had different ideas. He loved Fluffles and wanted to chase her. He loved Derek and wanted to ride on his back . . . and ride on his back some more . . . and ride on his back some more. He loved bedtime stories and wanted to hear *The Gruffalo's Child.* "Again!" he said when I finished.

So I read it again.

"Again!" he said when I was finished, but there are limits.

"You have to go to sleep now," I said. I'd made him a nest on the floor in the corner of my room with a folded blanket and the puffy pink tulip comforter from my bed. I covered him up with another blanket, kissed him, and said good night.

He wailed as I left the room.

Derek and I set a timer for ten minutes. "If he doesn't stop crying in ten minutes, I'll go comfort him and tell him all is okay," I said confidently. "Then I'll leave the room again." I had watched old episodes of "Supernanny" on TV and knew exactly what to do.

He did not stop crying in ten minutes. I comforted him and left again.

We waited another ten minutes. He did not stop crying.

Finally, Derek grabbed two Oreos and went in. (Like Mom, I always have a stock of Oreos in the cupboard for emergencies.) "Skyden, if you quit crying, you can have these. If you don't quit crying, you can't."

He quit crying.

Derek gave him the Oreos and left.

"You are ruining his teeth, you know," I said.

"But I'm saving my nerves." He turned on the television, and we settled down to watch HGTV, the sound turned low. A tedious couple looking for a new home rejected two places I'd love to own because the light fixtures were "dated" and they couldn't possibly live without an en-suite or marble counters in the kitchen.

After fifteen minutes, I quietly opened to bedroom door to check on Skyden. "Derek!" I called.

Holding an upside-down bottle of liquid soap was a two-year-old in a sea of toilet paper.

By talking to Skyden and using the powerful detective skills we had developed, Derek and I later reconstructed what must have happened. Skyden had twisted each Oreo apart, as any normal person would have done, in my opinion, but then somehow managed to sit or step on one of the halves and mash the chocolate into my comforter. When he saw the mess he'd made, he made his first decision—to go into the bathroom and get some soap to clean it up. (Maria always makes him help clean up his messes.)

He found a bottle of liquid body wash sitting on the edge of the bathtub and decided to use that. I always leave the flip-top cap up on the soap so that I don't have to fumble with it in the shower, so it was easy for him to take it and turn it upside down on my comforter. A lot more soap than he intended came out, so he went back to the bathroom, took the end of the toilet paper and walked with it to the bed to clean up the mess. He used up a whole roll, trying to wipe up the mess but grinding it into the comforter instead. That's when I came in.

Both Skyden and my comforter were soaked with bath wash, so I stripped off his clothes and carried him to the tub while Derek worked on the mess.

"It's like he made one decision after another with good intentions, but none of them turned out well—and eventually led to this mess," said Derek, picking up wads of toilet paper and putting them in the wastebasket he'd brought from the bathroom.

After I'd cleaned Skyden up in the tub, I used Maria's key to look for some clean pajamas while Derek changed his diaper. We all worked together to make a new nest with dry blankets. Finally, we put an extremely clean Skyden into the nest, but this time we read to him until his eyes started to droop. When Foster came home at 10:00 to pick him up, he was snoozing peacefully.

I did not snooze peacefully. For one thing, I missed my cozy comforter, which was wet from all the soap and stretched on a couple of chairs to dry. Also, I couldn't stop thinking about what Derek had said about decisions. Was there some way that one bad decision after another could be related to the murder at the Juniper Theater?

I was beginning to think so.

CHAPTER 32

THE KIDS WERE, to put it mildly, thrilled to see me on Wednesday. After hugs all around, they had to tell me about Mrs. Markham. She was crabby, not nice like me. She messed up the lunch count one day, and Mario had to have a yogurt plate instead of a hamburger. Nathan was really mean to her, and she yelled at him. She wouldn't let them do story time after Joseph and Carlos put crayons in their ears and pretended they were antennas and started talking like robots.

I had to cut them off. We moved to the rainbow rug, and I asked, "Who can tell me something *good* that happened since I've been gone?" Hands flew up.

Victoria's little brother learned to roll over. Jeremy's mom turned 40 and they had a party. Emily's nana was coming to visit. Shelby's dad bought her an "Elsa" pillowcase. Joseph got to go to a Rockies game with Uncle Lou. Colin's dad tied dental floss around his tooth and a baseball and then dropped the baseball to pull out his tooth.

I was very sad to learn that Antonio and his cousin Valeria were missing. Amelia told me later that no one knew what had happened to them, but their home had evidently been abandoned. They were gone, leaving no forwarding address. Were they avoiding immigration authorities? Were they safe? I would likely never know. I hate that fact of life about teaching—that children we learn to care about move on, and we don't get updates about how they are doing. It's hard to let go. It's hard not to worry.

Luckily, the staff had been warned that there was going to be a lockdown drill in the morning sometime. The school has periodic lockdown drills, tornado drills, and fire drills, but I hate lockdown drills the most. The kids aren't too young to have heard about school shootings, and it's always hard to help them take the drill seriously without also scaring them to death. We'd practiced before, but when the principal came on the intercom and said, "Lockdown. This is a drill," they looked alarmed.

"Everyone—No talking *at all*." I put on the no-nonsense, evil eye that all good teachers have at their disposal. "Go immediately to the restroom farthest from the door." The kindergarten has two restrooms right in the room. As I spoke, I immediately went to the door and shut it, knowing it would lock automatically. I shut off the lights and quickly pulled down all the shades. Then I herded the stragglers into the tiny restroom, silently reminding them with the 'shhhhh" sign that they were to be absolutely quiet.

It was crowded. I gave hugs to frightened children and dirty looks to those who started to push or shove. Victoria started crying, but I showed no sympathy. I mouthed "No!" and gave another "shhhhh" sign, and we huddled together, waiting for the all clear announcement that would come from the office.

We were quiet, but the auto-flush on the toilet was not. The toilet flushed again and again and again while the kids looked terrified that it would alert the bad guys. I tried moving kids away from the sensor, but it was impossible in the close quarters. It kept flushing, over and over. I realized that, along with everything else, I now needed to remember to bring in a yellow sticky to cover up the sensor during drills. One more thing to worry about.

We spent less than ten minutes in the bathroom, but it seemed an eternity. Finally we heard the "All clear" announcement over the intercom, and I could speak normally. "Okay, friends, we can leave now. Everything is fine."

"There are no bad guys?" asked Victoria.

"It was a drill. Remember, we *practice* sometimes so we know what to do if there is a fire or a tornado or a bad guy."

"How would a bad guy get in?" The kids know about the buzzer at the entry, which requires that a person in the office push a remote unlock button to let someone in. I didn't want to say, "Miss Evelyn might make a mistake and let him in." Instead, I said, "All the teachers and all the people who work here do everything they can to keep you safe."

I didn't mention that a staff member herself could possibly be the bad guy or that windows can be broken and door locks shot off, or that one of the students might be a shooter or, as had happened once, a first grader might, without her parents' knowledge, put her dad's handgun in her backpack for show and tell.

It's a dangerous world we live in, but I hate, *hate* that five-year-olds have to know that.

I was glad to be back at work. The people who had avoided me before were now friendly, but I remembered how they had treated me, and I resented them. How could they know me and think that I might have murdered someone? It was hard to accept how the parents had behaved as well. "My mommy told-ed me that we had a substitute because you might have done something really, really bad," Macy said.

"Like kill someone. That's what Daddy said," said Joseph. "Did you?"

"Of course not. It was all a big mistake. I would never intentionally hurt anyone."

"What's is intentionally?"

"On purpose. I would never hurt anyone on purpose."

"But you might on accident?"

"*By* accident. Sometimes people do hurt others without meaning to. Remember when Hailey turned around fast and stabbed Raymond in the arm with her pencil? She hurt Raymond, but she didn't do it on purpose. She didn't do it *intentionally*."

"And I still have the lead in my arm," said Raymond. "See?" He pulled up his sleeve. "Mom said it might be there forever."

"I have a scar on my arm," volunteered Sylvia. "I tripped on our back steps, and hit that thingy in the cement that you scrape your boots on."

I winced.

"See my Dora the Explorer Band-Aid?" Rosa thrust out her knee.

"I got a *cast*," said Max.

He had obviously won the jackpot in the injury department. I quickly decided to settle the kids down with a story. They were supposed to be working on the letter "M" this morning, but first they needed to take themselves into a nicer, sweeter world where everything turns out fine. I quickly went through my closest plastic bin of books and chose *Llama Llama Red Pajama*.

At lunch, I saw an email from Garret's mother, Mrs. Conley. Just what I need, I thought. I don't get a break from her, even on my first day back?

Mrs. Conley was quite concerned because Garret didn't want to go to school anymore, but it wasn't because of me. That was a relief. He didn't want to come because he was afraid of Nathan. No matter how carefully anyone watched, Nathan managed to find ways to poke, pinch, hit, shove, or otherwise torment Garret. Mrs. Conley thought something was wrong with Nathan, and he should be removed from the classroom for the safety of the other children.

I decided to do what I would do if the problem child were anyone but the principal's child. I took the note to Seraphina Conway and suggested we set up a meeting after school. I could tell she was upset, but I tried to sound calm. "I'm sure the three of us can figure out how to deal with this."

Nathan was on his best behavior that afternoon. In fact, he was so good that I felt his forehead to see if he might be coming down with something. He went to the listening center when asked, turned on the tape recorder, and listened to a story without reaching his legs over to kick Alissa. He went to the game center and played the letter sound dice game with Max, not once throwing the dice across the room or refusing to give Blake a turn. He took a counting assessment with a parent who was helping out, and he counted cheerfully to 100.

But as the kids were lined up to go to afternoon recess,

he shoved Garret, hard, causing him and the three kids in front of him to go down, one after the other, like dominoes. Howls erupted, and I helped the four on the floor get up. I made sure they weren't seriously hurt, then looked up to see Amelia, across the hall, lining her kids up. She could see I was fuming and said, "Would you like me to take your class to recess with mine, Miss Polansky?"

"Yes, please!" I said. Then I took Nathan firmly by the arm and led him to the office.

"Sit," I said, pointing to the chairs in front of Evelyn's desk. I went into the principal's office and said, "Your son is outside. I just picked up four kids, including Garret, off the ground because of his shoving. He is *not* going to recess with me." I turned to go, then added. "I'm sure this is not going to help things with Mrs. Conley, either." I left.

Mrs. Conley met with us after school in the principal's office. Seraphina started the meeting by thanking Mrs. Conley for sharing her concern. She wanted to hear what Mrs. Conley "understood" had happened.

"You mean happened again and again," she said. "Nathan is out of control. Despite Miss Polansky's best efforts, he still manages to poke and pinch and shove behind her back. And on the bus. And on the playground. And after school."

Seraphina bristled. "Kids commonly poke and pinch and shove one another. Part of what we do here is help them learn more acceptable behavior."

"Nathan isn't learning it. My child comes home crying almost every day because of something Nathan has done."

"Kids exaggerate," she said. "Sometimes when we react strongly to something a child tells us, we encourage the child to continue that kind of behavior. You could be rewarding him by your concern, so he exaggerates."

Mrs. Conley gave her an icy stare, and I felt insulted on her behalf. Still, Seraphina continued. "I'm sure Nathan wouldn't intentionally hurt anyone."

"You're wrong. He does." Mrs. Conley was firm.

Seraphina looked at me. "Miss Polansky, you spend most of the day with Nathan. I know you have had issues with him, but you wouldn't say his behavior harms others, would you?"

I took a breath. "I have to say that we have had many incidents of children hurt or upset by his behavior." I wasn't thrilled to be put in the middle here, but I had to be honest.

Seraphina did not look happy with me. "Perhaps we can monitor Nathan a bit more closely and put him on a rewards system, where he receives tokens for a day with good behavior. Miss Polansky could monitor him carefully and determine when he gets the tokens."

I was monitoring him as closely as humanly possible. I did not want to add token monitoring as part of my duties.

Luckily, Mrs. Conley was having none of it. "Tokens aren't going to cut it. I want Nathan removed from Miss Polansky's class."

"Well…perhaps we could move *Garret* to another classroom," said Seraphina.

"No, he loves Miss Polansky, and I don't want his year interrupted. Having Mrs. Markham as a substitute was hard enough on him."

"Moving Nathan would interrupt *his* year," Seraphina said, an edge to her voice.

"Then so be it. He is the one causing the problem. In fact, I believe he should be removed not only from Miss Polansky's class but from this school. Garret says he tells other kids that he can do what he wants because his mom is the principal."

"That is ridiculous."

I had to speak up. "Unfortunately, I have heard him say the same thing." Seraphina glared at me.

Mrs. Conley said, "I don't believe it is a healthy environment for the principal's son to be in the same school, at least when the principal's son is a problem and the principal refuses to recognize the problem."

"I do recognize that Nathan is a strong-willed child."

"Strong-willed, yes. Also downright mean," Mrs. Conley said. I tended to agree but fought to keep my face neutral.

At that, Seraphina's professionalism went out the window. "My son is not mean! He is a normal five-year-old who acts up at times!"

Mrs. Conley was not to be deterred. "Even if he's moved into another classroom in this school, that doesn't take care of recess and before and after school. The school has a duty to protect children from harm, and Nathan needs to get some special help. I am prepared to go to the superintendent with my request and file a formal complaint."

They were at a stalemate. The mama bears stared at each other, each with her back up and willing to do about anything to protect her child. As the silence dragged on, Paula came to my mind. Like them, was she willing to do just about anything to protect her child?

I admired Mrs. Conley's calm. She stated what she

wanted clearly, didn't apologize, and was immovable in her conviction. I could learn from her.

At that point, I had to excuse myself because of a previous appointment. My previous appointment was a rehearsal with the Streusels and didn't take place for another two hours, but I decided it was best that I remove myself from this situation.

When Derek picked me up, I checked my phone for email and found a message I'd somehow missed from the day before—a note with "Your Carnival Crew" in the subject line:

It has been pointed out that, although many of us have sent meals and flowers to Judith's children, her estranged husband is also suffering and deserves compassion. If you can contribute a small dish or food item and bring it to Wednesday's rehearsal, we will drop everything off Thursday morning, which we understand is Jared's day off. (Band members, I know you don't rehearse on Wednesdays, but if you can swing by with your donation and sign the card, it will be appreciated.) Please use the refrigerator and the long counter beside it for your donations. The card will be on the table.

Thanks,
Your Carnival Crew
Tess, Becky, Paula, Caleb, Noreen

I sighed. I most certainly was *not* going to contribute a darned thing. But what if my name was missing on the card? Would that be even more fuel for his anger toward me? Would others think that pointed to my guilt? I decided to risk it.

I did stop at the theater on the way to rehearsal with the Streusels. I needed to pick up my music stand LED lights so I could see better in Otto's basement. His printer cartridge was running low, so music he had been handing out lately was very faint and hard to read. I knew from past experience that he would continue using the cartridge until the print was almost invisible. He was not one to spend money unless it was absolutely necessary.

After I grabbed the two clip-on lights from my stand, I stopped quickly in the greenroom and took a peek in the refrigerator to see if people actually had contributed food for Jared. They had a Mexican meal going on—a Pyrex dish of burritos, a small foil pan of enchiladas, two packages of guacamole, a bowl of fruit. On the counter was a bag of Doritos, a jar of salsa, and a chocolate cake.

I looked at the card, pretending I was going to sign. Becky had written, "The Lord bless you and keep you. The Lord make his face shine upon you and give you peace. (Numbers 6:24-25)." Tess had written, "Like a bird singing in the rain, let grateful memories survive in time of sorrow—Robert Louis Stevenson." There were also some "Our thoughts and prayers are with you" messages, as well as, mostly, just signatures.

I had no messages for Jared that were appropriate to write on a sympathy card, so I didn't.

CHAPTER 33

The Streusels were thrilled that I had been publicly vindicated. "I love you guys," I said. "I wish all my colleagues had reacted the way you did. You never questioned my innocence for a moment."

"I did," said Otto, winking at me. "So have you ordered a new accordion yet?"

"The insurance will only pay about 90% of what I paid for Tillie. Some nonsense about depreciation. She never depreciated. She just got better!"

"Of course she did," Moriko said.

"I've put my name in at the company for another used, female-sized one. In the meantime, I'll start saving again. It will take a while."

'How's the murder investigation going?" asked Allan, getting right to the point, as usual.

"We've pretty much reached a dead end. I'm now imagining possibilities everywhere. Yesterday, I even started thinking it could be this twit named Helena. Or maybe Herb, our security guard. Nothing makes much sense."

"Why the twit?" asked Allan.

"She is so self-centered she'd probably be willing to whack anyone who accidentally spoiled one of her selfies."

"And Herb?"

"Maybe he has a connection to the theater that we don't know about. Who hired him? I heard that it might have been Tess, which makes sense, since she's the director now. Maybe they were in cahoots for some reason." I sighed. "Anything is possible. Anyone is a possibility."

"Speaking of possibility, you said once you wanted to know more about Feleesha," said Leroy. "I found out my daughter-in-law went to school with her. Shayla is a year older, but she remembers her. Maybe she could tell you something helpful."

"That would be great. Can you set something up?"

"Absolutely."

When I finished rehearsal, Derek was more than ready to go. He said his headphones were not effective enough in blocking the polkas.

It was early, so we decided to stop in and see how Sammie was doing. Sam was there, of course, and I noticed Mennen shaving cream and an extra toothbrush in the bathroom.

All of us, except for Sammie, had a glass of wine. I decided there would be no talk of murder. Even though we hadn't nabbed the murderer yet, I was feeling much happier now that I had been vindicated. I was looking forward to playing in the show again on the weekend. I had my job back, and I was beloved by 23 children—now 21 with Antonio and Valeria gone. Detective Dan had given me several looks that were distinctly non-official, and I was going to be playing for the general public downtown in a non-senior center, non-Moose, non-Veteran's Club venue for another Octoberfest celebration next week. Yes, Jared was still a danger, but I still had Derek's protection. Life was good.

"Maybe someday I'll go to Germany and see a real Octoberfest celebration," I said, after reminding them of the event next week.

"If I were going to Europe, I wouldn't choose Germany," Derek said. "It would be Spain."

"Actually, I'd go to New York City long before I'd go to Germany," I said. "Musicals!"

"The Mets!" said Sam.

"Museums!" said Sammie. "I'd love to go again, this time without a teacher breathing down my neck."

Sam looked thoughtful. "I need to build up some more vacation time with this new job, but how about if we go to New York this spring?" he asked. "Maybe the end of May when it's warming up, but too soon for tourist season?"

This guy is looking to the future, was my first thought. *Sammie will be having a baby around then* was my second.

Sammie acted like he was joking. "New York, New York! It's a helluva town," she sang.

Derek and I tried to help out by launching into "Give my regards to Broadway. Remember me to Herald Square."

Sam smiled. "I'm serious. I'd love to take you to New York."

Derek, Sammie and I froze. There was a long silence.

Sam frowned. "What? You don't want to commit to something so long from now? I'm not going away, babe. It's going to be hard to get rid of me." He hugged her.

She paled. Then she took a deep breath and said, "We need to have a talk, Sam."

"Derek, I think we can go clean up the dishes," I said, grabbing his arm.

"Oh, lord, this is it," I said softly when we got to the kitchen and closed the door. Instead of doing the dishes, we sat on the floor beside the door, unabashedly eavesdropping. They spoke quietly, but we could make out most of the conversation. Sammie told him she was pregnant, and by another man.

There was silence.

"You didn't think to maybe mention this before I started falling in love with you?"

"He's falling in love with her!" I said softly.

"Big surprise," Derek answered. "Shhhhh."

"Who is the guy? You neglected to mention that you were seeing anyone else."

"I wasn't." There was silence for a moment, then, "It was a one-night stand. Before I met you."

We heard a smack—not a hitting-a-person kind of smack but more like a slamming-a-beer-down-on-the-table kind of smack. "Great. A stranger," Sam said.

"No, a guy I've known for a long time. We go dancing together, but we've never been a couple."

I fervently wished we could see their faces. I tried to ease the door open just a crack.

"But you hooked up," I heard Sam say. We tried to peer through the crack, but the angle was wrong.

"Just the once."

"For any particular reason?"

Sammie's voice trembled. "I don't know. Mostly because I had a little too much to drink."

"You don't drink . . ." Then he realized. "Oh."

"I'm human, Sam. I got, um, restless."

"She means horny," whispered Derek.

"I *know*," I whispered back.

"I know how 'restless' you can get," Sam said. "You've been restless a lot with me."

"But this time, with Donald, I just thought it wouldn't…"

"Donald?"

"Oh dear," I whispered. "Don't give him a name."

Sammie continued. "This time, I just thought, why not? Maybe it will be nice…It wasn't. Haven't you ever had a one-night stand?"

"Never."

Derek blew out a breath and looked at me. The remark certainly gave Sammie pause. Us, too.

"I wouldn't do that," Sam continued.

More silence. Was he really so perfect? Derek and I gave each other looks that said we were doubtful.

He finally spoke again. "I did sleep with a woman I knew was way more into me than I was into her."

"Once?"

"Okay, several times." More silence. Then, "So are you going to marry this guy?"

"Of course not! I wouldn't marry someone I'm not in love with."

"But you would sleep with him. I'm glad you have standards."

"Don't be mean," I whispered, as if he could hear me. Sammie was sobbing now.

"When did you plan to tell me?" Sam asked. "When I started noticing you were wearing maternity clothes?"

She was doing that gulping thing she does when she

cries. "I didn't know . . . how . . . I liked you more than . . . anyone . . . I've ever dated. I just wanted to enjoy you while . . . I . . . could . . . before you disappeared . . . forever."

"So this Donald is now going to be in your life forever? Being a father, but not a husband?"

"No!" she cried. She managed to control herself. "Donald has already signed away his rights." I guessed that Sam probably looked pretty shocked at that piece of news. If only I could see him.

"My mother will provide child support," Sammie went on. She had gained some control and wasn't gulping now. "Donald will be persona non gratis until the child turns 18 and *might* want to look him up. My brothers and my stepdad will provide plenty of male influence."

More silence.

"And I've always wanted kids," she sobbed again. "Lots of kids."

"Me, too," he said. "My own."

"I'm sorry I didn't tell you. I just couldn't have an abortion. And I just didn't want you to go away…yet."

I was crying now too. It was like listening to a soap opera, only worse. It was real, and it was my best friend suffering.

"I need to go," Sam said. "This is a lot to lay on me. I need to process it. Alone." His voice sounded cold. Or maybe hurt. I couldn't tell. "Bye, Sammie." I couldn't help noticing the note of finality in his voice. Then I heard the door close.

And then another.

Derek and I went out. Sammie was in the bedroom. I knocked. "Sammie . . ."

"Go away."

I'd never heard her cry so hard and so long, even when she told me her parents were getting divorced. Or when her grandma died. Or when her dog Buster got hit by a car. I tried to go in anyway, but the door was locked.

"Go away."

We didn't.

Derek got out blankets for the couch and found Sammie's sleeping bag in a closet. There was no way we were leaving her alone. He crawled into the sleeping bag to stay the night, and I curled up on the couch—both of us miserable, feeling Sammie's pain. We had known this was bound to happen, but that made it no easier. "She'll have to come out to go to the bathroom," I said. She has a bladder the size of a walnut, and pregnancy hadn't helped the frequency of her bathroom trips.

An hour later, Sammie did indeed unlock the door and go into the bathroom. While she was there, I crawled into her bed, grabbing her old Mr. Fuzzy bear off the chair.

She crawled into bed, and I gave her Mr. Fuzzy.

"We listened in," I admitted.

"Of course you did," she said. Then I rubbed her back while she cried. And cried. And cried.

Finally, we fell asleep.

CHAPTER 34

My cell phone alarm went off, so I slipped out of bed to go home and shower before school. I tried to be quiet, but Sammie woke up, too. She looked like hell.

"I'm sorry," I said. "Go back to sleep."

"It's okay," she said. "I've got to get going. I've got a store to run." She headed for the kitchen.

"It's your store. You could take a sick day," I pointed out, following her. Derek had woken up and was right behind me. For once, I was grateful for the Keurig and all the little pods. They were fast, and all three of us needed a cup of coffee badly—and quickly.

"I'm going to have to do a lot of things I don't want to do when I'm a mom," Sammie said. "Like go through labor, for one thing." She grimaced. "Might as well start practicing now."

She is tough, and I knew that. Her pattern has always been to allow herself to wallow in misery for an allotted period of time and then move on. My guess was that last night had been the allotted period of time.

She handed me a coffee and put in another pod. "I'm running a business, so I will run it. I have a baby inside of me, so I will take care of her. I have a man to get out of my system, so I will get rid of him. I will move on."

"Here," said Derek. He handed her some cold tea bags for her eyes. I poured my coffee into a to-go mug and rummaged around for another while we waited for Derek's coffee to finish.

"I'll check on you later, after I get Ella to school," Derek said.

"I'll call later," I said. Holding our mugs, we each gave her a one-armed hug and took off.

After a shower at home, I dressed quickly and was opening a carton of yogurt when I felt my phone vibrate. I looked at the screen and frowned. It was Seraphina Conway. Reluctantly, I answered.

"I'm afraid I have some bad news again, Ella," she said. "In light of what's in the paper this morning, I have to put you on paid leave again. You don't need to come in today."

"What? What on earth is in the paper?"

"It's an account of Jared Pence following you and grabbing you," she said.

"I think you have this backwards. I was the victim, not the perpetrator." Derek gave me a questioning look, then handed me a fresh cup of coffee.

"I know, but it seems that your situation is putting you in danger. Since you are in danger, the kids are in danger. For the safety of all, you need to stay away from the school until all this is resolved. I'm sorry."

With that, she hung up before I could even reply.

Could she possibly be right? Was I putting others in danger by just, well, being me? Or could Seraphina's anger and frustration about my support for Mrs. Conley have influenced her decision? I wondered.

I sat down at the kitchen table and stared at nothing. I was exhausted.

Derek sat down beside me, and touched my arm. "You okay?"

I told him about my suspension. Then he sat and stared at nothing with me.

"If you're thinking of going for a run this morning, forget it," I said. "There's no way I'm going with you."

"I wasn't thinking of it. I was thinking of breakfast at the Uptown Grille. My treat."

"I can handle that." I finished my coffee and we went to my car. There was a note under the windshield wiper:

YOU ARE GETTING AWAY WITH MURDER!

I crunched the paper in my fist and tossed it in the backseat. "I'm going to kill him."

Derek found the crumpled note and smoothed it out as I started the car. "You might want to be careful about your terminology," he said.

I backed out, coming a little too close to the mailbox at the curb. "You mean 'kill'? Let me reword it then. I *want* to kill him. Jared Pence. But I won't. Because *I am not a murderer!*"

"I think this note is something you might want to save for Detective Dan," he said.

After Denver omelets, we felt a bit more energetic. We lingered over even more coffee, finally alert enough to discuss Jared.

"His anger is obviously escalating," Derek said. "I'm

worried that he might actually try breaking into the house now, or seriously try to hurt you."

"He's already tried."

"I mean something more serious than grabbing you. I'm going to set up the game camera again, for evidence."

"That will help a lot," I said. "When I'm dead, you'll at least know who did it."

"We're also getting a dog," he said, taking his credit card receipt and getting up. "Bianca is home with the kids. We're going to stop in and borrow Poquito."

I started to argue, then gave in. We headed for his brother's home, where we hoped his wife would be understanding about our need to borrow the family dog.

Poquito—Spanish for "little one"—is a pint-sized mutt from the pound, not exactly scary looking with his sweet face, curly brown hair, and enormous black eyes. He does, however, have a ferocious bark, which he offers at the drop of a hat. He *sounds* pretty mean and might scare off Jared if he didn't get a look at him.

Fluffles was not thrilled to meet him. She leapt on top of the coffee table and hissed while Poquito happily tried to make friends.

Then she leapt to the back of the sofa and hissed. She moved to the back of the easy chair and hissed. Finally, she took a flying leap toward the bedroom and sprang onto the bed as Poquito merrily gave chase. She balanced on top of the narrow headboard and hissed.

Derek grabbed Poquito. "Maybe Fluffles can live in your bedroom for a while."

"She has to be able to get to the cat box." I keep her litter box in the unfinished basement with the door slightly ajar so that she can go downstairs.

"Then Poquito can stay in the den with me."

"And what do we do when we go somewhere?" I pulled Fluffles from the headboard and held her. I was not detecting a purr.

"The yard is fenced. He can stay out there," he said.

"You mean where he might lap up antifreeze????!!!!"

He gave up. "I guess he goes where we go."

Great. Now I had a bodyguard *and* a dog shadowing me. I'm a cat person.

When it was time for lunch, I made grilled cheese sandwiches with tomato basil soup. I knew Derek loved grilled cheese sandwiches with tomato basil soup. For good measure, I added a big kosher pickle to his plate.

Derek sat down with Poquito at his feet. I waited until he had eaten a few bites and looked content. Then I said, "I think we should not be so passive about Jared. We need to act."

"We have a game camera, motion detector lights, a gun, and a barking dog," he said. "What more do you want to do? Rent a tank?"

I took a deep breath. "I know this seems crazy, but I want to go talk to Jared."

"You're damn right it seems crazy. It seems *completely* frigging crazy."

"That's why I want you to go with me. With your gun."

He didn't hesitate for even a second. "You're out of your mind. No way." Poquito scraped a paw against his leg, and he put him in his lap, scratching his ears with one hand while spooning up soup with the other. Poquito looked so happy I almost expected him to purr.

Fluffles did not look happy. She crept cautiously into the kitchen toward her bowls, keeping an eye on Poquito. Poquito's ears flew up at the sight of her, and he sat up in Derek's lap, panting happily. "A friend!" said the look on his face.

Derek kept a firm hold on him. Fluffles stood stock still and stared. Then, ever so slowly, she crept toward Poquito and finally stood at Derek's feet, sniffing.

Poquito leaned down and sniffed back.

"It's okay, Fluffles," I said in my sweetest voice.

Fluffles decided Poquito was unworthy of her attention, at least for the moment. She went to her dish and ate some dry food.

"Progress," I said. "Now back to Jared."

"We are *not* going to see Jared. Period." He went back to his soup and sandwich.

"I don't want to just sit around waiting for whatever Jared might do next. He said he wanted to talk, so I'd like to talk." I reached behind the Snoopy cookie jar and pulled out a paper I'd hidden there. "I want to show him this." I handed him a receipt.

He stared at it. "Jesus! You spent $10,000 on an accordion?"

"Does everyone have to act like that is so weird? Tillie is a great accordion!"

"*Was* a great accordion. But what's that got to do with Jared?" He handed the receipt back as he bit into his pickle.

"I want to explain to him, personally, how much I loved

Tillie. I want to tell him how many years I saved up to buy her, and I want to show him how much she cost. I want to ask him if he seriously believes someone on a teacher's salary would destroy something she paid $10,000 for in order to murder someone she didn't even hate?"

Derek chewed his pickle, thinking.

Was he bending? I continued. "We would go in broad daylight. You would have your gun, *and* you're clearly really in shape—you know, in case you needed to get physical." It couldn't hurt to throw in a little flattery.

"We can't go in broad daylight. He'll be at work," he said.

"Nope. I know from the meal collection the cast is doing that Thursday is his day off. They were going to drop off the food this morning because they knew he'd be home."

"Great. If he's home all day, he's probably been drinking. We'd be going over to see a crazy drunk guy who hates you." He shook his head again. "Bad idea. Very bad."

"Doesn't showing him the receipt make sense?"

He didn't say anything, so I pushed on. He was weakening. "And he doesn't know me at all. Really, could you look at me, face to face, and think I'm a murderer?" I gave him what I hoped he'd interpret as a sweet and endearing look.

"He could look at you and say you're crazy."

By 1:30, I had worn him down. He wanted to work on his book. He knew he'd never be able to as long as I had this crazy notion in my head.

He gave up and agreed to take me. I suspected that, deep down, he thought I might be right about the receipt.

As we cleaned up the kitchen, Poquito tried to play with Fluffles. That was going too far, as far as Fluffles was concerned. She swatted his nose, and he yelped and ran into the living room. Fluffles leapt to the counter. I reached for her, and there was a crash.

Rocky was on the floor, broken.

I wanted to cry, but I didn't.

Derek gave me a little hug and went for the broom.

CHAPTER 35

"You have your gun?"

"Check." He pulled aside his jacket, and I saw it in a holster at his waist. "You have your receipt?"

"Check." I pulled open the side pocket in my purse and showed him. "Cell phone?"

"Check."

"Let's go."

I picked up Poquito and put him in the back seat. He immediately jumped into the front. I sighed and put him in my lap, and we drove to Jared's home and parked in front. The garage door was wide open, but his car was there. "Looks like he's home," I said. "Let's do this."

Derek cracked a window for Poquito, and we went to the door and rang the bell. I tapped my fingers against my jeans nervously.

There was no answer. We rang several times and pounded on the door, but nothing.

"Let's try the door inside the garage." We went inside and pounded on that door, too, but there was no answer. I took a look at the shelves along the garage wall. "Look at that. Antifreeze." I whipped out my iPhone and took a picture.

"Can I help you?" A jogger ran in place at the garage door.

"We're looking for Jared," I said. "There was no answer at the front, so we decided to try this door. Have you seen him?"

The jogger was wary. "And you are?"

I didn't want to give him my name. "We just want to talk to him."

"I think you need to get out of his garage."

"We were just going," I said.

At that, Derek's phone rang. As he reached to get it out of his back pocket, his jacket fell open, revealing his gun. The jogger looked at the gun and started jogging backward, unzipping the pouch around his waist as he went. When he reached the porch of the house next door, he began tapping his cell phone.

Wisely, Derek declined his call, and we headed for the car.

"That went well," he said, opening the car door. Poquito jumped out and ran into Jared's garage.

"Poquito!" I shouted.

The jogger saw me going back toward the garage. "Stay out of there!" he called.

"We're going, but I need to get our dog." I hurried after Poquito and scooped him up, then rushed back to the car.

"Great," Derek said, pulling away. "I'm sure that guy has called the police."

"It's not against the law to knock on a door. But you might want to step on it."

At 3:00 I kept my appointment with Carl's granddaughter-in-law Shayla at a coffee shop near her office. Derek said he was thoroughly sick of not getting anything done, so he chose to sit at a table nearby and work.

I'd met Shayla once before at an Octoberfest performance, so we recognized each other. We ordered drinks, and she got right to the point. "So Granddad tells me you want to know more about Feleesha Farnsworth."

I nodded.

"I went to high school with her." She used a careful, neutral tone of voice."

"Same class?"

"I was a year behind her. I remember her because she had a part in *Oklahoma*, but she dropped out three weeks before the show because she got a better part in the community theater production of *Little Shop of Horrors*." She looked at me as if she still couldn't believe that Feleesha had done such a thing. "Who does that? Leaves a group in the lurch without an understudy? We were so mad."

I shook my head sympathetically. "Who could blame you?"

"And get this. When she told Mrs. Gutierrez she was dropping out, she brought her *mother* along. Didn't even have the guts to tell her by herself." Shayla shook her head, obviously still annoyed about the injustice of it all. "We were all going to boycott *Little Shop of Horrors*, but our friend Jeremy got a part in the chorus, so we had to support him."

"Wasn't he bailing on you, too?"

"Jeremy wouldn't do that. He wasn't a lead, so his rehearsals started later, after our show was over."

"I'm curious—how *was* Feleesha in the show?"

"Not all that great, but maybe I was prejudiced against her—you know, because she bailed on us. Also, because of the scandal. Jeremy told us some older guy and Feleesha were fooling around. I think the old guy was even married."

I perked up. This was not only interesting gossip but possibly relevant gossip as well. "Really? Do you remember the guy's name?"

"Actually, I do." She sipped her latte and got foam on her upper lip. "Every time I see an ad for Jared's jewelry on television, I think of him—because that was his name."

Suddenly I focused. "Jared?"

She gave me a look. "Certainly not 'jewelry.' Red-headed guy, kind of ordinary looking but a good singer. He played Mr. Mushnik." She finally wiped her mouth, but then she took another sip and foam reappeared. "We all joked that she probably brought her mother along when she was meeting him."

How could she not feel that mustache on her lips? "So what happened? I mean with the red-headed guy?"

"Who knows? It was great gossip, but when the show was over, Feleesha disappeared, and I never saw her again."

"Disappeared?" This gossip was getting better and better.

"Not disappeared like we were looking for her body or anything. She just dropped out of school and went to an acting school in Connecticut—Zander Academy of the Arts."

I couldn't believe she remembered a detail like that. "How the heck do you remember the name?" I did some quick figuring. "That was at least fifteen years ago."

"My aunt's sister-in-law went there, too, and she named her first kid after the school, if you can believe it. Zander, not Zander Academy of the Arts."

That was indeed very interesting—and not only because

someone would name a child after an academy. She smiled. "Weird, I know."

"Yes, weird," I agreed, "but also very helpful."

Shayla didn't have any more to say about Feleesha, so we chit-chatted a bit about her dad's new girlfriend. "She's so much like my mom," she said, "but not in a good way." I knew that Carl thought the same thing, but I kept my mouth shut. In Carl's opinion, his son and daughter-in-law's divorce had been ridiculous. Why leave one woman and then date one so much like her?

As soon as Shayla left, I decided to give Zander Academy of the Arts a call. I googled the number and looked at the time on my phone—3:20. It was two hours later in Connecticut, but maybe the admissions office would still be open.

I took a moment to marvel at my courage. I was not only making a phone call to ask for something again, I was doing it under false pretenses. Was this growth? I punched in the number, and a woman answered.

"This is Cornelia Sorenson of Spotlight Theater Productions," I said. I have no idea how that name came so quickly to my tongue, but for a second or two, I had to admire my brain a little bit. Then I continued. "For employment purposes, we need to verify that someone attended your school. The name is Feleesha Farnsworth. It's an unusual spelling: F-E-L-E-E-S-H-A."

I heard her computer keys clicking as she searched her data base. "We have three Farnsworths who have attended Zander, but they are all males. . . . Oh, I'm so sorry. I shouldn't make assumptions like that . . . and I shouldn't have assumed Feleesha is a female."

"No worries. I do believe Ms. Farnsworth is a female, as she arrived for her interview in heels and a pencil skirt. Although, like you, I guess I shouldn't make assumptions." I chuckled, doing a bit of long-distance bonding.

She chuckled back. Or at least I assumed it was a "she" who was chuckling. I thanked her and hung up.

Whatever Feleesha had been doing in Connecticut, it wasn't attending Zander Academy of the Arts.

CHAPTER 36

THURSDAY NIGHT'S BRUSH-UP DRESS REHEARSAL before our last three performances went relatively well, considering how much people can forget in just a few days. Even after the walk-through on Wednesday night without the band, people were still forgetting lines. "That's why we rehearse," said Tess, upbeat as always. She stood on the stage for a moment at the end of rehearsal to thank us all for the contributions to the meal for Jared. "Paula and Becky and I dropped off an entire Mexican dinner this morning, as well as some other dishes, and he seemed very pleased. You guys are super!"

I slid my eyes toward Gordon and he shook his head slightly. He hadn't contributed anything either.

Tess told us all to go home and get a good night's rest. "We have a big weekend ahead of us," she said, "and we all want to be at our best! Three more successful shows, coming up!"

As I stood up and stretched, I turned and looked out into the theater. Noreen came down the aisle from the light booth and stopped to pick up a 7-11 cup someone had left on the floor. "Damn pigs," I heard her say. I quickly turned around and picked up the Ziploc bag of gorp that I'd kept beside my chair during rehearsal. I fished through it for a couple of M&Ms and then stuck the bag in my pocket.

Gordon stood up and said, "Let's go, partner. I can't leave you alone down here. Who knows what someone might push off the stage onto you?"

I looked up at the stage, considering. Was the puppet theater up there light enough to toss? What about the suitcase Lili carried? Or even the concertina Aiden used in the opening? We *were* rather vulnerable sitting below the stage. Why had Gordon brought that up? I shivered, remembering that someone here had no problem shoving large objects onto people.

Gordon snapped the locks on his trombone case, and I followed him up to the greenroom. He looked around and said, "Just look at the potential weapons in here. Someone could hurl Paula's portable sewing machine in to the pit. Or her iron . . . or . . . "

"Shut up, please," I said.

"Just saying . . ." He gave my arm a friendly punch. "See you, kid. I'm outta here. Car's right outside."

He left, and I found myself looking around at all the other potentially lethal items in the room—a coffee pot, a small microwave, even Helena's make-up case, if she put all her stuff into it. I wished Gordon hadn't mentioned tossing things into the pit.

Then I heard a sound from the dressing area. Was someone crying? I walked back and found Feleesha sitting on a bench in one of the cubicles, sobbing. The curtain wasn't drawn, so I walked on in.

"Feleesha, what's wrong?" I sat down beside her and put my arm around her. "Are you okay?"

"She's okay," Paula snapped. She had approached and was standing by the curtain holding a couple of costumes on hangers. Ignoring her daughter's sobs, she told her, "I need your harem pants. The hem on the right pants leg is coming out." She turned and took the other costumes to the repair rack beside her sewing table.

Not a lot of sympathy there, I thought. I stepped outside and pulled the cubicle curtain shut. "Hand your pants out to me," I said. "I'll take them over to your mom and be right back."

Still sobbing, Feleesha handed me the pants, and I took them to Paula's table. I went back to talk to Feleesha, but she was gone.

What could have upset her so much? I had no idea.

I realized I hadn't told Derek that I was ready to go, so I texted him.

TEN MINUTES, he texted back. AT THE GYM.

I looked around idly as I waited. Could there be any clues here, hiding in plain sight? I looked at all the counters full of make-up, curling irons, curlers, costume parts, hats, a couple of pairs of tights. I walked by the refrigerator and peeked inside, just for the heck of it. I tried to open a cabinet marked STAFF ONLY, but it was locked.

I walked over to the dressing area again and looked down the line of dressing cubicles. The three-quarter length curtains were drawn at only one section. Visible under it were two sets of male shoes, facing each other closely.

Very closely.

I recognized one of those sets of shoes.

I stood, frozen for a moment. What the . . .?

I decided I couldn't handle any more looking around and hurried out to wait at the stage door with Herb.

I was quiet, but Herb wanted to talk.

"Feleesha sure seemed upset tonight," he commented.

"I know. Any idea what was wrong?"

"Nope. But she didn't leave with a buddy, like I told her she was supposed to. She just ignored me and screeched out of here in her Toyota." He opened the door a crack for some air and pulled down the little door stop so that it would stay.

"Not good," I said.

"Should I have shot her?"

I looked at him in horror.

"Kidding," he said. "Security guard humor."

"Security guard humor needs some work," I said.

Becky and Aiden joined us at the door, so Herb stepped out and opened it all the way for us. I followed Becky and Aiden outside, where Derek had just pulled up.

Becky did not seem pleased with Aiden. "Just do as I say," she was saying in that voice all mothers use when they mean business.

I didn't want to interrupt, but it seemed rude not to say goodbye. "See you," I said.

Becky gave me a little wave over her shoulder, then stopped beside the Dumpster. As I got in the car, I heard her say, "I don't care if they are chocolate chip. You're not keeping them. I told you to stay away from Feleesha." Then she stood by as Aiden opened the Dumpster and dropped in a paper plate full of cookies.

"That's weird," I said to Derek, buckling my seat belt. "Who throws away chocolate chip cookies?" I told him about the interactions I'd seen between Aiden and Feleesha, and Becky's reactions.

"Seems Becky is not too fond of Feleesha," he said.

"You think?" He didn't need to state the obvious. "But to throw away cookies? You just don't do that, even if someone you don't like made them."

"You would if you thought they were poisoned."

"Oh." I thought about that. "No. I've seen him throw away other stuff from her, too—non-food stuff."

"Any idea why?"

"I don't know. Maybe Becky knows something I don't." I thought a moment. "You know, I've seen Feleesha reaching out to Aiden several times, and I thought it was sweet—that she was just being kind to him. But maybe not. " I hesitated. "I guess I can be wrong sometimes."

"Yeah?" He stopped at a red light and looked over at me, raising the eyebrow over his green eye.

"Yeah." I decided I might as well own up to my mistake. "I saw something . . . um . . . eye-opening tonight. Stanley's shoes were entangled with another guy's in one of the dressing rooms."

"Legs attached?" he asked.

"Yep."

The light changed and he drove on. "So you've finally caught on."

"You knew?"

"Of course I knew. I wasn't going to out him, though. That's up to him."

I leaned my head back on the headset and looked out the window. I'd really thought Stanley had a thing for me. I'd been wrong. I wondered what else I might be wrong about.

As we got home, a police car pulled up in front of the house, and Detective Dan and another officer got out. Detective Dan did not look happy.

"We have some questions for you," he said. "Can we go inside?"

I looked at the curtains twitch at Mr. McConnell's window. "Sure."

"I understand you were seen at the home of Jared Pence this afternoon," he said, standing just inside the door. I motioned to the sofa, but both officers shook their heads.

"Yes, I wanted to talk to him." I explained my theory about the accordion receipt.

"Did you go inside?" Detective Dan asked. The other officer just stood by, looking stern. Did they think I was going to try to flee?

"No. We did go inside the garage, which was open, and banged on the door to the house. His car was there, so it seemed like he was home. But he didn't answer."

"A neighbor reported your license plate and said you looked dangerous and were carrying a gun.'

"I have a concealed carry permit," said Derek. "Jared has assaulted Ella in the past, as you know, and it seemed wise to take it along."

Detective Dan turned to me. "Why on earth would you choose to go see a man who had assaulted you?"

"I *told* you already! I wanted to show him I couldn't be the murderer because I would never want to ruin a $10,000 accordion!" Didn't he listen? I was becoming frustrated with Detective Dan.

"But you never went inside?" he asked again.

"No! I already told you that, too!"

After more questions, the detectives turned to go. Detective Dan lingered at the door a moment. "Jared Pence was found near death late this afternoon. It appears to be attempted murder. It's not good that you were seen there."

I couldn't believe it. Another murder? Or attempted murder? I watched the two officers go down the walk, then shouted, "Wait. Maybe this is important." I hurried down the sidewalk towards them. "Just so you know, Feleesha was sobbing uncontrollably tonight after rehearsal. Maybe she'd heard about Jared somehow."

He shrugged his shoulders. "So? Was she close to Jared?"

"I don't know . . . for sure."

"But you know something." He looked at me hard.

"Okay. This is gossip, but I think it's reliable information, considering my source. I heard she had an affair with Jared when she was about 15 or 16."

There was a pause. "The guy does get around. But a fifteen-year-old?"

"I know. Creepy. But maybe she still has feelings for him. Or maybe she even started up with him again. Really, she was a mess. I tried to talk to her, but by the time I delivered her harem pants and came back, she was gone."

The other officer looked puzzled. "Harem pants?"

"It's a costume thing," Detective Dan said. "Thank you for the information, Ella. We'll look into it." They left.

I looked at Derek and tried not to cry. "Am I a suspect in another murder now?"

"I told you that going there was a bad idea."

CHAPTER 37

After a night of tossing and turning, I pulled up the *Juniper Times* on my phone. There was no information about Jared, so I turned the radio to a Denver news station and kept it on while I showered and dressed. Eventually, I heard it: *Jared Pence, husband of the woman murdered at the Juniper Theater, was found near death at his home Thursday afternoon. Foul play is suspected.*

I suspected something more—that soon a follow-up report would mention that Ella Polansky had been seen at the house before the murder was discovered. And newspaper and television reports would undoubtedly include the same ugly picture of me.

Poquito was sitting at the back door staring at me as if to say, "Don't you *see* me here?" I looked around for stray cups of antifreeze, just to be on the safe side, and let him out. Then I called Detective Dan.

"So what happened with Jared?" I demanded. "How did he almost die? . . . This is Ella Polansky."

"I know who it is, and it's 7:00 a.m." He sounded groggy. "I was out until 3:30. Can't this wait?"

"You're awake now."

He sighed. "Give me a sec." I heard some rustling sounds

and imagined him pulling aside the covers, revealing what I guessed would be a very nice chest, hopefully un-tattooed.

"Since I'm probably going to be blamed, I deserve to know," I insisted.

The rustling had stopped. "Okay, here's the deal—and I'm not telling you anything that won't be released later this morning. Jared was found with two almost empty bottles beside him. It *appeared* he had almost drunk himself to death."

"So how is drinking yourself to death attempted murder?"

"Appearances were deceiving. It turns out that both bottles were tainted with antifreeze."

That gave me pause. "Just like Ginger…But it didn't kill him?"

"I found out from the hospital that alcohol interferes with the absorption of antifreeze." I heard him shuffling papers. Was he reading from notes? "Something about the ethanol blocking the harmful metabolites of ethylene glycol and counteracting the effects of the antifreeze. In years past, booze was even used to treat antifreeze poisoning, before Fomepizole became the standard treatment."

"Wow," I said. "Jared's probably sorry it's not the good old days of treatment." I realized how callous that probably sounded. "I'm sorry. I didn't mean to be disrespectful to the dead. I mean the almost dead."

He just went on. "Incidentally, they put something in antifreeze nowadays to make it taste terrible."

"Really? Why would Jared drink the booze then?"

"The liquor undoubtedly masked the taste, at least somewhat. Or maybe he was so drunk he didn't care what it tasted like."

I wondered, briefly, why Ginger had lapped it up, but I tried to stay on track. "So putting the antifreeze in the alcohol actually saved him instead of killing him?"

"It slowed down the effects of the alcohol. If the antifreeze had been put in, oh, lemonade, he'd be dead."

"Except that he wouldn't have drunk lemonade," I said.

"Probably not."

"Thanks for telling me," I said.

"Are we done here? I'm going back to sleep."

"Wait." I was thinking hard. There had been burritos and enchiladas in the theater refrigerator for Jared on Wednesday. And Tess had mentioned how he had been pleased to get the Mexican meal they delivered. Maybe, just maybe, someone had donated a bottle of margaritas to make it a complete Mexican meal. "What kind of liquor was beside Jared?"

"Ella, enough. I can't give you those details. Let me go back to sleep. Please."

"I'll bet one of them was a bottle of margaritas," I continued. "The kind of mix with everything in it, including the tequila."

"Let it go. The police are investigating."

I persisted. "You didn't answer. Does that mean that it *was* a bottle of margaritas?"

"Goodbye, Ella. Leave it to the police. Don't call back."

I decided that Derek and I would do some investigating. I opened my phone and pulled up a map of liquor stores in town. I noted ones close to Jared's house and ones near where Tess, Paula, and Becky lived. They were the ones who were supposed to have delivered the food. Maybe they had delivered something else as well.

I made mushroom omelets for breakfast, with little

Boulder breakfast sausages on the side. Then I went to the den and motioned for Derek to pull out his ear buds and come eat. He was immediately suspicious when he saw the food. "What do you want me to do now that I don't want to do?"

"As soon as it's 10:00, we're going to go have a drink at the Rusty Nail."

"Seriously? Get a grip, Ella. We are *not* going drinking at 10:00 in the morning."

I continued. "After we do that, we're going to canvass liquor stores." I told him what I'd learned from Detective Dan about the poisoning. "So here's what I think: the people delivering a Mexican dinner also delivered a poisoned bottle of margaritas. Paula, Tess, and Becky delivered the meal, so it must have been one of them."

"Or someone else who left the margaritas in the refrigerator for them to take over, along with the food. Didn't everyone contribute things? Well, except you?"

I sighed. He was always so logical. "But surely no one would leave a poisoned drink in a refrigerator used by the whole cast. He—or she—might have accidentally poisoned someone else who snuck a taste."

"We're talking about a murderer here. Do you really think a murderer is going to worry about that?"

"Yes," I said, feeling stubborn. "The murderer wanted to kill Jared, not some fifteen-year-old who might see the stuff in the fridge and sneak a drink."

He gave up, at least temporarily, and moved on. "How is having a drink at the Rusty Nail going to help? This omelet is really good, by the way. You could do this every morning."

"I could, but I won't."

"Again, how is having a drink at the Rusty Nail going to help?"

I thought it was obvious. "We'll find out what Jared's drink of choice is. You know, by questioning the bartender. Don't they know everything?"

"On TV maybe. In real life—maybe, maybe not. But, more important, *why* do you care what his usual drink is if you think it was the margarita mix that was poisoned?"

"Detective Dan said there were two bottles beside Jared. I think the poisoner knew about how they put stuff in antifreeze to make it taste bad. So she diluted the bad taste by spreading the antifreeze out into two bottles—the margarita mix and a bottle of his favorite drink. You know, so it wouldn't taste as bad but would still be potent. They knew he'd probably drink both."

"Why not just use two bottles of margaritas?"

"Because she didn't know for sure that he liked margaritas. She only knew for sure that he liked…well, whatever he liked. Which is what we're going to found out."

"This is *such* a stretch," Derek said. "You are constructing an elaborate fantasy here, based on no evidence at all…"

I interrupted. "Based on *some* evidence, not *no* evidence. There was antifreeze in both bottles."

"Okay, based on *some* evidence." He looked at his empty plate. "Could you make more toast? And warm up my coffee?"

"You're pushing it," I said. But I did it.

At 10:05, we walked into the Rusty Nail and sat down at the bar. Already there were two men sitting there, and it appeared that the drinks they were having were not their first of the day. I ordered a Coke, and so did Derek.

The bartender brought us our drinks, then got right to the point. "So you two are clearly not here to drink. What do you want?"

"Just one thing," I said, looking at him in what I hoped was a winning way. I wasn't very good at the whole feminine wiles thing. "You must know Jared Pence, since he's here a lot." He nodded. "What does he drink?"

"Yukon Jack," he said readily. "Always Yukon Jack." Then he smiled at Derek. "Want something to eat with that Coke?" Derek smiled back. "How about some chips?"

Honestly, how could he eat more? We had just eaten a huge breakfast. Then I caught the look that passed between him and the bartender. I guessed my feminine wiles were useless.

"Progress!" I told Derek when he *finally* finished his potato chips and we left.

"If you call knowing a guy drinks Yukon Jack progress." He didn't start the car, just sat, resigned to listening to whatever was coming next.

"So we're going to visit liquor stores and ask if they remember anyone buying margaritas and Yukon Jack recently."

"Like anyone would remember that," he said, starting the car.

"They *might,* if it was a woman, especially one with a big cross around her neck."

"You think it was Becky?" He backed out.

"I don't know. But I'll bet it was *one* of the three bringing the food to Jared. You have to admit my theory makes sense."

"Kind of."

"Drive."

We pulled into the first store on my list, Family Liquor. "How could someone come up with that name?" I wondered. "What's 'family'-ish about alcohol?…Unless everyone in the family is an alcoholic… But 'family' implies little kids as well as grown-ups, so that…"

Derek interrupted. "Are you going in or not?"

I went.

There seemed to be only one man in the store. So much for "family." He was tearing down cardboard boxes and flattening them. He glanced at me as I walked toward him.

"This is a weird question," I said, "but it really could be kind of a life and death thing. Do you happen to remember anyone from the last few days coming in and buying Yukon Jack and a bottle of pre-mixed margaritas?"

"What if I did?" he shrugged. He had a bandanna tied around his head. I wondered if he really thought that was a good look for him.

"I'd just like to know if it was a male or a female," I said.

"That's it?"

"That's it." He continued tearing down boxes.

"So?" I pressed.

"So I don't remember anyone." He turned and grabbed another box, dismissing me.

We tried two more liquor stores with no luck. At the third, the woman behind the counter looked barely old enough to drink, let alone sell liquor.

"Sure, I totally remember someone," she said. "It was first thing Wednesday morning. Yukon Jack and Coyote Gold. She was older, maybe, like 50 or 60. I remember because it just seemed like a weird combination for someone like her."

"Why?"

"Usually older ladies buy wine," she shrugged. "Unless they are the half-wasted ones buying cheap bourbon."

"Was she wearing a cross?"

"What? Like around her neck?" I nodded. "Not that I could see. If it helps, she had gray hair, in a bob. Shortish."

"Thank you," I said.

"That's Paula then!" I told Derek in the car. "Tess isn't anywhere close to 50 or 60, and it would be pretty hard not to see Becky's cross."

"Becky could have been wearing a jacket that hid the cross," Derek said. "And if I remember Becky correctly, she has short gray hair in a bob as well."

I smiled. How many guys would know what a bob is? "Okay, *maybe* it was Paula," I conceded. "Or maybe it was Becky."

"And maybe, if it was, she bought the liquor but didn't do the poisoning. Or maybe it was just some stray lady who wandered into the store and happened to want Yukon Jack and Coyote Gold."

"And happened to have a gray bob?" I didn't hide the scorn in my voice.

"I admit it seems promising, but I don't think you have proof of anything, Ella." He headed toward home.

"Maybe not, but I might. I'm going to call Detective Dan."

I pulled out my phone. I had Detective Dan on speed dial now. "Ella Polansky again."

"I know. Do you have me on speed dial?"

I paused. How did he know? I went on without answering. "You've had several hours of sleep now, so listen up. Here's what you need to know: a woman bought Yukon Jack and Coyote Gold Wednesday morning at Cal's Liquor."

He didn't say anything. Aha! I thought. That means something to him. I continued. "And she was older, 50 or 60. Gray hair. Cut in a bob. I wanted you to know, just in case it was Coyote Gold and Yukon Jack used in the poisoning."

"Ella, you told me you and Derek did not go into the house." Now he sounded mad.

"We didn't."

"Then . . ." I think he realized he had just confirmed that Coyote Gold and Yukon Jack were the poisoning agents of choice. "Thank you for the information, Ella. Now leave this case to the police. Really."

"Good luck," I said. I wasn't about to promise anything.

I waited. Finally he asked, "What's a bob?"

By the time I reached the theater Friday night, everyone knew about Jared's poisoning. The 4:00 p.m. news had featured an interview with Jared's neighbor, who told about seeing two suspicious people—a male and a female—in the garage shortly before Jared's son discovered him. I was glad my name evidently hadn't been mentioned, but I was very sorry to hear that Jared's son had been the one to find him. Detective Dan hadn't mentioned that.

Cast and band members were on edge, and understandably so. Jared hadn't been one of us, but he had been married to one of us. We were all suspects since we had all sent food over to him.

Well, not all of us. "I guess you and I are in the clear," Gordon said as we sat down in the pit for a sound check before the show. "We didn't contribute anything." He warmed up by playing a scale and a lip-loosening exercise. Then he turned to me again and said, "Next you'll be telling me you were one of those suspicious people seen in Jared's garage."

He was joking. I didn't say anything.

"Son of a sea biscuit!"

"I can explain," I said.

I couldn't, though, at least not right then. Caleb was ready for the sound check, so Becky had us begin playing "Cirque de Paris."

Maybe it was my imagination, but it seemed Gordon had moved his chair ever so slightly farther away from me.

After the show, which went surprisingly well, Gordon said, "My wife came to the show and is waiting for me outside. Believe me, I can't wait to hear your story, but it's going to have to wait." He hesitated before he left. "Do you think you can stay out of trouble getting out of here?"

I nodded miserably, then texted Derek. I went to the greenroom and sat down beside Marco the Magnificent. He was capeless, to my surprise. In just a moment, Aiden sat down on the other side of me.

"I think tonight was my best," he smiled. It was nice to have him speaking to me.

"You're absolutely right," I said, giving him a high-five.

Feleesha sat down on the other side of Aiden, giving me a look I couldn't interpret. "Want half my Coke?" she whispered to him. She was holding a plastic glass and a can. "I can't drink it all."

"No, thank you." Aiden jumped up and hurried away immediately. Feleesha looked hurt.

"He seems kind of afraid of you," Marco the Magnificent said.

I thought of telling Feleesha that she shouldn't take it personally, since Aiden is a very shy guy. But I didn't. I knew she would probably take anything I said wrong, given the way she had behaved toward me lately.

It turns out it didn't matter if I spoke or not. She still turned on me. "It's your fault," she said.

Before I could respond, Paula was beside her. "Your voice, honey. Remember your voice." She nodded toward the door. "Sorry, but we've got to get going."

She didn't sound sorry at all.

Helena and Reagan had observed the scene. Helena said, "What was *that* all about?"

"I have no idea."

Helena shrugged. "She's so, like, psycho."

"Yeah?" I was interested.

"She's always shadowing her, like she's *part* of her or something."

"Oh, you mean *Paula* is psycho?"

"Like who else would I mean?" She did that little "duh" click of her tongue and looked over at her friend.

Reagan spoke up. "She acts like Feleesha is a kid. She tells her when to make tea or have a snack, and she makes her, like, stand and model before she goes onstage, to make sure she hasn't, like, forgotten any of her costume. Weird."

"Totally." Helena freshened her lipstick. "Feleesha just lets her boss her around. If it was *my* mom, she'd be outta here. Or else I would be." She tossed her hair and added, "Paula is worthless anyway. She never *did* fix our costumes. We had to get our friend Josie to do it."

"Thank God for Josie," I said, hoping to keep them talking. "I wonder why she's like that."

"Paula or Feleesha?"

"Paula."

"I told you! She's psycho!" Helena picked up her giant make-up bag and left. Reagan followed.

I decided to go commiserate with Herb while I waited for Derek. "What do you think, Herb? Helena and her friend think Paula is, to quote them, 'psycho.'"

He shrugged. "I'd just call her nuts."

I raised an eyebrow.

"She's a little controlling, don't you think? Poor Feleesha can't walk three steps without Paula breathing down her neck. You ought to see things backstage during the show. You'd think Feleesha was the star or something, the way she treats her."

"She *was* the star, originally."

"Oh yeah. Well, I think her mother thinks she's got to protect her from getting kicked out of being, uh, whatever she is now."

"Harem girl."

"Whatever. I feel sorry for her."

"Feleesha?"

"I sure don't mean Paula. She's out-of-control nuts." He made a little circling motion at the side of his head with a finger.

"Or psycho," I said, "depending on your point of view."

He opened the door for some cast members leaving, then stood against it to keep it open. I stood with him on the landing.

He shook his head. "Speaking of out-of-control…" He nodded toward Helena and Reagan getting into Joe's car. "Helena treats her friend—whatever her name is—kind of like Paula treats Feleesha. Bosses her around, makes her do stuff for her. And fooling around with Joe? He must be close to 20 years older than her!"

"She's fooling around with Joe?" I guess I miss a lot sitting in the pit. "She *is* eighteen, right?"

Just then Derek walked up. "Couldn't get in the alley when I pulled up. We're parked in front of Sammie's."

"Bye, Herb," I said, and we walked to the car. "Herb thinks Paula is nuts. So do Helena and Reagan."

"I'm sure they are all qualified psychologists," he said dryly.

"Are we going up to check on Sammie?"

"No. I stopped by earlier, when I dropped you off. She was going to go to bed early. She's okay. I mean her heart is broken, but you know Sammie. She'll move on."

"Maybe we could go out to the Rose next week. Dancing always cheers her up."

"I already suggested that. She says she can't go there because she might see Sam. She can't go dancing in Denver because she might see Donald."

"She's got to go dancing *somewhere*. Sammie has to dance." I looked at Sammie's store. "What the heck?" The store windows were covered with 8.5 X 11 pieces of paper, from top to bottom. Dozens of them. I was going to take one off and look at the other side when a police car pulled up in the space beside Derek's car. It was Detective Kendrick, and I certainly didn't want to do anything to draw her attention again. I got in the car, and Derek and I drove off.

"What's up with all those sheets of paper?" I wondered.

Derek shrugged. "Maybe she's doing some re-design of the place and wanted to cover things up while it was going on. You know how she needs a project when she's upset. She probably didn't have any butcher paper."

"But these were taped on the *outside* of the place. Wouldn't she have done that from the inside?"

He thought a moment. "Right. Maybe we should go back and see what's up."

I hesitated. "No. It's just paper, and I seriously do not want to attract Ms. Bad Cop's attention again for any reason whatsoever. You made sure Sammie set the alarm when you left?"

"I set it myself."

"Okay then. Let's leave it. We'll let her sleep and find out tomorrow."

CHAPTER 38

Sometimes, on the mornings that Derek made me run, I was starting to kind-of-sort-of like it, though I wasn't about to tell him that. As we ran on Saturday morning, it actually felt good to push myself and let go of tension.

As I waited for him to use the shower first so he could get right to work editing, I opened my laptop and stared blankly at the wallpaper image of my youngest nephew Barnaby as a newborn. Since he is almost six now, I thought vaguely about replacing the photo with something more current, but, as usual, didn't feel like going to the trouble. I just stared.

I was depressed. There were only two performances of *Carnival* left, and I still didn't know who had used Tillie as a murder weapon. Was it the same person who had poisoned Jared, or someone different? And how was I ever going to prove the poisoner wasn't me, since I had been seen at his house right before he was discovered?

I was out of ideas. I stared some more at the computer screen. Eventually, bored, I stared out the window, then at Poquito doing his business in the yard, then at the rug that definitely needed vacuuming, then at the bookshelf.

My eyes fell on my collection of Sue Grafton novels. What would private detective Kinsey Millhone do? I remembered that she always puts information on note cards and shuffles them around to see connections and come up with ideas. I decided to do the same. Enough staring.

For two hours, I made suspect cards, one person's name on each card. I added each person's primary connections, as far as I knew them, to people in the show other than Judith. (Everyone had a connection to Judith.) I added a possible motive for each person, even if I made it up out of whole cloth and even if it seemed ridiculous. I wrote, for example, that Helena's motive for murder might have been a smoldering resentment of Judith. Maybe she was mad that Judith hadn't chosen a photo of her for the *Carnival* show poster. Her motive for using Tillie? Maybe she found an accordion too offensive to be allowed in the same building with her. Her motive for trying to kill Jared? Maybe she was mad that he hadn't had an affair with her, too. Or that he actually had and she didn't want it to be over. Or that he had and she didn't want him to tell anyone about it because she was embarrassed to have succumbed to someone as uncool as him. Yes, I was making things up, but maybe my imagination would knock something real loose.

Ridiculous as it was, I found the exercise therapeutic. It made me look at the situation with new eyes. It even gave me ideas that might not be ridiculous.

Participating in the last evening performance of *Carnival* was magic. A large, responsive crowd helps create energy. Cast members suck up the energy from the audience and perform at their best. A confident cast, in turn, helps the audience relax and immerse themselves in make believe. Band members respond to the confidence and happily lose themselves in the music. Being a part of such a show is a real high, and Saturday night was such a show, despite underlying tension about the murder and despite Stanley getting the flu and barely making it to the end of the show.

Gordon hurried off immediately to drive Stanley home. "I'll be back for my stuff," he said. I knew he wouldn't leave his beloved trombone overnight, even though we'd be back tomorrow afternoon for the last show, a matinee.

I hoped I hadn't touched anything Stan had touched—a selfish thought, I knew. Still, I thought it would be a good idea to wash carefully later. I wondered about Stanley's "friend" and whether he would be washing carefully, too. Who could it have been? I had been looking at shoes for the last two nights but hadn't seen anyone wearing the right ones.

I didn't leave the pit right away. I sat for a while, savoring the feeling of being in such a successful show.

Then I heard, "Auntie Bellella, that was awesome!" I turned to see my ten-year old nephew Owen and his little brother with my older brother Alexander and his wife.

"You came!" I said. I don't know why I said that with such surprise. Even though they live in Denver, they always come to any show I'm involved in.

"How could we miss it with all the publicity the show is getting?" Alexander said. I reached over the railing and hugged Owen, the nephew most likely to follow in my musical theater footsteps.

Then I reached for six-year-old Barnaby. We have a routine: He stands rigidly. I hug him and call him my sweet little Barnaby-Boo. He grimaces elaborately and draws back. Then he can't help letting a bit of a smile leak out.

"We can't stay," Alexander said. "Early morning soccer game, but we wanted you to know we came." He gave Barnaby a warning look. "And we really enjoyed it."

Barnaby started to protest, but his mother took his arm firmly to propel him toward the lobby. Barnaby isn't a musical theater fan.

I made my way out of the pit to walk them out. I knew they had to drive back to Denver, and I wished, not for the first time, that they lived right in town. I felt tears come to my eyes as each of the boys hugged me goodbye in the lobby—Owen enthusiastically and Barnaby at his father's insistence. I wished I could see them more often.

As I walked back through the auditorium, I thought about how much I loved hearing "Auntie Bellella." When Sammie's baby was born, I'd soon be able to hear it more often. She would be as much a niece to me as the boys were nephews, and she would be living close by. I smiled, looking forward to it.

"Hey," someone called. I turned and saw my other brother Christopher coming out of a restroom. He gave a friendly punch on the harm. "Good show," he said. "I was sitting with Alexander and the kids. You can thank me for helping silence Barnaby's piteous moans."

I smiled. "Thank you. And I'm glad you came out of your cave." Christopher is not exactly a people person.

"Mom made me." He smiled, knowing that I knew he had come on his own. We're family, and, like Alexander, he comes to all my performances—except for polka gigs. "There are limits," they both have told me.

Of course he didn't invite me out afterward, but I wasn't offended. That's just Christopher. We talked for a few minutes, and he actually gave me a hug before he left. He wasn't generally a hugger.

Derek had texted that he had to get gas and would be a little late, so I sank into a chair in the greenroom. Cast and band members wouldn't be going out tonight. Everyone needed to save some energy for tomorrow's matinee, our last performance.

I watched the place empty out, wondering if any of my brainstormed motives might eventually turn out to be true. I didn't bother to get up and watch for Derek. Herb knew him well enough to let him in to get me if I wasn't out front to meet him. I just wanted to sit for as long as I could. I was tired.

Then I remembered that I had left my tote bag under my chair in the orchestra pit. I sighed, realizing I'd have to summon the energy to go back for it, as my purse was inside it. I got up, went down the stairs to the auditorium, and then down the steps into the pit. As I made my way across the tangle of cords, I was careful not to bump any music stands or—heaven forbid—Gordon's trombone. After I picked up my purse, I stood for a moment looking out over the theater and saw Tess at the back talking to Caleb. I called, "Great show tonight!"

She smiled and gave me a thumbs up. Her voice rose in pitch as she sang out, "Thank you. Wasn't it *great*?!" Then it slid back down as she said, "*So* much fun."

I sat down and was reaching under my chair for my bag when I heard Paula's voice. "I found your water bottle," she said. I turned and saw her going up the aisle and holding out the green metal bottle Tess had been looking for.

"You found it! Thanks so much, Paula," Tess said. "I've missed my Gatorade." She lifted the bottle to take a swig.

Without thinking, I yelled, "No!! Don't drink it! She poisoned it."

Tess looked at me like I was crazy for a second. Then understanding dawned.

As I looked out into the theater towards her, I suddenly froze. Memories began clicking into place. I noticed the stray kernels of popcorn in the aisles, the empty drink containers, the napkins that had fallen on the floor. I felt the chill in the air now that the heat had been turned to the overnight setting. Then, somewhere in the building, I heard a toilet flush.

Suddenly I knew who had killed Judith.

Tess took a step back from Paula, looking frightened. At the same time, Feleesha rushed down the stairs from the stage. She stopped in front of the pit and turned to me. She spoke softly but her voice was ice. "Leave my mother alone. Keep your nose out of things."

I looked at her and spoke without thinking. "You did it," I said simply.

That may have not been my brightest move.

Feleesha looked at me for a moment, steely-eyed. She didn't speak again, just bent down over the railing and yanked Gordon's trombone from his stand. Standing up, she took a baseball-batter-like stance and swung the trombone at me, hard. She hit me in my right arm with the bell, and I screamed in pain.

When I could catch my breath, I yelled, "What is wrong with you?" As I clutched my arm, she took another swing, but this time I managed to duck out of her way. I let go of my arm and with both hands grabbed the end of the trombone and tried to wrestle it away from her. She had greater leverage, though, standing on the higher auditorium floor. We weaved back and forth, knocking over Gordon's music stand and coming dangerously close to my accordion. My arm was throbbing, but I held tight.

Suddenly, Feleesha let go, and I staggered backward, falling into my music stand and knocking it over. I struggled to get back up, hanging on to the edge of my folding chair. When I finally made it to my knees, I saw that Feleesha had picked up the trombone again and tossed it aside. She was coming down the steps into the pit and taking something out of the bag she wore crosswise over her chest. I couldn't believe it. Was it an ice pick? My stomach lurched. Why would she be carrying an ice pick? I looked at the needle-like point, and the room spun. I could feel myself starting to black out.

I struggled to focus. No, it wasn't an ice pick. It was her mother's awl—the one she used to poke holes in leather—and she was pointing it at me. I heard Paula, now at the railing, saying softly, "Feleesha, you need to calm down. Everything will be okay if you put down the awl."

Feleesha ignored her and continued moving toward me. She didn't speak, just kept her steely gaze on me. Luckily she tripped over the direct box used to plug in the amplifier for the bass guitar. That slowed her down, but only momentarily.

My breathing was quick and shallow, but I tried to control it. I needed to remain conscious and think fast. Could I climb over the railing to get out of the pit? No, I couldn't turn my back on Feleesha. I also couldn't reach the steps because she blocked the way. Looking around frantically for protection, I settled on the drum screen surrounding Stanley's drum kit. Used for sound control, the screen had three connected panels, each about five feet tall and made of some kind of acrylic. Maybe it would protect me. I squeezed behind it just as Feleesha climbed over my fallen music stand. She held the awl raised in the air, ready to strike.

Paula continued speaking softly. "Stop, Feleesha. No."

Feleesha ignored her and struck the drum shield hard with the awl. The screen shuddered as I cowered behind it. She struck again and again. I became dizzier and dizzier with each strike but took deep breaths and tried not to look at the needle-like awl aimed at my body.

Suddenly the panel of one shield separated from the others, and the whole thing fell against me, knocking me into the rod that went through the center of the cymbals. I groaned in pain. I'd fallen on the arm that had already been injured. I swayed, grabbing Stanley's stool for balance before righting myself. The separation of the three panels had knocked Feleesha off balance, and she had fallen into my accordion. I couldn't help thinking "Not another one!" but didn't take time to look for damage. Instead, I picked up the two panels that were still connected, folded them together for added thickness, and held them in front of me, like a shield. As Feleesha righted herself and aimed again, I worried about my exposed hands grasping the shield, but I knew I had to hold on.

I heard a shout. "Stop!" I tore my eyes away from Feleesha for a second and saw Derek looking down at us from the stage. His gun. Where was his gun? He crouched, then dropped into the pit. He landed hard, grunting, but quickly righted himself and grabbed Feleesha around the waist, yanking her back from me. The awl dropped and rolled under Gordon's chair.

As I tried to process what I was seeing, Poquito trotted across the stage, saw Derek in the pit, and jumped in after him. He recognized Feleesha as the enemy and began growling and biting Feleesha's harem pants, tugging at them menacingly and stopping every few seconds to spit out sequins.

Herb just stood on the stage looking confused.

When I saw that Derek had a firm hold on Feleesha, my vision cleared, and fury took over. From behind the screen shield, I yelled, "Tie her up!"

"With what?" Caleb had run from the sound booth, and Tess was right behind him, looking terrified.

"Let me deal with Feleesha," Paula said.

"Tie her up, too!" I ordered.

Caleb didn't question me. He grasped Paula firmly by each arm and held onto her. I looked over at Derek. Feleesha was putting up a good fight, but he had her pinned on the floor.

"What the hell?" It was Gordon, who had come back for his trombone. A horrified look crossed his face when he saw it lying in front of the pit, but I didn't let him linger. "Get down there and help Derek hold onto Feleesha. She tried to kill me." He did as he was told.

Becky and Aiden appeared on the stage, undoubtedly attracted by the noise. "Becky, get down here and help Caleb hold on to Paula," I said. She hurried down the steps.

"Aiden, call 9-1-1," I said. "Tell them it's an emergency at the Juniper Theater, and tell them that Detective Dan Sherman should be notified." He looked scared. "Now."

Caleb pulled Paula to a chair in the auditorium and pushed her into it. Immediately Becky sat on her. Herb finally came to life and sat on Becky. Tess pinned one of Paula's arms to the chair, and Caleb pinned the other.

I held my bleeding arm and thought quickly. We needed to tie them up, but with what? I saw Noreen coming into the back of the theater from the lobby. "Noreen!" I yelled. "Bring us some gaffer tape. Hurry!" Gaffer tape is used by production crews in theaters to tie down cables and handle other short-term set-ups. It peels up without doing any harm to whatever it is applied to, and it doesn't leave a residue.

Noreen stood for a second, shocked as she took in the scene, then went to the light booth and came out with two rolls of tape. She pitched one down the aisle to Caleb, then hurried down to the front carrying the other. I couldn't help thinking that I would be recruiting her for the Whitney's-sponsored softball team this summer. What an arm!

Caleb let go of Paula to pick up the tape, then tossed it to Derek. He took the other roll from Noreen and began taping Paula to the chair. Herb got off Becky and went down to the pit to help Derek.

I was still trapped behind the sections of drum shield and having trouble moving because of my arm. I tried to ignore the blood pouring onto Stanley's kettle drum, but I wasn't about to move until Feleesha was safely tied up. I watched as Derek and Herb managed to wrap her feet and hands with the tape. She struggled mightily but was oddly silent.

Paula was not. "You've got this all wrong," she said, more than once. "This is ridiculous! We're going to sue!" When she started using foul language, calling us all filthy names, Becky pulled a scarf from her jacket pocket and stuffed it in Paula's mouth.

"There is a child in your presence," she said. "We do not need to hear that kind of talk."

"I'm not a child, Mom," Aiden said, predictably, as he came down the steps to join his mother.

That's when Feleesha—at last—spoke again. "You are *my* son, Aiden. Not hers. *My* son."

Aiden stopped in his tracks.

"Ignore her," said Becky.

"But why is she saying that?

Becky cut him off. "Later. Help Ella."

Aiden reached down and was able to help me extricate myself from the drums and pieces of drum shield. I stood on a chair and, with a hand from Aiden, managed to climb out of the pit.

I sank into a theater seat. Feleesha had really whacked me hard, and the cut was deep. I was feeling a little faint and put my head between my knees. As the group gathered around me, Becky had Aiden take off his hoodie. She handed it to me and said, "Hold this tight against the cut."

"Another hoodie bites the dust," I said, and all but Caleb looked puzzled.

Herb spoke up. "So I get why we tied up Feleesha. She was trying to kill you. But why did we tie up Paula?"

"Because she tried to kill Jared," I said.

Suddenly Feleesha came to life again. "No!!!!!!" she screamed from the pit. "My mother wouldn't do that! I love him!!!!"

No one addressed that odd proclamation because noises were coming from the lobby. We looked toward the back of the theater and saw Detective Dan, Officer Mildred Kendrick, another officer, and two EMTs entering the auditorium. Detective Dan looked around at Paula taped to her chair, the trombone on the floor, and the mess in the pit—toppled music stands, my accordion on the floor, the broken pieces of drum screen, and a taped-up Feleesha lying across power cords. "What the blazes is going on here?" He looked at me.

I gestured toward the pit with my un-hoodied arm, pointing to Feleesha. "Feleesha whacked me with a trombone and then tried to kill me with an awl." The ungaffered people around me nodded. Officer Kendrick gave me a look that clearly said, "This woman is bonkers."

But Detective Dan, to his credit, just nodded at me and asked for more information.

"Okay. So why is she tied up?" He nodded at Paula.

"She tried to kill Jared."

"Mom would not do that!" Feleesha shouted.

"Feleesha killed Judith, and Paula tried to kill Jared. Trust me on this," I said. I winced as an EMT applied a compression bandage to my arm. "And she tried to poison Tess."

Detective Dan pointed to Paula. "Untape her," he said to the officers. As I watched, I secretly hoped it pulled her arm hairs at least a little. When Detective Kendrick pulled the scarf out of her mouth, Paula let loose a string of obscenities. Ms. Bad Cop said, "Sit quietly, or we'll cuff you."

Paula continued, and not quietly, so she cuffed her. Then she led Paula away so the rest of us could hear ourselves think.

Detective Dan nodded to the other officer. "Arrest the other one," he said. Then he began directing witnesses to different parts of the theater, to be interviewed separately. When he got to Derek, Derek interrupted. "Before I go,

you might want this. It's the awl that Feleesha was using."
Standing only inches from me, he held up the awl.

I took one look and passed out.

I must not have been out long. "I wasn't thinking," Derek
was saying as I opened my eyes. "She hates needles. I mean,
she *really* hates needles."

"The awl must have gone over well then," said Detective
Dan.

"No shots!" I said to the EMT beside me when I saw he
was opening his bag.

"We're not giving you a shot," he said calmly. "We're
going to take you to the emergency room for treatment."

"No. I want my mother," I said, and Detective Dan had
to smile.

"Her mother is a nurse," Derek said. "Let me call her
instead."

"Yes," I said. "I'm not leaving here until I tell Detective
Dan what happened." Oops. I hadn't meant to call him that.

He smiled. "Call her mother," he told Derek.

I was a little woozy, but I heard the third officer reading
Feleesha her rights and Detective Dan explaining to Paula
that she needed to answer some questions. He then sent
Officer Kendrick to the lobby with her, presumably to play
the Bad Cop role she played so well. The EMTs left, seeing
that no one was seriously injured.

Then Detective Dan took out a small notebook and sat
down beside me. "I'll start with you. Are you able to answer
some questions?"

"Yes," I nodded.

"So start at the beginning."

"The *beginning* beginning, or the beginning of tonight's mess?"

"The beginning of tonight's mess." Poquito jumped in his lap and he gave me a questioning look.

"My protection," I said. "Poquito is his name."

Detective Dan scratched the dog's ears and got ready to listen. Poquito licked his face.

I began.

CHAPTER 39

"IT STARTED WITH THE WATER BOTTLE," I said. "I saw Paula give Tess the bottle she had been missing, the one she used for Gatorade. I knew Paula must have swiped it and doctored it with antifreeze."

"And you knew this how?"

"She was the one who had tried to poison Jared with antifreeze. Antifreeze seems to be the thing lately."

"You *think* she was the one who tried to poison Jared with antifreeze. Why would she want to kill him?"

"Because she hated him. He is the one who impregnated Feleesha when she was just a teenager, and she found out he was fooling around with her again—while at the same time trying to get back together with his wife. She knew he was bad news, and she figured the only way to protect her child was to get rid of him."

"How did you come to this conclusion?"

"I've been learning a lot lately about mama bear syndrome. And bad choices."

He made some notes. "I'll try to confirm all this. I mean about the affair and the pregnancy. Let's get back to Feleesha. When I was coming in, I heard her yell that Aiden was her son. Why would she think that?"

"Because Aiden has red hair, and he is the same age as

the child her mother made her give up fifteen years ago. That must have been why Becky didn't want Feleesha close to Aiden. She had figured out that Feleesha thought he was that child."

"Have you figured out why Feleesha wanted to kill *you*?"

"Yes. Aiden had a crush on me and was leaving me little gifts. Feleesha picked up on this and figured, in her twisted mind, that I was trying to lure him away from her."

"He had a crush on you?" He smiled with his kind brown eyes. "At one point, I thought you thought he hated you, and that's why he used your accordion to kill Judith, whom he also maybe hated because she was making him do the opening fake concertina bit."

"It's so nice to hear the correct use of 'whom,'" I noted. "Thank you."

"I let go of that theory about Aiden a long time ago."

"It's hard to keep up," he said. "So you say Feleesha hated you because of Aiden. Did she hate Judith, too?"

"I don't know if she hated her, but she wanted her dead. And she killed her. I'm sure of that."

"Hang on." He put Poquito down, stood up, and took out another note pad from his back pocket. Poquito waited patiently for him to sit back down, then jumped back. He used the dog's back as a desktop as he wrote. "Okay, so *why* do you think Feleesha killed her?"

"One of the reasons was that it was pretty apparent that Judith was going to replace her with the understudy. Then she would have to deal with her crazy mother and her disappointment, yet again. "

"But she got replaced anyway."

"Yes, but she hadn't thought Tess would actually do it if Judith was gone. Tess is, well, a lot nicer than Judith was. Kinder. She did come through, eventually, on what was best for the show, but she tried to help Feleesha save face."

"You said that was 'one of the reasons' she killed her. What was the other? Or others?"

"The *real* reason was so she could keep Jared from going back to Judith. Feleesha had made the bad decision to have another affair with Jared after fifteen years. She compounded that bad decision with all the decisions she made as a result."

"Wait. I thought Jared left Judith for Darla Oglesby."

"He did. But that didn't stop him from having an affair with Feleesha, or from wanting his wife back. It had happened before, and Judith always took him back. Feleesha didn't want that to happen again."

"Okay, I think. So have you figured out how Feleesha did it?".

"Of course." I smiled at him. "This is the part I *know*."

"Let's hear it." At that point Mom arrived. A policeman escorted her to me, and she nodded at Detective Dan.

She looked at me and sighed. "Can I work on her arm while you talk?"

He nodded. I did, too. Mom is practical, so she started right in. I continued.

"Tonight as I was saving Tess from the poisoned Gatorade, I looked out at all the trash in the audience, and I had the fleeting thought that at least Noreen wouldn't yell at us about it since the audience had made the mess, not us. I suddenly remembered how she had yelled at us about not cleaning up after ourselves the night the murder was discovered." I winced as Mom pulled off the compression bandage. "And while I was remembering that, I heard a toilet flush from somewhere, and I remembered what else she yelled at us about."

"What?" Mom couldn't help herself.

"Three toilets upstairs in the balcony area that hadn't been flushed. She was grossed out and pretty ticked."

"Still not putting the pieces together," said Detective Dan.

"And then I noticed it was chilly because they turn the heat down at night."

"Okay . . . ?"

"And then a memory flashed before my eyes . . . not literally, but you know. It was a picture of Feleesha sitting beside me eating carrot sticks and string cheese just before the murder was discovered. She took the cheese out of a little cooler, and she had a Bronco blanket over her shoulders." I gave him a triumphant look.

He disappointed me. "I still don't get it."

"Me, neither," said Mom.

I tried to make it simpler. "She planned the murder. Instead of leaving like everyone else the night before, she hid in the restrooms with the lights out. Then she camped out in the theater all night so that she would be here the next day at 4:00 p.m. when Judith took her usual spot. She had a cooler so that she had food. She had a blanket to keep warm. There were bathrooms up there, so she had that, too—but she didn't want to flush because the office manager and the ticket sales volunteers would be in the building during the day. She couldn't risk having them hear a flush from upstairs. So she didn't flush."

"But why your accordion? Why use that and not, oh, the ice pick she had tonight?"

"It was an awl," I corrected him. "An *awl*."

"Okay, an awl. Why not stab her with the awl?"

"Because she was jealous of me because of Aiden's crush, remember? Why not get rid of Judith and hurt me at the same time? Another of many bad decisions," I noted.

He gave a "get on with it" motion with his hands.

"So she hauled the accordion up the stairs during the night, positioning it above where Judith would sit, but right below the ledge so it couldn't be seen. Then when Judith came in, she made sure the straps holding the bellows closed were snapped—so it wouldn't make noise—then picked it up quietly. She put it on the ledge and then pushed it over onto Judith."

"I know—another bad decision."

"Certainly for Judith. Then Feleesha went down, unlocked the stage door, and sat down and calmly started eating her gluten-free carrots." I remembered the oh-my-god, oh-my-gods after the murder had been discovered. "We seriously underestimated this woman's acting ability."

Detective Dan nodded thoughtfully. "It all makes sense . . . kind of." He looked at his notes. "Why would Paula want to poison Tess, *if* she was trying to poison her? Have you got that figured out?"

"Maybe she was just mad about her replacing Feleesha with Celeste. Revenge, you know. It's a thing."

"I'll have the bottle checked." He had a lot more questions, but I didn't mind. It was nice to spend time so close to him. I tried hard not to think about that attractive woman I'd seen him with at the show.

Mom sat quietly beside me listening when she had finished with my arm. When Detective Dan was finished, she said only, "Thank God you are okay."

And then I saw the tears in her eyes.

Eventually, Mom left and Derek and I were allowed to go home. We took Poquito and didn't speak until we were outside the theater. Then I turned on him. "So where the hell was your gun?" I asked. "She could have killed me."

"Did you maybe forget that I jumped in the pit, tackled her, and saved your life?" He stomped ahead of me to the car. "Get in."

I did.

He didn't start the car. "One of the things they taught in my concealed carry class is that you should never draw a gun unless you intend to use it. I don't think I could ever shoot someone."

"Holy moly! So you weren't forgetting your gun all these times?"

"No."

"Don't you think you might have been able to use one to save *me*?"

"Maybe, maybe not. I didn't want to test the idea, so I usually left the gun in the trunk." I didn't say anything, thinking back to all the times his gun had been missing. He continued. "To be fair, Herb didn't draw his gun either."

Derek still didn't start the car. Maybe he was waiting for my apology, which I knew I owed him. "I'm sorry. Thank you," I said.

He must have accepted, as he changed the subject. "How's your arm?"

"Sore. How are you?"

"Bruised. Damn, but that woman can kick."

He started the car, but before we could leave, Becky was tapping on the window, Aiden beside her. "I need to talk to you," she said. 'Can we go to Whitney's?"

He looked to me, seeing what I thought. "I could use a drink," I said.

"Me, too." He nodded at Aiden. "Will they let him in?"

"They will if he doesn't drink," I said. "I think."

"We'll give it a try."

We cracked a window for Poquito and went into the bar.

CHAPTER 40

IN LIGHT OF THE CIRCUMSTANCES, Eric, the bartender, agreed to let Aiden sit quietly and have a Coke. He saw my bandaged arm, and he had seen the ambulance and police cars. I think he hoped he could overhear something good.

Becky, of course, had ordered only a soft drink. I asked for a chardonnay, and Derek asked for a Crow Hop IPA. Then he saw Aiden's concerned look and changed to a Coke. "I forgot that I'm driving," he said nobly.

"I want to fill in some pieces that might be missing for you," Becky said. "I've told all this to Detective Sherman, but I thought you should know, too. You are the one who's gotten the most grief over this whole situation."

I listened as I sipped my chardonnay.

"I was music director for a Harper Springs Community Theater production 15 years ago. *Into the Woods*, not that it matters. One night I caught Feleesha and Jared making out in a dressing room. Feleesha was just 15 years old, and Jared was a married man!"

I shook my head. "I just don't see that guy's appeal—for a female of *any* age." I did realize that his attacks on me could have colored my view a little, though

"Oh, he has a way about him," she said. "I could see that." She realized what she had said and hastily added,

"Not that *I* was attracted to him, but I could see why others might be. It's the way he looks at a girl, all soulful-eyed, and pretends to listen—like she's the only person on earth."

"I'll take your word for it. So what did you do when you discovered him with Feleesha?"

"I didn't want to hurt Judith by spilling the beans, and I knew how psycho Paula could get about Feleesha, so I didn't want to tell her either. So I prayed about it." She touched her cross and looked down at it reverently.

I tried not to roll my eyes. In Colorado, a person in authority is required to report suspicious activity of child abuse or child molestation to authorities. They are not supposed to make judgment calls.

Becky looked up and continued. "I finally decided just to talk to Feleesha myself. I hoped to give her some guidance and help her see how foolish she was being." She sighed. "But Feleesha was not the sweet, quiet thing I'd always observed. Instead, she became openly defiant and told me she was pregnant and happy about it, and she and Jared were going to elope. She had no sorrow or shame at all!"

Aiden was hanging on every word. I'm not sure his mother usually mentioned things like affairs and unplanned pregnancies.

Becky used her straw to fiddle with the ice cubes in her drink. I decided not to tell her that straws are a blight on the environment, and she shouldn't use them. Now was not the time.

"I pointed out that you can't elope with someone who is already married, but she said his divorce was in the works." She shook her head. "The kid was so naive. I wasn't sure what to do, so I decided to keep quiet and let the Lord guide the future."

What I wanted to say was, "Maybe if the Lord had told you to protect that child, she wouldn't have become a murderer 15 years later." But I didn't. Again, I kept my thoughts to myself.

Becky continued. "And then, 15 years later, I couldn't believe it, but Jared was fooling around with Feleesha again! I felt guilty for not blowing the whistle on them 15 years ago."

"How did you know they were fooling around again?" Derek asked.

"I noticed Jared hanging around near the theater area a lot—sitting in the coffee shop, going into Whitney's, lingering in the parking lot. I talked to Noreen about it, and she thought he was just trying to find chances to talk to Judith so he could get her to come back to him. Maybe. But I saw Feleesha talking to him a couple of times, and others in the cast, too. Especially Helena. I suspected he was grooming her for an affair. And maybe her friend, too."

"Reagan," I said. "Her name is Reagan."

Becky nodded and continued. "I prayed some more." Again the touching of the cross, but this time she grasped it in her hand. "Finally, I decided to talk to Judith. It turns out she knew all along that Feleesha was fooling around with Jared. And here's the really nasty part. She knew that Feleesha could never handle a major role, so she gave it to her just so she could kick her out later and humiliate her. That had been her intention all along."

"Wow," said Derek. At that moment, the music on the sound system switched from "You Can't Always Get What

You Want" to "Witchy Woman." I looked at Derek and cast my eyes up towards a speaker. Had he noticed? He must have. I could tell he was trying not to smile. "That was pretty evil," he said to Becky.

"She was an evil kind of woman." She looked at her son. "Some people really are evil," she pointed out.

"Like Paula," I said. "She's evil, too. I think she's the one who tried to kill Jared. She knew Feleesha would never give him up, and she wanted him out of the picture." I tried to wrap my brain around the idea that some people turn to murder as a solution to their problems.

Then Aiden looked at his mom. "Why did Feleesha say I was her son?"

She sighed. "Because she thought you were. She'd had an illegitimate child and given the baby up for adoption."

"All babies are legitimate," I interrupted. "She had a baby, and a baby is a baby, no matter if the mother is married or not!" I may have been thinking of Sammie a little with this defense.

Becky didn't argue. "Okay, she had a baby." She looked at Aiden. "Jared has red hair. You have red hair. You're adopted. Her baby was adopted. She had him fifteen years ago. You're fifteen. I think she just jumped to the wrong conclusion. At least that's what I figured when she started wanting to hang around you. That's why I didn't want you to encourage her."

Aiden looked thoroughly confused. "My dad lives here in town," he said. "And my biological dad lives in Wyoming. I've met him. But I don't know my biological mom. Is it Feleesha?"

"No. Absolutely not," she said. "You are not her child,

and thank the lord for that!" Again, she fingered the cross. "What I've told you before is the truth. Your mother was a young girl from the church I went to when I used to live in Wyoming. She was just getting ready to go to college, and having a baby was not something she wanted to do. Our minister arranged for a private adoption, and she moved on with her life. She showed her love for you by giving you to loving parents who would love you and take care of you."

"Until they got divorced," he said, his bitterness obvious.

She paused, then went on. "Your biological father wanted to know about your life, though, so your dad and I agreed to show him pictures, tell him about milestones, and even meet you once in a while." She bent toward Aiden, almost willing his eyes to hers. "A child can't have too many people to love him."

I nodded. That was the truest and best thing she had said all evening.

CHAPTER 41

AT NOON MOM CALLED to tell me to put on the coffee. "We let you sleep in, but now we're all coming over," she said.

Who was "we"? I wasn't sure, but I made a pot of coffee. Not long after, in walked not only Mom, Baba, Geraldine, and Sammie, but also Derek's stepfather Jake and—wonder of wonders—Sam.

Jake gave me a hug first. "This is the trouble you get into when I'm not around, young lady? How do you think I feel, getting home from West Papua at midnight and finding that my favorite girl—next to Sammie, of course—has been attacked by a trombone and an ice pick!"

"It was an awl," I said, hugging him back.

Baba threw her arms around me. "Bellella! You poor baby!" She fingered my bandaged arm.

"Here," Mom said, handing me a package of Strawberry Shortcake bandages. You can put these over the Steri-Strips."

"Thank you so much," I said sarcastically.

"Are you in pain?" Baba asked.

"Not with the pills I have."

Baba looked alarmed. "Opioids?"

I smiled. "Advil."

She breathed a sigh of belief. "I can't believe that monster hit you with a trombone."

"Neither could Gordon when he found out. And I was a lot more concerned about the awl, frankly."

"Hence the fainting," Derek said.

Geraldine insisted that Derek and I recount all that had happened the night before. They pulled up chairs around the table, and Mom poured coffee. I looked at Sammie with a "What the . . . ?" look and a tiny gesture toward Sam. He caught it and spoke up.

"Before you interrogate Ella, let me say something to all of you and get it out of the way. The elephant in the room and all."

Baba looked around, then caught herself.

Sam continued. "Sammie and I have agreed to keep seeing each other and see how it goes. When she starts showing and people assume the baby is mine, we'll just go with it. See how I feel."

"*What????*" said Jake. "Sammie is *pregnant?*"

"But you're not married," Baba said to Sammie.

"I'm pregnant," said Sammie. "And I'm not married. And the baby isn't Sam's."

"Sorry, dear," said Geraldine, looking at Jake. "There hasn't been time to fill you in, and I thought that Sam was history."

Baba gave me a look that told me I'd be hearing about this later. Why hadn't I told her?

"I'm not history," said Sam. "This pregnancy doesn't make it easy, but I've done a lot of thinking. My sister has an adopted child, and I realized that I could not love her even an iota more than I do if she was related biologically to me. She's my niece, and I adore her. I love kids, and my guess is—despite the unfortunate beginning—that I will love this child, too, especially with the sperm donor out of the picture."

"Sperm donor? Unfortunate beginning?" Jake was looking very confused.

"Later, dear," said Geraldine. She looked at us. "Terrible cell phone coverage in West Papua."

"I think I know how that 'unfortunate beginning' took place," muttered Baba.

"Shhhh," I said, touching her arm.

"I just wanted to get that out of the way," Sam said. "That's all."

Sammie glowed. "He papered my store with pages of notes to me, all saying he was so sorry he left me." We all smiled, except for Jake. I imagine he wanted some background but gamely put his questions aside to concentrate on Derek and me.

We told them everything that had happened the night before, and we tried to answer all their questions.

Baba seemed the most upset about my injuries. "I can't believe someone would do this to *you!* But thank God Derek saved you."

"Hey, I was involved, too," I said. "I tried to wrestle the trombone away from her and then wielded a drum screen like a shield. All Derek did was pull her off as she was about to stab me."

"Some might call that saving your life," Mom said, giving me a look.

I relented. "Okay, yes, he saved me. But I helped."

Mom had a question. "You said that Paula kept really close tabs on Feleesha. So how did she manage to arrange an overnight in the theater without her mother noticing? For that matter, how did she manage an affair with Jared, under Paula's watchful eye?"

"Tess figured that out," said Derek. "She remembered that Paula had to go to Junction City for a funeral. She was gone three days, but Feleesha couldn't go because of the show and being the lead and all. She checked the dates, and they coincided with when Judith was killed."

"How about the affair?" asked Geraldine. "How did she manage that?"

"No answers there yet."

The doorbell rang. Mom answered the door and ushered Detective Dan into the kitchen. "I'm sorry for interrupting," he said, "but I need to ask Miss Polansky some questions."

"How are you?" He looked at me with his kind brown eyes, like he really wanted to know.

"Other than the gash in my arm and a little soreness, okay," I said.

"I talked to your director earlier, and she said they canceled today's show," he said. "So don't worry about that."

"I hope this doesn't put us in the red," I worried.

"Evidently there was a donation that covered the shortfall," Detective Dan said. I looked at Geraldine, whose expression revealed nothing.

Detective Dan continued. "I do need to ask you some follow-up questions." Everyone sat tight, gripping their coffee cups and looking eager. "Alone," he added. "Given your injury, I thought it would be smarter to come here than to have you come to the station."

"No problem," said Jake. "I just got back from overseas and haven't even had a chance to talk to my family." He looked at Sammie. "And it seems there is a lot to talk about. Let's go to our house. You, too, young man."

"I think you're finished with your bodyguarding, Derek." Geraldine said. "We'll return Poquito."

"I'll be over in a few minutes," he said.

"And I'll call you later to check on you," said Mom.

Everyone left, except for Detective Dan and Derek, who was packing. I offered Detective Dan a cup of coffee and then, feeling that coffee was somehow inadequate, several Oreos. He accepted. "It was a long night. It's been a hell of a mess trying to sort this out," he said.

"Did you get any sleep?"

"Yes, I didn't have to come in until late morning."

Derek came out of the den, and Detective Dan held out his hand. "I'm glad you were there last night. You saved Ella's life."

"I held Feleesha off with the drum shield," I pointed out.

"Okay, *helped* save her life."

Derek smiled. "And I did it even without my gun." He glanced at me. "That's kind of been an issue with Ella."

"You acted wisely, and I doubt that a gun would have helped the situation."

"Okay, fine," I said. "Again, I'm glad you helped save me, and without a gun. And I'm glad you tied them up with gaffer tape, like I told you to. And I hope it hurt at least a little when the officers peeled off the tape."

"She does have a sadistic streak," said Derek.

"Only when attempted murder is involved," I said.

Detective Dan took a sip of coffee and glanced at my

cup. Wonder Woman. Sammie had given it to me to replace Rocky. "Your efforts at the liquor store have also proven to be key," he said. "I can't say any more now."

Derek kissed the top of my head gently. "See you later, roomie."

"Former roomie."

"And former bodyguard. Woo-hoo! I'm free!" He left.

Suddenly I was nervous, alone with Detective Dan. "So what's with the antifreeze?" I blurted. "Did you check the bottle Paula gave Tess?"

"There wasn't any antifreeze in the water bottle. You were wrong about that." He twisted an Oreo apart and ate the half without the filling, then the other half.

I couldn't believe I had been wrong about the water bottle. He noticed my disappointed look. "But so far you are turning out to be right about everything else."

I was pleased but a little fixated on the antifreeze situation. "Was I right about Jared poisoning Ginger?"

"Probably. Antifreeze has a long shelf life, so he might have used some old stuff he had around. Or he might have used a newer bottle. I was reading a recent study that shows that deaths of cats and dogs and even people from antifreeze poisoning have not gone down since the additive was put in antifreeze. Maybe cats get enough to kill them before they realize it doesn't taste good. Or maybe they just don't have very discriminating taste."

Fluffles took that as her cue and jumped in my lap. "You don't know cats," I said. "This one knows in an instant if I substitute Friskies for Fancy Feast, and she refuses to eat. She just whines and whines until I give her what she wants. Not the best parenting technique . . . not that that's parenting

. . . exactly . . . I'm not a parent, but I'm a teacher, so maybe I should say *teaching* technique . . ."

"I get it," he said. "We may never know about Jared and the cat."

"Except that he poisoned her."

"Almost certainly."

"Is he going to be okay?" Fluffles lifted her chin up for me to pet underneath it. I obliged.

"He'll recover from the poisoning, but with his drinking problem, I doubt that he's going to be okay."

"And he will be informed, in no uncertain terms, that I am not the one who killed Judith?" That was the important thing. "And he'll believe it this time?"

"Absolutely. I will make sure of that. Maybe I could borrow that $10,000 receipt of yours, just as an extra bit of proof?"

I smiled. It had been a good idea after all. I changed the subject.

"How the heck did Feleesha manage to carry on an affair with Jared with her mother keeping such close tabs on her?"

"How did *you* manage to do things you didn't want your parents to know about when you were in high school?"

"I was a good Catholic girl."

He raised his eyebrows.

"Okay, I sneaked out, like kids everywhere do. In my case, I used the door from the laundry room to the garage, and then the side door."

"No dramatic second floor window escapes down a tree?"

"No second floor." I thought a minute. "So Feleesha and Paula both *attempted* murder but didn't succeed."

"You're forgetting Feleesha. Yes, she *did* murder Judith, and she's proud of it. Your theory is correct about how she hid in the theater overnight in order to kill Judith. The woman is . . . well, she seems a little, no, a lot . . ."

"Unhinged."

"Yes. Her mom defended her by giving us a history of her hospitalizations. She suffered some kind of breakdown after she gave up the baby and realized Jared wasn't about to leave his wife or even admit to the affair, since she was underage. Paula eventually brought her back here, and she relapsed, going to the hospital again. Paula may go overboard, but she really is a mama bear trying to protect her kid."

Mama bear syndrome seems to be universally recognized, I thought, and everywhere. "Paula is the one who drove Feleesha to *being* nuts, though."

"Probably. But that didn't stop her from trying to protect her, and to keep others from knowing her problems. She may have been a rotten mother in many ways, but I think she does love her daughter fiercely."

"Not the kind of love most of us go for. Not every mom tries to kill her daughter's bad choice of a boyfriend." Fluffles turned over in my lap, wanting her stomach rubbed now. I obliged. "So what's going to happen?"

"Feleesha will be charged with murder and attempted murder, and my guess is her lawyers will use the insanity defense, especially since she's already confessed. Paula wouldn't talk at first, but when Mildred—I mean Officer Kendrick—expressed sympathy and understanding, she pretty much couldn't shut up."

So Ms. Bad Cop could also play Ms. Good Cop. I

wondered if Detective Dan could also play Bad Cop. Then I remembered that he was Curly in *Oklahoma*. He was an actor. He probably could.

"Paula will be charged with attempted murder," he said.

"I suppose I'll have to testify?"

"If there are trials for either or both of them, yes. I think there is a strong likelihood of a plea bargain, though."

I sighed and drained my Wonder Woman cup. "Two deaths are a hard thing to absorb."

"One, you mean. Jared really is expected to recover."

"No, two. Everyone forgets Tillie."

"Of course, Tillie." He patted my hand. "Two deaths."

We were silent. Then he cleared his throat and said he had to go.

CHAPTER 42

SUDDENLY I WAS ALONE. It was over. I looked around, at a loss for what to do. I checked my email.

There was a note from Tess, explaining to those who hadn't been there what had happened after the show. The matinee was canceled but the cast party would still be held at 5:30 at Whitney's. Feleesha and Paula were in custody and would not be attending. We were all safe.

I didn't feel like answering a bunch of questions again. No party for me.

I called Sammie. "How did Jake take everything?" I asked.

"Under the circumstances, pretty well. I'm sorry I had to tell him before I told Dad, though. I'm meeting Dad this afternoon. Jake really likes Sam, by the way."

"Everyone really likes Sam," I said. "He seems like a good guy. And I like his shoes." I wondered if I'd ever learn who owned the shoes I'd seen entwined with Stanley's.

"There's something I've been meaning to tell you," Sammie said. "Yesterday afternoon a woman came into the store to drop off some things, and I got to talking to her."

"Which you're good at. What did you find out?"

"It seems she first heard of Second Chance when she was downtown to see *Carnival*, which she loved.

"That's nice."

"But guess who she was."

"No idea."

"She was that good-looking woman Detective Dan was with on opening night."

"Way to bring a person down." Couldn't this have waited? I was already dealing with a lot.

"She was there because her *brother-in-law* wanted someone to go with."

It took me a minute to process this. Why did she sound so happy? Why was she telling me this?

Then it hit me. "Her brother-in-law is Detective Dan!"

"Yes!"

I felt as happy as I had when Derek tackled Feleesha and made her drop that awl.

I decided to take a nap, but I couldn't sleep. I tried to read, but I couldn't concentrate. I went for a run—Derek had definitely had an effect on my health—but I didn't enjoy it.

I took a shower and started to get out my blow dryer. Then I stood in front of the mirror a minute, looking at my long, wet hair. Little strands had already started to spring out as they dried. "The hell with it," I said, and I fluffed it with my fingers, bringing out the curl and letting my hair do what it wanted to do. Soon I had a mass of golden brown curls floating around my head.

I put on jeans and the green sweater that brought out the gold in my brown eyes a lot better than the lavender eye shadow I had bought. Then the doorbell rang.

It was all of the Streusels, as well as Moriko. "Your mother called me," she said. "We're so happy you're okay."

The guys positioned themselves in choir formation on my patio.

"What in the world . . . ?"

Moriko continued. "Otto wrote this little song the guys want to sing for you. You know, instead of sending you flowers."

"We didn't have much time," Otto said. "So take that into consideration."

Carl blew into a pitch pipe, and they sang, to the tune of the "Bellella Polka:

Bellella, Bellella. Glad that you're okay.
Can't think of another rhyme, so Hey! Hey! Hey!
Bellella, Bellella. Glad that you got through it.
Most of all we're happy that Bellella didn't do it!

Then all of the guys started beat boxing—the lamest beat boxing I have ever heard. By the end, I was laughing so hard I was in tears. Foster, Maria, and Skyden had come out on the porch and were applauding, especially Skyden. He immediately tried it himself, spitting with enthusiasm.

Mr. McConnell and his wife stood on their porch frowning.

I invited everyone in, but Moriko held them back. She looked me over carefully. "You look nice," she said. "Were you going out?

"Well . . ."

"You go ahead. We only came to sing to you and tell you that we're happy the case is solved."

As they got in the car, I gave a little wave to Mr. McConnell. "They're family," I called.

I heard him say to his wife, "No wonder they're nuts."

I took a deep breath, got in my car, and drove to the police station.

"I would like to see Detective Sherman," I said firmly at the front desk.

"Name?" the police officer asked.

"Ella Polansky."

The police officer called him. "Someone is here to see you." He looked at me. "He said he'll be right down."

I took a few more deep breaths, waiting, but he was there in just a minute.

He seemed surprised to see me. "Ella. What are you doing here? Is anything wrong?"

"Could we step outside for a sec?"

"Sure."

Outside the building I looked at him and asked for exactly what I wanted. "Would you like to have dinner with me?"

He didn't answer for a minute, and I thought he was going to turn me down. "Just to be clear," he said, "as in a date?"

"Just to be clear, yes."

He smiled. "Yes. How about tonight?"

"You're not too tired after last night?"

"I slept late."

"Me, too."

"I should be done here by 5:30," he smiled. "I'll pick you up as soon as I get off."

I smiled back and headed for my car.

"I love your hair," he called.

Two hours later, Detective Dan knocked on my door, and I let him in. I took my jacket from the coat tree, and he helped me into it. Then I picked up my purse and put it over my shoulder.

"Galoochi?" he asked.

The man had listened. "Galoochi." I smiled.

We were standing very close. Neither of us moved. Then I let Galoochi drop from my shoulder to the floor. Detective Dan pulled me to him and kissed me. I kissed him right back.

It was a good kiss. A very good kiss. In fact, I would give it a "ten" in the kissing department. We kissed some more. All tens.

"You want to stay in and order pizza?" I murmured against his chest.

"Sure," he said. We took off our jackets and sat on the sofa. He pulled up pizza places on his phone, and we decided on the only non-chain place in town that delivered.

He hesitated, then said, "I don't suppose you like anchovies?"

Could things get any better? I smiled at him and nodded.

We waited quite happily for the anchovy pizza, snuggling up on the couch with Fluffles and kissing some more.

And after we ate the pizza?

I'll just say that a disappointed Fluffles had to spend the night in the living room with the door to the bedroom closed tight.

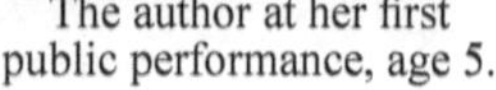

The author at her first
public performance, age 5.

Cheryl Miller Thurston is a Colorado writer, teacher, and musician. She has published articles, books, poetry, plays, musicals, and music on a variety of subjects, but this is her first novel.

An accordionist from the age of 4½, she is also the founder of Closet Accordion Players of America, a national organization that, with a sense of humor, encourages accordionists to come out of the closet and play proudly.

www.ClosetAccordionsOfAmerica.com